The Renovation
Elke Feuer

eBook Edition ISBN-13: 979-8-9896517-0-2

Paperback ISBN-13: 979-8-9896517-1-9

Cover design by Elijah Toten.

Also By Elke Feuer:

For The Love of Jazz

Deadly Bloodlines, Deadly Series Book 1

Deadly Race, Deadly Series Book 2

Deadly Family, Deadly Series Book 3

Persuading Lola

Dedicated to . . .

My fans: you've stuck with me through a lot waiting for the next book. I love and appreciate you all!

Contents

Chapter 1

T he air in the boardroom dropped several degrees when Sharon Donovan walked in. She'd been in several times over the years, but today was different. The five people seated at the table would make a decision that would change her life forever. One woman and four men were in the starkly decorated room, which was well stocked with snacks. She wished the woman was there to support her, but the opposite was true. One of the men was her father, Mark, but *father* wasn't a word she'd use to describe him.

Sharon sat upright against the uncomfortable chair and placed her hands on the table, rather than her lap—her way of exerting confidence she didn't feel. Confidence she never felt around her father and the other people in the room who, ironically, were mostly family.

"Your contract date is almost here," Robert, her uncle, stated. "And you still don't have a suitable person for a husband."

"You're not even dating," Virginia, her aunt, added snidely. "You should give the seat to another member."

"Absolutely not!" Mark interjected.

"She has less than six months," another member added. One she knew had someone in mind for the seat.

"I want to petition again to remove the marriage clause of the contract. I believe I've proven myself over the years by bringing more money to this company than anyone else." *Not to mention it's not the 1800s.*

A resounding, "No!" came back from everyone.

"The clause is there to ensure the family bloodline continues," Mark stated. "The only reason your contract time was extended was because of Patrick calling off your engagement. No more extensions and no more talk of removing the marriage clause. You must be married if you want this seat." He gestured to where Virginia sat. "We've already made allowances by making the seat available to you, and not just your husband."

"There's no chance of her finding a husband before the deadline, so we should move forward and vote for a different candidate," Robert pressed again.

"Your idiot son is not a suitable candidate," Mark bellowed.

Robert's and Virginia's face flushed red, but neither responded. Everyone knew they only wanted more control that they could gain through their son having a seat.

"I've been too busy making this company money to find a husband. And all I'm asking is for the same curtesy you'd offer your sons. What is my birthright," Sharon said firmly.

Mark snorted. "If it were up to you, you'd stay single, and we'd lose this seat and our family legacy."

"Don't you mean *my* family legacy, Mark?" She used the name he'd asked her to address him by whenever they were at work. "You married into this family. You weren't born into it."

Where had the courage to say those words come from? Sharon never confronted him in front of others, especially at work.

Mark's face expanded like a puffer fish and Sharon swore the dark, thin strands on his head stood at attention. "I made this company what it is today! None of you had the guts to take the risks I did." He pointed to the other members of the board who were born into the business but had been merely happy to ride on its existing success.

"Then why not take another risk and release me from the marriage clause? I've more than proved that I deserve this seat without it, and it gives me more time to find a husband instead of a contract marriage like the rest of you."

The faces around the table blistered, but no one responded. There were no love marriages in their circle—only marriages of convenience, political, social, and business gain.

"No more extensions. No more changes. Make your match or I'll choose for you," Mark offered.

"No!" Sharon wasn't about to give away her right to decide. Mark's choice would be to his advantage and not hers. If she were forced to marry, it would be on her terms. If only she hadn't lost Patrick as an option. He was not only a childhood friend, but knew how much being a board member meant to her and would've been a wonderful companion. But he was no longer an option.

"You have three months, Sharon. Miss this deadline and you'll lose everything, including the remaining charities your mother established," her father threatened.

Mark had made threats before, but not like this. The charities her mother established meant everything to her.

He already reduced them after she died. The ironclad wall she put up over the years cracked a little, since the man who caused all the pain throughout her life was someone who was supposed to love and protect her. *Stop the pity party, Sharon!* The thought echoed loudly like a bad tune from her childhood that played every time she tried to express her feelings.

Sharon stood, wishing she could walk out the door and not come back, but she'd worked too hard to get here, and she wasn't about to back down.

"Let us walk you out." Robert and Virginia followed closely behind.

Sharon resisted the urge to roll her eyes. They'd hardly been an ideal aunt and uncle once she turned eighteen and realized she wasn't going to step aside, like her mother, but fight for her seat on the board.

"There's nothing more to say." Sharon headed straight to the elevator and pressed the button, not bothering to turn around to face them.

"You insolent little brat! Don't turn your back on us!" Virginia shouted. She exuded a dislike Sharon had always sensed and never known why.

"Don't be unreasonable, Sharon. This is the way it's always been. Your mother understood that. Why can't you?"

"By giving my seat away to someone who isn't family? Where's the logic in that?" Sharon asked, stepping into the elevator.

Robert and Virginia closed the small space between them, and Robert grabbed her arm. "You'll get to keep your title, the house, money, and charities. What do you care about a seat? A seat you could control with the right husband."

Sharon glanced at Virginia. "I don't want my control that way. I deserve it because I earned it." The calm of her tone was from years of suppressing her reactions.

"Don't speak to your aunt that way." Robert gripped her arm tighter. "Besides, she doesn't control me!"

Sharon remained silent as she watched the anger erupt on both their faces before the elevator door opened onto her floor and Robert abruptly released her arm.

"Think about what we said, or you'll regret it," Virginia taunted before the door closed.

What the hell did Uncle Robert see in her? He was no saint, but Virginia was a snake with legs. Her mother had never tried to defend her brother because she always understood the pressure that came from being part of their family, and only said they deserved each other.

Sharon headed to her office. She had bigger issues to worry about than their threats. She had to find a husband or lose everything she'd loved and worked so hard to build.

Chapter 2

D aniel Stanley knocked on the door again. *So much for a punctual client,* he grumbled, checking his watch. Josie, his friend and occasional business partner, had recommended him to Sharon Donovan for a renovation. He wasn't sure why, since Sharon was once engaged to Josie's fiancé.

Josie mentioned Sharon was a business consultant from a wealthy family and suggested he wear nice clothes. Danny snorted. Jeans and a shirt were good enough for his other clients. Money didn't make her special. Not in his eyes. If she didn't hire him because of what he wore, that was her loss. *"Stop being a stubborn ass!"* Josie's voice scolded. Danny chuckled.

The door opened. In the doorway was a stunning blonde who was assessing him with the sharpest blue eyes he'd ever seen, making him feel like he was back in high school standing before the principal. *Not a good start.*

"Daniel Stanley?"

Danny cringed. Only his father called him by that name, and only when he'd done something wrong. "Danny," he offered. The last thing he needed was a client addressing him so formally the whole time.

Brows furrowed, as if she was deciding to use the alternate name or not.

ELKE FEUER

"Sharon Donovan?" He wanted to make sure he was dealing with the client directly and not pawned off to some assistant.

"Yes. Please come in." She stepped inside and closed the door behind him. "You're not what I expected," Sharon said when she faced him.

You're exactly what I expected. Danny looked around a room that belonged in the pages of *Architectural Design*. Perfect lines and precision, but it lacked a warm human touch. The spaces in her home were as cultured and cold as the living room. Sharon's appearance was the same. Nothing out of place. He bet she could drive in a convertible with the top down and come out looking the same.

"What did you expect? A male version of Josie?" he said with a grin.

Sharon's lips pursed, but it wasn't to hide a smile. "Not exactly."

She didn't expect him to show up in jeans. That was obvious from the once-over she gave him at the door. *Is she regretting letting me inside?* While a job from her prestigious family name would beef up his business, he wasn't desperate. Business would be fine with or without Miss Snooty Pants. *"Don't be such a snob!"* A twinge of guilt stabbed him for making assumptions about Sharon, the way she appeared to be making about him.

Sharon led him through the home until they reached a bathroom, the room she wanted renovated. He hadn't known what to expect with Sharon. The voice on the phone was soft with a sexy edge, even with the professional tone.

Two doors led from the bathroom. One to what appeared to be a closet and the other to her bedroom. Everything

8

looked great to him already, but what did he know?
Rich people were always renovating their already-fabulous
homes. "What changes did you have in mind?"

"The separate rooms feel disjointed. I want them to flow
into each other organically between the closet and the
bathroom, and I also want to expand the closet."

Danny peeked inside her closet. It was bigger than his
first apartment. Any bigger and it'd take up the entire
bathroom space, which was enormous too. He listened as
she continued explaining what she wanted. *Does she plan
to have a designer involved?* Based on her comments, he
suspected she'd do the designing herself.

"What do you think?"

"Do you have a timeline in mind?" Danny asked as he
finished jotting down notes about the changes she wanted.
He snapped a few pictures with his phone.

"Before Christmas. I'm hosting a party and want the
changes done in time."

Christmas was three months away. *Is she going to host
the party in her closet?* "I'll need the house plans to see
where expansions can be made, but it's possible." He didn't
ask the undecided question hanging in the air. Was he hired,
or merely one of the contractors she was considering?

Sharon circled the bathroom, as if deciding if she wanted
more changes. "The plans are on the kitchen table, but I
want them back in two days. That should give you enough
time to get the information you need to prepare a quote. You
can drop them by my office." She headed to the kitchen.

Danny didn't bother pointing out that two days from now
was a Saturday, suspecting she planned her days down to
the millisecond. The plans were placed in his hands, along

with her business card. He pulled a card from his back pocket and handed it to her. She plucked it carefully from his fingers, as if touching him would be distasteful. He checked his fingernails. They were clean. Ms. Donovan was a piece of work, and he was certain she was going to be the biggest pain-in-the-ass client he'd ever had. "I'll be in touch," he stated.

Sharon followed him to the door, but he didn't glance back until he got in his car. A quick look at the front door confirmed she still stood in the doorway, watching him. Danny didn't know whether to be annoyed or flattered that she watched him leave.

Sharon's family were from old money, like her ex-fiancé Patrick Pullman, which explained why she was guarded, and borderline rude. Patrick had turned out to be a nice guy, once he realized he wasn't romantically involved with Josie. Maybe Sharon wouldn't be a bad client after all. However, he'd been wrong before.

Daniel-Danny was wrong in believing she expected a male version of Josie. The truth was, she knew everything about him. No one came into her home and worked for her without getting their business and background checked. What surprised her was his age. It was in his file, but those weren't details she concerned herself with. Another surprise was how attractive he was. Not heart-stopping exactly, but he was tall, lean, and nice to look at, even though he needed a haircut.

Most men found her attractive and didn't hesitate to ogle her, but Danny hadn't taken that opportunity. He appreciated her face, but his glance hadn't explored any further, even when she wasn't looking—she was certain of it. He wasn't gay. The way he studied her face said so. He didn't flinch when she asked him to drop the plans off at her office on a Saturday, nor did he inquire about her company or change his facial expression when he read the title on her business card. Most people commented on the fact she was CEO, whether it was asking a question or assuming it was her family's business. That alone was enough to make Daniel Stanley intriguing.

When Josie recommended him, Sharon suspected it might be to set her up, but his reaction said either he wasn't interested...or didn't suspect Josie's intention. While on paper he might be a somewhat suitable candidate, his in-person appearance was another matter. Not that he didn't look good in jeans, but he had a rough edge about him that said he wouldn't be caught dead at cocktail dinners, or attend a ballet performance.

Seeing Patrick and Josie together last year gave her the closure she hadn't realized she needed. It also made it painfully obvious she needed to move on and that she desired what they had: romance with spark.

She loved him, but it was always missing something. Something he knew right away. Something she hadn't realized until she saw the way he watched Josie with raw passion and a deep affection and love. The moment she saw it between them, she desired it for herself.

Getting it was another matter. The men in her circle, and her parents' circle, didn't fit the bill. No one had. But the tingle at the base of her spine when Daniel stood in her doorway was promising, and the most emotion she'd experienced in a long time. She grinned, remembering the grimace on his face at being called Daniel. While he did look more like a *Danny*, she suspected calling him by his real name would be more fun.

She'd hire him no matter what price he came back with.

Chapter 3

D anny glanced at the envelope containing his quote and Sharon's house plans, wishing he was the type to use a messenger for deliveries. Enduring another moment of Sharon's snooty glare made his stomach turn. If she did choose his company, at least she wouldn't be home while he was working.

Why did her condescending stares bother him? He knew why. Bad memories. Danny took a U-turn from where his thoughts were headed. Sharon was just another client, and this job would be over before Christmas.

Sharon's smile greeted him as her assistant ushered Danny into her office. She had a beautiful smile, even if it appeared fake. Danny had glanced around when he reached the area the receptionist said was Sharon's office. Behind the desk was a young man. The sign on the door with Sharon's name and title told him was in the right place.

The urge to laugh tickled his chest. She had a male assistant. Why wasn't he surprised? Danny introduced himself and tried to leave the drawings with him, but he insisted Sharon wanted to speak with him first. *Damn!* Danny nodded and entered the office. Like her home, her office was sterile and painfully modern. Danny took the seat she offered. There was the token family photo on the glass shelf behind her, but the only inkling of her were the business awards and framed photos of her with who he assumed were important businesspeople.

"Thanks for getting back to me so quickly."

"All part of the service." Danny grinned.

Sharon's eyes raked over his face before taking the envelope from his hand. She sat and opened it.

Danny expected her to flinch at the price, rich or not. She didn't.

"Can you start on Monday?" Sharon asked, not looking at him.

"Sure."

Her gaze met his. "Great!" Sharon reached into her desk drawer and pulled out a set of keys and placed them before him. "I leave for work at 8:00. I'll turn off the alarm so you can get in. See you on Monday."

Danny glanced at the keys.

"Is there a problem?" Sharon's sharp blue gaze searched his face.

Danny grabbed the keys. "No problem. You know where to find me if I try to steal something," he joked.

Sharon didn't laugh. Not that he expected her to. She didn't even crack a smile. *Tough audience.*

Danny stood.

"I'll expect daily updates on your progress." Her gaze remained on the paperwork before her.

Danny gritted his teeth. So much for the common curtesy of eye contact. He headed toward the door.

"Mr. Stanley."

Danny turned.

"Thank you." A slight smile curved the edges of her mouth, softening the roughness of her pale face.

He nodded before leaving.

Well, that was unexpected. Danny headed to the elevator. The soft tone of her voice and the brief flash of vulnerability in her eyes followed him down the hallway, and left him pondering about Sharon's thank you and the keys in his hand. He hit the elevator button. *Get a grip, Danny!*

A man's frame nudged him when the door opened. "Watch it," the man hissed. "You bumped into me."

Judging eyes raked over Danny's attire. "You were in my way."

The man stormed off before Danny could respond, leaving him to glance at the back of an expensive-looking suit. "Jackass," Danny grumbled. The man strode into Sharon's office and closed the door. *Figures. Is he a coworker, or something more?*

Danny punched the L button in the elevator and tried to tune out the horrible music on the ride down.

Chapter 4

———◆———

"Come in, Carlton." Sharon called as politely as she could muster. "It's all right, Ryan," she assured her assistant, who followed closely on his heels.

"What can I do for you?" She gestured for him to take a seat. He sat on the couch on the other side of the room.

"Give me the Janson deal," he said casually, as if asking for one of her pens and not the biggest deal she was in the middle closing.

"If you found your own clients, you wouldn't need mine."

"I find clients."

Sharon raised an eyebrow. Most of the clients he attracted weren't worth a second glance.

"You've been in this business longer. You know more people." Carlton pouted.

Sharon pushed her chair away from the desk and stood. "I look for clients, not expect them to fall into my lap."

Carlton was guaranteed a seat on the board when he turned twenty-five. Sharon gritted her teeth to keep from seething with anger and frustration. He wasn't stupid, but certainly not Board of Director material, in her opinion. She'd already made the company millions and was responsible for two teams by the time she reached his age. He was the product of Robert and Virginia, spoiled and entitled. Sharon had the misfortune of calling him *cousin*.

"I–I need your help," Carlton stammered.

What trouble has he gotten himself into now?

"My father is threatening to extend the age at which I can take a seat on the board."

"Why?" Sharon asked, although her mind churned with questions given the encounter with his parents who clearly wanted him to take his seat sooner rather than later. Maybe Dan had come to his senses and realized Carlton wasn't ready. But why give up the control he'd have with Carlton on the board?

"He feels I haven't earned it," he mumbled, raking a hand through his sandy colored hair.

Sharon knew Robert and Mark were disappointed with Carlton's performance. Sharon had tried to assure her father that Carlton was young and needed more time, but he barked back all the accomplishments she'd achieved by his age. The only time he acknowledged them. Carlton annoyed her, but she felt sorry for him for the pressure being put on him by the men in the family. Taking this drastic step surprised even her. "How can I help?"

"You know more about the contractual requirement for a seat on the board. Can he really do that?"

Sharon smiled. "Yes, he can."

"What about Uncle Mark?"

"Unfortunately, his decision–making is limited when it comes to you." *Not to mention he thinks you're an idiot.* "You should have a lawyer look at the contract to know exactly what it says and what options you have." *If any.*

"Is that what you did?"

"My situation is different."

"But you have a seat already, don't you?"

Sharon sat next to him on the couch. "No, not until I'm married. And I must do so before the end of this year, otherwise I lose my seat on the board." She neglected to add, "...and everything else."

"Harsh."

Sharon adjusted her jacket. "See how easy you have it?"

"I suppose."

"Take my advice about the lawyer. Ask Bradley, he's been with the firm a long time and might be able to shed some light. My father likes and trusts him. Maybe Bradley can change his mind."

Carlton contemplated her words.

"Maybe you can find something else in the company you enjoy, and are better at?" Sharon suggested.

Carlton's jawline jumped.

"I'm done trying to make you feel bad, and if you found something you exceled in, it might change Robert's mind."

"I thought if I were like him...and you."

Sharon rested a hand on his. "You're not like us. You're you. Be yourself. Trust me on this one."

From his expression, Sharon couldn't tell if he understood her meaning or if he chose to ignore her.

He stood. "Thanks for the advice."

"Good luck."

Carlton left her office quieter than he entered.

What was Dan up to? Was he simply trying to scare Carlton straight, or was there something more to the threat?

Chapter 5

"Your father is on his way to your office. Bradley Rumson's with him," Ryan announced when she answered the phone.

Sharon glanced at her watch. Not enough time for her and Ryan to concoct an "unexpected meeting" excuse. Her father and Bradley would be waiting for her at the doorway. She organized the papers and folders on her desk and stacked them to one side.

The knock came moments later. Mark and Bradley strolled in when she answered, their frames and egos eating up the space in her office.

"We have something important to discuss with you," Mark stated.

Sharon adjusted her jacket. "Please have a seat," she said, gesturing to the chairs in front of her desk. Was her father thinking of having them work together again? God help her. Bradley was nice enough, but not her favorite person to work with. His ego wasn't as big as most men in the office, but not by much.

"I want Bradley to work with you on the Janson merger."

"May I ask why?"

"He's better suited to handle the legal aspects."

Sharon relaxed. Bradley had been hired for being a good lawyer, not for closing deals, but with her father, she never knew his true intensions.

This wasn't the first time her father made this move, but thankfully Bradley was only handling the legal side of things. Mark claimed she had to play the game if she wanted more men in the company to respect her and not feel intimated by her. Ironically, her father intimated people all the time.

"I'm happy to work with Bradley, but I don't want this deal falling apart with wasted time bringing someone up to speed."

"I'm a fast learner," Bradley interjected.

"I'm sure you are, but this is an important and time–sensitive deal. The next team meeting is Monday at 9:00 a.m." Sharon pressed a button on the phone.

"Yes, Ms. Donovan?" Ryan answered.

"See that Mr. Rumson gets a copy of everything pertaining to the Janson deal by lunchtime."

There was a short pause. "Right away, Ms. Donovan."

She hung up the phone. "Was there anything else? I have a full schedule today." Sharon glanced between the two men.

"How about dinner on Saturday night to review the plan of attack?" Mark added.

"Of course."

Mark turned to Bradley. "Join us. I'll leave it to you to make the arrangements."

Shrewd, Father—very shrewd. Another attempt to set her up on a date. "Can I speak with you alone for a moment?"

Bradley took the hint. "I'll send Ryan details about dinner."

Sharon tipped her head and waited until the door closed before speaking.

"Why do you keep doing this?" Sharon said bluntly.

"Doing what?" Mark asked, clearly miffed.

"Undermining my authority by taking away deals I start or trying to set me up with every man in Chicago."

"Not every man."

Sharon rolled her eyes. "You didn't answer my question."

Mark sat on the couch, obviously expecting her to join him. She remained behind her desk. He shifted his tall, thick frame until he found a comfortable position. "I'm just trying to help you."

Sharon pushed the chair away from the desk and stood. "Would you help another employee in your company, or would you expect them to do their job?"

His winkled face studied Sharon. "You're not another employee."

"Exactly. I'm the CEO and I didn't get this position just because I'm your daughter, but the Board of Directors will think so if you keep sending men to seemingly bail me out, especially when I don't need them."

"They're not there to bail you out."

"You're right. The men you assign to my projects think they're there to run things and I'm just a pretty face and your daughter. It completely undermines my authority with them and the rest of the office, and causes me nothing but trouble with clients. And when you schedule dates, you're doing nothing but implying I'm part of the deal, like you're pimping me out."

Mark's face turned bright red. "I'm not pimping you out!"

"You don't think so, but that's the impression the men have."

"This is the way business is done."

"Maybe in your day, Father, but things have changed." The number of rules he'd enforced on her as a child was crushing, or so she thought until she started working for him. His expectations of women in the workplace were downright archaic, and playing along was exhausting.

Sharon did it to please her mother, before she died years ago, and then to keep her father happy, but she was fed up. Trying to please him had sucked enough life out of her. She'd lost herself and Patrick because of it. She wouldn't lose anything else.

"I'm just trying to help. Your deadline is approaching."

That got her thinking about Carlton's visit. "Did you know Dan's thinking of changing Carlton's contract?"

"How did you..."

"He told me. Was looking for advice." Did her father have something to do with it? But how? He didn't have that kind of control over Dan and Virginia. Or did he?

Mark snorted. "Advice my ass. Worry more about your own contract, Sharon."

Sharon cringed at his harsh tone. When she found out about the clause to claim her seat on the company's board on her eighteenth birthday, she thought it was a bad joke. She should've known better—Mark did not have a sense of humor. Not when it came to business or family.

"You haven't pursued another relationship since Patrick, and you don't like the men I introduce you to."

Introduce? You mean shove down my throat. "I don't like the situation."

"I know you don't, but it's the only way to ensure our company's and family's legacy."

Sharon wanted to be part of her family's legacy, but the circumstances were ridiculous.

"Bradley is a good candidate."

Sharon cringed internally but knew he was right. While Bradley wouldn't be easily controlled, he might be open to an arrangement if the price were right. "Yes, he is."

Mark's face brightened as he smiled, providing a glimpse of the younger man he once was, before his tall frame gained extra weight and his smooth face winkled from time and the stress. A few of those lines were thanks to her.

"Don't worry about your usual excuses for missing dinner. I'll go to dinner alone with Bradley and scope him out for myself."

Mark stood. "Good. You've never shied away from a challenge, and I know you'll rise to this one."

If only I could pry myself away from it, Sharon thought as the door closed. There was no way around it without walking away empty-handed, and she'd worked too hard and sacrificed too much already.

She called Ryan into her office.

When she hired him, it'd been to stand out. Everyone else in the office had a female assistant. The other men in the office gossiped that she wanted another man to boss around, but truthfully, Ryan turned out to be the best candidate. She hired him five years ago, and it was the best decision she'd made.

Ryan strode into her office, a young model straight off the pages of a high-priced men's magazine. The type of man who didn't get his hair cut by a barber and put aside money for manicures.

Younger than she would've liked, but what he lacked in experience, he made up for with dedication, a willingness to learn, and going above and beyond. Ryan's best trait was he didn't mind working for a woman. If it bothered him, he hid it well.

"Please make dinner reservations for me and send an invite to Bradley Rumson." Her father had asked Bradley to make the arrangements, but she wasn't about to give him the upper hand in anything. She might find herself having dinner in a dark secluded corner being pawed at.

Ryan's eyebrow rose, but he jotted down her request.

"And also find out as much as you can about him. Where he went to college, his family, if he or his family has been associated with any type of scandal." Sharon was certain her father had checked into his family, but unlike him, she knew there was more to someone than their family.

Her final statement caught Ryan's attention. "Do you want this information before or after your dinner date?"

"After is fine." Sharon didn't glance up from the computer, too embarrassed to see the expression on Ryan's face. Thankfully, he knew better than to question her requests. Especially when it came to her personal life.

"Anything else?

"That's it for now."

"Oh, I almost forgot." Ryan darted from her office and returned moments later with a package in his hand. "This came for you." He set a long gold box with a big red ribbon on her desk.

"Thanks." Sharon sat down and started working on her computer.

"Are you going to open them?" Ryan asked when he paused at her office door.

"Not right now." He was hovering because he wanted to see who the flowers were from, which means the card envelope was either sealed or inside the box.

"You sure?" Ryan prodded, a grin spreading across his face.

Sharon glared at him. "Don't you have work to do?"

"Of course, Ms. Donovan."

Guilt pinched her when the door closed. Ryan never asked about her personal life, but he did have an occasional peek inside when she had dinner or lunch dates, and he knew about her broken engagement with Patrick, and that she'd had no second dates since then. Ryan's interest in the flowers was likely curiosity and the hope that she'd found someone new.

Sharon snuck a peek at the large gold box. The size and quality of the box said *expensive*, piquing her interest. Grabbing the box, she looked for a card. There was none. She tugged on the bow, her pulse thumping in excitement as it unraveled. *Are they from Daniel? No! Too expensive looking. Probably from a client.* Sharon lifted the lid, but it fell from her hands.

Inside were black roses, but not the fashionable kind. These roses were dead on purpose. *Who the hell sent me dead flowers?* Her conversation with Dan and Viginia and her threat came to mind. Was it them? Sharon couldn't see Dan being so petty, so it had to be Virginia.

She yanked the box closer and searched through the dead leaves for a card. Nothing. A chill raced up her back. She suppressed it. If they planned to scare her, they'd have to do better than that.

"Who delivered the flowers, Ryan?"

"I don't know. They were on my desk when I returned from the file room."

Just as she suspected. A delivery service would've wanted a signature confirming the package was received. Sharon grabbed the box and stormed out of her office. She dropped the box on Ryan's desk. "Please throw these away."

Sharon didn't wait around for Ryan's response and returned to her office. She had better things to do. A deal needed closing and she had home renovations to oversee.

A groan escaped when she remembered her pending date with Bradley, hoping he'd have enough manners not to grope her. He'd never made gestures before, but then they'd never been to dinner together. *Alone.* Sharon made a mental note to meet him at the restaurant so she could drive herself home if things ended badly. Not a good start for the man she was considering as a future husband.

Chapter 6

T he alarm was turned off as Sharon promised when Danny arrived at her house. The place seemed eerie without her there. The urge to explore her home without prying eyes pricked him. Did she have a home office, or somewhere else she enjoyed her time alone? *That's not creepy at all, Danny.*

"Hello? Where is everyone?" A woman's voice called from the front door. "Is it safe to come in?"

Danny grinned as he headed to the woman's voice. "I hope you bought coffee?" Coffee was the fine for a foreman who showed up late. Laura was someone he hired to help after Patrick's renovation opened the door to more clients.

Laura lifted the containers in her hand, chockful of coffee cups. She technically wasn't late, but because Danny always arrived on site before anyone else, especially with a new job, Laura took it upon herself to bring coffee. It made her a hit with the crew.

Danny grabbed the one with his name on it. "What? No muffins?" he teased.

She snorted. "I'm not Josie. Besides, you'd probably break a tooth on mine."

Danny laughed. He was hesitant to hire Laura, not sure how the guys would handle it. They'd worked with Josie, but she was a restoration architect and they'd worked together as a team. Laura had put them at ease from the first day and fit in with no problems. After working with Josie, he found women brought something different to a site. It was something he needed when working with high-end clients.

Danny led Laura through the house to the space being renovated, filling her in on the rules of the house. Sharon hadn't laid them out, but he knew the drill and believed in leaving the home clean and clear.

"Sounds like the typical client," Laura said, glancing around the space, her eyes resting on the exorbitant amount of shoes. Danny wondered if she was thinking the same or wishing she had them for herself.

Sharon had moved all her things out of the closest, including all the drawers, which lay open and empty. The bathroom counters and all the cabinets and drawers were also bare. The only thing that remained was the furniture, so that would save them time. Minutes later, the rest of the crew streamed in, hauling plastic and other prep material. After the crew prepared the space, they got to work removing bathroom fixtures and knocking out walls. By lunchtime the space was bare and ready for them to start the next round.

Danny was sitting on the outside steps eating his lunch when a BMW pulled into the driveway. Shoving plastic containers into his icebox, he stood just as Sharon reached him.

"I didn't expect to see you until this afternoon."

Sharon strode past him. "I was excited to see the changes."

You mean, checking up on me. Danny followed her inside.

Sharon's sharp gaze shifted about the room, but her expression remained solemn, making it impossible for him to tell if she liked what she saw. She hadn't said a word or commented on the layers of plastic hanging from the bedroom door.

Everything in her closet, bathroom, and bedroom had been removed, except the large pieces of furniture.

"What do you think?" Danny asked, hating the silence.

"You've made a lot of changes in a short time."

"You made it easy, and it's a fairly simple job."

Sharon nodded and headed back to the living room. Danny followed.

"I didn't mean to interrupt your lunch," she said quietly.

Danny shrugged. "I was almost finished."

She strolled behind the large onyx granite countertop. "How many guys are working with you?"

"Just two, and Laura, for now. I'll add another if I need to, but I think that's enough. The fewer people parading through your home, the better," Danny joked.

"Laura?"

"Yes, she's part of my team."

"A-a woman?" Sharon stuttered.

Danny grinned. "They do exist."

"I know, it's just…"

"You didn't expect me to have one."

Sharon's gaze combed over his face, as if seeing him with new eyes. Danny didn't know whether to be pleased or terrified.

"Good for you," she said before grabbing a bottle of water from the fridge, giving Danny a glimpse inside. The only thing inside was bottled water and neatly stacked containers of food. No doubt perfectly prepared and portioned.

Are her cupboards bare, or do they have neatly stacked spices and condiments no one has ever heard of, and that have never been opened?

"I don't cook," Sharon offered as she twisted the top off the water bottle and took a long, deep drink.

"I didn't think so."

"Why not?" Sharon asked, clearly offended.

"Because you're a busy successful businesswoman. And you don't have a family, so why cook?" Danny offered.

Sharon's harsh gaze softened. "I bet you cook."

Danny chuckled. "That's because I can't afford to have food delivered to my house. But if I could, I'd do it in a heartbeat."

A small smile tugged at her lips. "I figured a guy like you had a girlfriend cooking for him."

Danny's smile vanished. "A guy like me?" *What the hell does she mean by that?* Old memories pinched him.

"Attractive..."

She thinks I'm attractive? If Danny didn't know better, he'd suspect Sharon was flirting with him. It was then he noticed her eyes roaming over him from head to toe before settling on his lips. Excitement shot up his spine at the intensity of her gaze.

Something sparkled in her eyes when their locked. If he knew her better, he could name it, but she was so guarded he wasn't certain if the look was the urge to kiss him or just curiosity. Whatever it was, the air in the kitchen sizzled.

"Hey, boss." Laura's voice sliced through their moment.

Danny cleared his throat and the fog in his head.

"The infamous Laura," Sharon said.

Laura's gaze shifted between him and Sharon.

"Don't worry. Only good stuff," Sharon assured her.

Laura grinned and gave Danny a cutting glance. "He'd better."

Sharon studied them both, making Danny wonder what thoughts churned in that head of hers. It was better he didn't know.

"I look forward to seeing the rest of the renovations when I come home tonight." Sharon gave a polite smile.

Danny nodded.

"Did I interrupt something?" Laura asked when they heard the front door close. She wiggled her eyebrows.

Danny rolled his eyes. "Get back to work." He shoved Laura out of the kitchen. Her teasing was worse than the guys'.

When Sharon came home, he'd be gone. Danny hoped her popping home during the day wasn't going to be a regular thing. Seeing her was nice, but the last thing he wanted was a client hovering over his shoulders. He preferred meeting with them at the end of the day with a quick update. Sharon rattled him. He'd been rattled before—he didn't like it.

Danny cringed at how stupid he sounded. He'd just met her, for Christ's sake. She was beautiful and had a sex appeal he hadn't expected, so of course there was friction. *You're a grown man, Danny. Once you're around her more, you'll realize she's just another rich client who wouldn't dream of mingling with hired help.* Her icy smile and stiff posture said she didn't know how to have fun. The image of her gazing at his lips flashed in his mind, and he longed to know her thoughts at that moment.

What the hell were you thinking? Sharon scolded herself as she drove back to the office. Hiring him was a bad idea. She should've known from the moment he sent tingles through her. While she enjoyed them immensely, the source was the problem. She didn't like mixing business with pleasure. *What pleasure, Sharon? The only thing you've been up to lately is business. Even the dates you choose are business related, and the results remain the same. No spark, not even a blip of attraction.* They were good–looking, successful men, but being around them was like being in a business meeting with a coworker. They were dull, or so full of themselves trying to impress her.

Sharon had tried to give them the benefit of the doubt, knowing how challenging it was to be yourself in a business world where it was kill or be killed, but no one let their guard down. She couldn't blame them, since her own wall remained. Too many years of keeping it up.

When she saw Patrick—or *Paddy* as she'd affectionately called him since childhood—the night of his parent's annual fundraiser, she got the closure she didn't realized she needed. She'd been hurt when Patrick broke off their engagement, but it hadn't devastated her. That spoke volumes about their future together. She'd thought a marriage like her parents was a good idea, but Patrick wanted more. He said they both deserved more. She never imagined ever wanting anything profound, but when she saw the loving way Patrick gazed at Josie, she realized she wanted it for herself. Getting it was another matter.

If only Danny was someone else. It wasn't just his profession. She needed someone to fit into her circle of friends, business, and family, and unfortunately Danny wasn't that man. Middle class was written all over him, and that wouldn't matter if he was cultured and dressed nicely.

Taking him to a family event might prove entertaining, but work? Not so much. She wanted to be taken seriously when she gained a seat on the Board of Directors. Bringing someone like Danny into her world wouldn't get her there any faster. While her attraction to Danny was a nice distraction, it was one she couldn't afford.

She'd called him attractive, and to his face. Would those words come back to haunt her? Danny seemed genuinely surprised. Was it because he didn't think he was attractive, or because she thought he was? It didn't matter.

The lunchtime visit was because she didn't like people in her personal space, and wanted to make sure everything was going well. From now on she'd stick to seeing the progress after she got home from work. Especially when words like *attractive* and other inquisitive comments to find out whether he was dating or not came out of her mouth. Keeping their relationship professional was a must, especially when he had such kissable-looking lips.

Chapter 7

Another blind date. Danny forced a smile for the woman across the table from him. How the hell did he get roped into them? *'Cause you love your mom.* The voice was right—and the only reason he continued to say yes—but she had no clue what kind of women he liked. That was obvious from the dates she found for him. The last one had spent the entire time on her phone, taking photos of every drink and plate served, including taking a selfie with the waiter.

If taking photos of food and drink was part of her profession, he could've let it go, but she was a teacher. By the end of the night, he expected to have to take a final photo of them in the parking lot next to the restaurant sign and ask to tag him on social media. Her expression was worth the bad date when she learned his only social media account was for his business.

She wasn't just glued to her phone—she hadn't stopped talking since they sat down. Not that he minded listening, but it'd been an hour, and she hadn't asked one question about him. She rambled on about her job and how much she hated it. He longed to suggest quitting, but there was no opportunity to jump in. When the food came, the plate remained untouched as she shared why she'd ordered this dish and all the nutritional benefits. Danny figured there'd be no benefits if she didn't eat it. Not to mention the prices. Danny nearly choked on his beer when he saw that an appetizer was almost twenty dollars. He wasn't cheap, but that was highway robbery.

At least the restaurant she picked was nice. Quaint, with amazing views of Chicago's skyline. Danny was adjusting his jacket coat when his gaze caught a couple walking into the restaurant. *Sharon.* The man with her was as impeccably dressed as she was. Her red dress clung to curves he hadn't seen behind her business attire. Her blond hair, although neat, hung in soft curls around her neck and shoulders. *Damn, she is beautiful.*

The man with her glanced obnoxiously about the room, as if assessing whether the place and the people were worth his time and money. Sharon also glanced around the room and her eyes found him. Danny lifted his glass in greeting. She nodded and checked out the woman with him before giving him a slight smile. The man with her extended his arm as the waiter led them to a table.

"Good evening, Ms. Donovan," Danny said warmly when Sharon paused by his table. Her eyes assessed him with approval, but then he was dressed in something other than jeans and a T-shirt.

"Good evening, Mr. Stanley." Her gaze shifted to his date.

Damn! I can't remember my date's first name. "This is Ms. Grumbly," Danny offered, grateful she'd stopped speaking.

Thankfully she smiled and offered, "Denise."

Sharon had the same reaction he had when he first heard her name. A smile tugged at the corner of her mouth. "Nice to meet you." She gestured toward the man next to her. "This is Bradley Rumson."

"Good to meet you." Danny held out his hand to shake it, but Bradley ignored it. Sharon's cheeks flushed with embarrassment.

"Would you like to join us?" Denise suggested.

"No, we wouldn't want to impose," Sharon countered. Her date's face lit up with horror.

"You won't be imposing. Right, Danny?"

Danny shrugged. "You're more than welcome to join us."

The waiter was pulling out the chair next to Sharon, making the decision for them.

Sharon sat. "Thank you."

Bradley was clearly annoyed, but sat anyway.

The waiter took their drink order, and the silence was painful after he left. Danny was relieved, considering the past hour had been nonstop chatter.

"So how did you guys meet?" Denise chimed in.

"I was handling a case for her father's business," Bradley offered. "I was a corporate lawyer at—" He rattled off the name as if it would mean something to them "—Soon after, her father hired me to work for him."

Danny couldn't help but notice Sharon stiffen at Bradley's words. "How about you two?"

"His mother set us up." Denise then proceeded to tell the entire story of how she'd met Danny's mother and every event leading up to this evening.

"What's your profession?" Bradley interrupted.

"I'm a general contractor." Danny waited for the smirk. *There it is.*

"Danny owns his own business," Denise added. Those were the best words she'd said all night. He could've said them himself, but there'd be no point. Bradley wouldn't give a damn if he owned a chain of construction companies.

"He's renovating my bedroom."

Bradley and Denise glanced at Sharon, and then him. A mischievous twinkle winked at him from the rim of the glass Sharon was drinking from.

The waiter returned and took their food order.

Denise barely spoke a word after Sharon's comment, and Bradley didn't brag once. Danny and Sharon chatted about mundane topics, before and after the food came, pausing occasionally to let their dates chime in. They didn't.

The longer he and Sharon chatted, the longer Danny wondered if Sharon and Bradley were dating or, like him and Denise, on their first date. While Bradley studied him with wary eyes, he didn't appear jealous. Bradley also didn't show any form of affection toward Sharon that normal dating couples shared. Relief trickled through him. Maybe they just weren't the PDA type. It didn't matter. Danny adjusted his jacket and regarded Denise. She might be a chatterbox, but she was his date, if only for tonight.

The waiter placed the check presentation folder on the table and Bradley reached for it. "Let me know what I owe," Danny stated.

Bradley didn't even glance at the check but took out a black credit card, opened the folder, and placed the card inside. "I got this."

Oh, hell no! "Thanks, but I insist." He reached for the folder.

"It's no problem."

"It is for me."

Denise and Sharon's gazes shifted between both men. Sharon grabbed the folder and handed it to Danny.

"Thanks." He glanced at the check and pulled out enough cash to cover his portion.

Bradley didn't touch the cash. Danny gritted his teeth. *Guess the waiter's getting a generous tip.* He longed to ask if his cash wasn't good enough, but Danny suspected that leaving the money was meant to impress Sharon.

The goodbyes were awkward. Everyone gave a polite but cool good night.

Danny drove Denise home. The moment they hit the road, she started chatting again, and this time, Danny listened intently, trying to see past the chatter to the woman underneath. If she included him in the conversation, he could chalk her chatter up to nerves, but when he reached her home and she still hadn't asked him one thing about himself, he knew this was their last date.

She kissed him on the cheek good night and said, "Let's do this again."

Danny didn't want to say, *No chance in hell,* but he didn't want to lie, so let silence be his response. Her disappointment was obvious, but she left without pressing for an answer.

As he drove home, Danny wondered if Sharon's night was faring better than his. She was stunning. In her work attire, with hair under control, she came across as unapproachable. Seeing her tonight in a dress, her hair in soft waves and smiling freely, made her feel more open. That woman was different from the woman he'd interacted with the past couple of weeks. The one he saw at her house

41

was nice enough, but the woman tonight was something else. This woman could drive him to distraction and make him dream about kissing her sweet lips. He'd sleep better knowing the other woman would be the one he'd see on Monday. Danny hoped she'd stay that buttoned-up woman; otherwise, he was in big trouble.

Silence followed her and Bradley to their cars. Although he hadn't complained about meeting at the restaurant instead of picking her up, she could tell it annoyed him.

Sharon didn't care.

The night hadn't gone badly, but he'd been rude and snobbish. Not that she expected more, but part of her had hoped. She was running out of time and didn't want to start over again. Start over? She hadn't even gotten started. No one appealed to her, and that's why she'd hoped Bradley was a smidgen nicer than the other men.

"How about a going for a drink?" Bradley asked when they reached her car.

He didn't say at his place or hers, which made her feel better. Maybe a drink was a good idea since they hadn't gotten a chance to talk at dinner. If she was going to scratch him off her list completely, she'd make sure it was a good decision. "Sure."

"We'll take my car."

Sharon didn't argue and got in when he opened the door.

The bar was intimate, but she didn't mind since she wanted to talk. After they ordered drinks, Bradley loosened his tie and seemed to relax. She did the same by leaning against the cushions of their booth.

"This is much better," Bradley commented, gazing about the room.

"I agree." Bradley was good looking, with his dark hair and striking brown eyes, but he didn't do anything for her. Maybe it was because their only interaction was at work, and her father seemed determined to push them together. That was enough to turn her off.

"You look beautiful tonight. I don't think I remembered to tell you." Bradley's gaze roamed over her in appreciation.

"Thanks. No, you didn't." Sharon smiled. "I suppose you're not used to seeing me like this?" Most of her dresses tended to be conservative.

Bradley grinned. "No, I'm not. I think I forgot because you left me speechless when I saw you."

"No need to lay it on thick."

He laughed. "Okay, but it's true. It took me a minute to recognize you."

Sharon smiled. "I don't always dress this way."

"You should. It suits you."

"Thanks."

His gaze shifted over her breasts before they found her eyes.

Change topics, Sharon. This wasn't the direction she wanted the conversation to go. Although he was looking better by the minute, and she was feeling more comfortable, she didn't want to get off track.

"How long has your family lived in Chicago?"

Their drinks arrived, and Bradley picked up his glass. "I would've thought your father gave you the rundown, since this was his idea."

Sharon grinned. "He did, but I want to hear directly from the source. My father tends to look at everything differently than I do." She reached for her martini.

"That's a good thing."

"I like to think so."

"They moved here when I was a kid. We lived in New York before then."

"New York. Did you adjust quickly, or did it take time?"

He shrugged. "I hated leaving my friends behind, but I made new ones."

Sharon took a sip of her drink and then rested her elbows on the table. "I bet you made friends easily."

"Didn't you?"

"What do you think?"

"I suppose making friends is difficult when your name is on half the buildings," Bradley reflected, as if he understood. "Making jokes made it easier for me."

"Jokes? Ladies don't tell jokes. They laugh politely at the men who do," Sharon answered quickly. She took a long drink from her martini.

"Sounds like something your father would say."

"One of many things," Sharon mumbled.

Bradley adjusted his jacket and position in the booth.

"Carlton came to see me the other day. Said you sent him."

Sharon was relieved he changed the topic. She didn't want to talk about her father. "Yes. Did you come up with a solution?"

"He asked to shadow me."

"Really?" *Carlton must've changed his mind about asking for help with the contract.* Not that she could blame him. Maybe shadowing Bradley would help him find his way. Carlton did seem lost. "What did you say?"

"I was surprised, but I don't see a problem with it. Hopefully it'll help him settle down and find his place in the company."

Sharon looked at Bradley with new eyes. She knew all about presenting one face to the world and having another, especially in their circle of people. Bradley might not be so bad after all. "I'm glad we did this."

Her comment surprised him. "Me too."

Bradley dropped her back at her car after another drink and surprised her by kissing her on the cheek instead of going for more. Another point in his favor. While there was no electricity between them, being around Bradley tonight was more comfortable than any of her other encounters which, in her mind, was promising.

Chapter 8

S haron adjusted her hair once more, making sure every strand was in place. She never wore it down at work. Her father lectured that it was too distracting to the men in the office. The hairbrush hit the bathroom countertop with a *bang. Are they grown men or teenagers with ranging hormones? Why should I change my appearance for them?* She wasn't distracted by the attractive men in the office.

Pushing away from the counter, she headed to the closet. The spare bedroom wasn't nearly as large as the master, but was sufficient until the renovations were finished—although finding her clothes wasn't easy. With little room in the closet, some were laid out on the floor.

Along with expanding her closet, she longed to take every piece of business clothing, throw them in giant garbage bags, and drop them at a homeless shelter or some other organization rather than continue to look at them. She wouldn't, but she'd continue to dream. Funny how she fought her father on so many aspects of her life, yet she couldn't accomplish the simple feat of dressing how she wanted.

Like the other habits and rules her parents had instilled, they were lessons she'd learned the hard way, along with how easily things could go wrong. The possibility of having to choose Bradley as a husband was one of them. After

handling a case for their company, her father had decided
to hire him. Sharon had seen right through her father.
He was a suitable candidate, and her time to replace
Patrick was overdue. Never mind that she thought Bradley
was a pompous arrogant jackass who treated her like his
secretary when they worked together and mansplained
anything she said in meetings. Bradley had been a partner
at his law firm and her father wanted to bring him into
their fold as more than just a business associate.

Sharon cringed with guilt, remembering their recent
date. She hadn't cared how attractive and successful he
was—she didn't like him. People thought she was frigid, but
she enjoyed sex, and attraction was a must. The attraction
with Paddy was good, along with the friendship, and why
she considered their marriage a smart move. Better him
than someone else her father picked out. Although after the
other night, Bradley had moved up a rung on the ladder.
There's no one else, Sharon. After dressing, she headed to
the kitchen. The coffee finished just as Danny arrived.

"Good morning."

The surprise on his face said he hadn't expected to see
her. She usually left the house by eight, but had lingered this
morning. *You wanted to see him, Sharon.*

"Morning."

"Coffee?"

Danny held up a coffee cup.

"Help yourself to whatever's left."

"Thanks."

"Denise seems nice," Sharon said, breaking the awkward
silence hanging in the air.

"Yes."

Danny didn't offer the same words for Bradley, and she couldn't fault him. Nice wasn't a word she'd use to describe Bradley's behavior when they met.

"The food was good."

Sharon smiled. "Yes, it was." *Safe topic.*

"Have you and Bradley been dating long?"

Sharon eyes snapped to his. Well, that was unexpected. Danny spoke his mind, but she never thought he'd ask such a personal question.

"Sorry. It's not my business."

"What about you and Denise?" Sharon countered, wanting him to feel her discomfort from his personal question.

Danny glared back boldly. "We're not. She was a blind date." A smirk tugged at his lips.

Sharon gritted her teeth. She longed to tell him it was none of his business, but the glint in his eyes challenged her.

"We're not dating," she mumbled. *Not exactly.* Although she was seriously considering it, dating wasn't what she'd call what they'd be doing. More like *searching for perspective partners.*

"I didn't think so."

"Then why did you ask?"

Danny shrugged. "Just wanted to see if I was right."

"What made you draw that conclusion?"

"He's too arrogant."

"You mean rich."

Danny disliked Bradley, or at least his arrogance and the way he flaunted his wealth.

"That too."

"Why?"

Brown eyes assessed her as if contemplating his answer. Was he looking for the right words so he didn't offend her?

"People who flaunt their wealth the way they do rarely regard the people around them. At least those who aren't like them."

Cryptic words. "Is that your way of saying your rich clients are difficult to deal with?"

"That's not the word I would use." Danny took a sip of his coffee, his gaze studying her.

"What about me?"

"You know what you want," Danny offered.

Was he saying I'm bossy? "Don't most clients?"

Danny's gaze shifted to her kitchen. "Not always." A pained expression creeped across his face, as if he were attempting to keep it at bay. He failed miserably.

Silence stretched out between them.

Someone hurt him. Was it a woman, or was he burned by a rich business partner? The words to ask tingled in her mind, begging to be spoken. Sharon pursed her lips together to keep silent. Their conversation and encounters were too personal already. Breaching this topic would open a door that shouldn't open.

"Clients aren't the only ones who give problems." Many people had trampled over her over the years. "Boundaries are necessary. No matter who you are." The words came out harsher than she meant.

Danny's brows narrowed, and his spine stiffened.

He thought she was talking about him. Before she could correct his misunderstanding, he interjected.

"You're right. Boundaries are important. Especially when you have a working relationship."

Sharon contemplated clarifying her statement, but the rest of the crew burst through the door. Their chatter stopped when they saw her.

"I was just leaving." Sharon grabbed her keys and headed out the door, the weight of her conversation with Danny pressing down on her. She should've left the house at her regular time. She intended to return to her usual routine tomorrow. The sooner the better.

Danny cursed silently when Sharon left. How had their conversation gotten off course?

He'd missed her car in the driveway, his mind focused on the day ahead and his head buried in his cellphone. The change in conversation, and his personal question, was a bad way to start the week, and a worse way to keep the peace while working on her home. The last thing they needed was an awkward situation. It'd happened to him before when he spoke his mind. In that case, he lost a client and a chunk of money he couldn't afford to lose.

Sharon was nothing like his other client, but he didn't know her. People had a way of hiding their true selves, a lesson he learned the hard way.

From today, he'd keep their relationship professional. She'd said as much with her boundaries comment. She didn't like people prying into her personal life. The way her lips tightened when he asked the question said as much. While no one in her family was in office, they were just as powerful, since they had political connections... Like Patrick's family.

She and Bradley weren't dating. Hearing the words sent an unexpected ripple of relief through him. Sharon was out of his reach in so many ways. *Stop dwelling, Danny!*

Talking about Bradley and her wealth made her as uncomfortable as him. Was it because of his comment, or for another reason? From the looks of her home and the way she lived, she was comfortable with her wealth, and while she didn't flaunt it obnoxiously—like Bradley—she enjoyed the spoils. *Was she burned by someone?* Danny had been so caught up in his own memories of the past, he hadn't considered her comment from that perspective. It didn't matter now. Their interactions going forward would be strictly business. He'd make sure of it.

The day raced by, and before Danny knew it, the crew was saying goodbye. He checked his watch and the task in front of him. Sharon would be home soon, and they hadn't planned to review the renovations today, so he didn't want to be here when she got home. The less they ran into each other, the better. Danny finished up and was clearing a few things out of the way when he heard the front door open. *Shit!* He could try to sneak around the kitchen and avoid her, but that seemed juvenile.

The sight that greeted him took him by surprise. The top buttons of her blouse were undone, and her jacket lay on a barstool. She was removing the pins from her hair and her eyes were closed as she raked her fingers through the locks, a sexy smile on her lips. The private moment was so exotic that Danny couldn't pry his eyes away. His gaze was still locked on her when her eyes opened. She was startled, but didn't shift her eyes from him. A charge jolted between them as they continued to watch each other, their eyes roaming over the other from head to toe until their eyes met again.

The ring of his phone pierced their moment. Danny scrambled to remove his phone from his pants pocket. "H–hello," he stammered. "Hey, Mom. Umm, I'm still at work."

Sharon's attention shifted to the mail.

"Sure, I can stop by for dinner." He checked his watch. It was almost 6:00.

"No, I'm not going out with her again." The heat from Sharon's gaze burned him. "We'll talk about it when I get there." Danny didn't want to talk about his date in front of Sharon. "Mom, I'm here with a client." Danny gritted his teeth at his mother's questions. "Yes, it's a woman." He shifted the phone from one ear to the other, wishing he could leave. "Yes, she's attractive. No, I'm not going to ask her out. Mom. I'm hanging up now." Danny punched the End button, cutting off his mother's questions. He shouldn't have answered the phone.

"Do you always hang up on your mother?" Sharon said with a grin.

"Only when she's grilling me in front of a client. I'll apologize when I see her."

Sharon's eyes softened, keeping them locked on him.

Danny cleared his throat. "Would you like to see the progress we made today?"

She chewed her bottom lip, contemplating her response. An incredibly sexy gesture he wanted to enjoy himself.

"Tomorrow is fine. You don't want to keep your mother waiting."

Danny started to say she could wait, but staying alone with her was a bad idea, especially seeing her nibble that lip. "Sounds good. Night, Ms. Donovan."

"Sharon."

"Sharon," Danny repeated, smiling.

Danny strode out as quickly as his legs would carry him.

Chapter 9

"**M**om?" Danny called after entering his family home. "Dad?"

"We're in the kitchen."

Danny grinned. His mother's favorite place to be. He kissed her on the cheek when he reached the kitchen. She graced him with a smile, a smile their father, John, stated still melted his heart. They'd been married forty years and still glanced at each other like newlyweds.

"What's for dinner?" Danny asked.

"Meatloaf."

"I came all the way out here for meatloaf?" Danny mocked. It was his favorite.

"You'll eat it and love it 'cause I made it."

"Your mother has spoken," John stated.

"You always take her side."

"And so he should. He knows his place."

"She's the boss."

"I thought you were the boss. The man of the house."

"I am, when it matters. But she cooks my food, remember?"

Rose pointed at her husband with a spoon. "And don't you forget it."

It was a running joke that if Rose didn't get her way, she'd stop cooking, or worse, put something nasty in the food.

"I've suddenly lost my appetite." Danny slumped on the barstool next to his father.

Rose hit Danny playfully with the dishrag before returning it to her shoulder. "Tell me about your date with Denise and why you're not going out with her again. She's such a lovely girl."

"She is, but she never stopped talking."

"You're a good listener."

"She didn't ask one question about me."

"That's because I told her everything."

"I'm sure you didn't tell her everything."

"Just think, son—you'd never have to speak again. No probing questions about your day or what you're thinking. Sounds like a good deal to me."

"Then maybe you should date her," Rose threw at him.

John shook his head. "I'm taken."

"And don't you forget it."

"Never."

A knowing glance passed between them, one he'd grown to understand and want for himself over the years.

"What about your new client?"

"She's a client," Danny said a little too quickly. His parents picked up on it.

"How long is this job?" his father asked.

"She's not suitable."

"Why not? You said she was attractive, and your jobs never last that long. In fact, that Pullman house was your longest job. The perk of doing renovations instead of building homes."

"She's not my type."

"I doubt that. If she wasn't, you would've said that first."

"What's her name?" Rose asked.

"Oh, no. I won't have you googling her and calling her up."

"I wasn't going to do that!"

John gave his wife a sideways glance.

"Not tonight," she clarified.

Danny and his father laughed.

"Trust me when I say she's not suitable. She's very wealthy and the men she dates are equally rich."

"How do you know who she dates?"

Shit. You should've kept your mouth shut, Danny. "She was on a date at the same restaurant I took Denise to." He tried to sound casual but failed.

"I see."

His mother did see and wouldn't let it go.

"What happened?"

"Denise invited them to sit with us."

"That must've been interesting..." John said.

"Not really."

"Why?"

"It was uncomfortable. We don't know each other, and her date was an obnoxious prick."

"Really?" his mother asked with a raised eyebrow.

"Yeah. Can you believe he wanted to pay for the whole bill?"

"Sounds like a nice guy."

Danny snorted. "He was an arrogant jerk who was just trying to impress Shar... Us."

"Did he?"

"Did he what?"

"Impress Shar."

"Her name is Sharon, and no, she wasn't impressed. Why should she be? She's got her own money."

"I guess that's good news for you then," John interjected.

"Why?"

"It means she's not influenced by money."

Danny snorted. "I couldn't care what influences her." *Liar.* "Can we drop the topic? No more blind dates, Mom. I mean it! I'll find my own dates from now on."

"Whatever you say, son." She turned her attention back to the stove. "Dinner's ready."

"Good. More eating and less talking."

His parents grinned and Danny rolled his eyes. If it were up to them, he'd be married off to Denise and expecting their first child before Valentine's Day. He knew they meant well, but he could do without their matchmaking.

Danny and John set the table. Danny made himself a plate and sat at the table. John made his wife a plate while she cleared up the kitchen and set it next to his seat. He kissed her and took his own seat.

As he watched his parents, he realized he longed for the respect, love, and support they shared in their relationship. His friend and occasional business partner, Josie, had found love, and he couldn't be happier for her, and he hadn't envied them. Until now. Seeing his parents share a knowing smile and laughter stirred something inside him. That kind of love wasn't easy to find, but he wanted it.

Maybe that was the reason he'd stayed single for so many years and never connected with other women on that level. He hadn't found what he was searching for. A kindred soul. There was one once, but he'd been wrong. Horribly wrong. Danny never told his parents about Teri. He had wanted to surprise them, but the only person who was surprised and grossly disappointed was him.

When Danny left his parents' house later that evening, his mother urged him again to consider asking Sharon out. He smiled and hugged her, but there was no chance in hell of that. He couldn't deny the attraction between them, but the last thing he wanted was another relationship like Teri, or worse, finding out she wasn't interested. Too heavy of a dose of humiliation for him.

Chapter 10

S haron checked her watch again. She should've left twenty minutes ago, but she was hanging around to run into Danny. *This is becoming a bad habit, Sharon,* her father's voice scolded. Bad habits were weaknesses to him.

Hanging around to catch a glimpse of Danny wasn't a bad habit; trying to form a relationship with him was. Not a habit exactly, but a bad idea. She grabbed the keys from the kitchen counter and headed toward the door. She cursed and returned to the kitchen when realized she hadn't made coffee. The ritual green juice she made before taking a shower was consumed, but she'd forgotten the cup of coffee she drank on the drive to work. The coffee was brewing, and its wonderful smell was wafting its way through the house when Danny walked in. He always arrived before the rest of his crew, including Laura. Laura was nice, and Sharon suspected she liked Danny. He was oblivious to the way Laura watched him. Was his lack of interest because of their working relationship, or because he didn't find her attractive? Sharon snorted. Their employee–boss relationship had to be the reason. Laura was very attractive.

Sharon and Danny's eyes met when he reached the kitchen.

"Morning."

"Morning." Sharon smiled politely even as her heartbeat thundered in her ears. How did he manage to make jeans and a ratty shirt look so good? It wasn't a bad boy thing. Danny didn't give off that vibe, and she'd never been interested in that type other than to piss off her father during her teenage years.

The vibe coming off Danny was the boy next door. The one you saw out your bedroom window and fantasized about because he was cute, mysterious, and hot as hell mowing the lawn on Saturday mornings. Sweat dripping down his bared muscled chest, and all the girls in the neighborhood drooling out their windows, mothers included, and he'd be innocent as to why.

"You all right?" Danny interrupted.

"Umm. Yes. Why?" *Oh god! Was I ogling him?*

"You had this strange look on your face."

"I was thinking about a meeting I have later today with a difficult client," Sharon mumbled. *Real smooth, Sharon.*

"Oh. By the way, would you rather I knocked before coming in when you're home? I don't want to invade your privacy."

"That's not necessary. I'm not staying in the rooms you renovate, and I don't walk around the house naked or anything," Sharon said with a nervous laugh. *Why the hell did I say that?* Sharon wasn't sure if the expression on Danny's face was horror or if he was imaging walking in on her naked.

Danny cleared his throat. "All right, then. What are your weekend plans?" His gaze darted about the kitchen, looking everywhere but at her.

Way to go, Sharon. You've made him uncomfortable. "I'm spending the day at the spa on Saturday and relaxing around the house on Sunday. Why?"

"I wanted to finish up some electrical work on Saturday so we're ready for the inspector on Monday."

"I won't be here for most of the day, so I don't mind."

"It'll just take a few hours."

"What are your plans this weekend?" Sharon asked.

Danny's gaze settled on her, as if contemplating whether to share the truth or give a generic answer.

"I'm helping my mom with a clothing drive Saturday morning, working in the afternoon, and then nothing on Sunday."

"A clothing drive?"

"Yes. At one of the charities she volunteers for."

"Where is it? I have clothes I was going to donate to the Red Cross, but I'd be happy to give them to your mother's charity."

"It's at a homeless shelter." He rattled off the address. "You can have them dropped off either today or tomorrow morning before 10 a.m."

"I'll drop them off myself." Did he think she was that much of a snob that she wouldn't drop clothes to a charity, or was it because of the neighborhood he mentioned?

"Uh, okay."

Danny's expression said he was clearly surprised. Tension and annoyance crawled up the back of her neck. "I'm not a complete snob, Danny."

"I didn't mean to imply you were."

"I've done my share of charity work."

"You mean donating money?"

"Yes, but I always volunteered during high school and college."

"Was it a required elective?" Danny mocked.

"No. My mother was passionate about hands-on volunteer work. She thought it built character and would help remind me how blessed I was to live the life I did." Sharon crossed her arms over her chest.

Danny cheeks flushed. "I'm sorry. It's just that..."

"People like me just donate money," Sharon offered.

Danny grinned sheepishly. "Yes."

"You're right. My father doesn't understand, but I wouldn't trade that lesson for anything."

Silence stretched out before them until the coffee machine beeped.

"Help yourself to the rest of the coffee," Sharon offered.

"Thanks." Danny shifted from one foot to the other. "I really am sorry for what I said earlier. I prejudged you and I shouldn't have."

Sharon's heartbeat banged against her chest as Danny's softened gaze crawled across her face before settling on her mouth, making her wish there wasn't a counter between them.

"It's okay. It happens all the time. I did it the first time I met you."

"Really? How did you misjudge me?" Danny raised an eyebrow.

"I thought your taste in clothes said low-scale contractor, and one who wouldn't give me the quality of work I wanted."

"Ouch. That's harsh."

Sharon smiled. "True, but now I know differently. You do clean up nicely."

Danny laughed. "I thought you were going to say you were waiting to see the quality of my work."

"I thought about it, but I didn't want to insult you. You're just tearing things apart right now, so it's difficult to say." She grinned.

"Jeez. Thanks!"

They laughed.

"Are you doing all the designing yourself?" Danny asked when their laughter ended, as he suspected when they met.

"I am. Does that surprise you?"

"No. Yes. I didn't think you'd have the time."

Sharon chuckled. "Maybe if I were redoing my entire home, but a couple of rooms, one being the closet, is something I can handle. I pretty much decided what I wanted before calling you so..." She took a sip of coffee. "That's makes it easier."

"Okay." Danny brows knitted together.

Sharon locked her arms. "What? You thought I'd hire some fancy designer to handle it?"

"I was prejudging you again. Sorry."

"I used to help my mother redesign the rooms of our homes." She shrugged. "I enjoy it. A bit like closing a business deal. It's the same thrill."

Danny started to lean across the counter but caught himself. "I guess that means we'll be spending a bit of alone time together picking out fixtures." He cleared his throat and straightened as if he didn't expect the words to come out so seductively.

"I guess so."

"They're looking for volunteers at the shelter over the holidays if you have time. I'm sure you have other ch–charities and all," Danny stuttered, changing the subject.

"I do, but I always set aside more time during Christmas for volunteering, as I know that's when they need it the most. Well, time I can spare around the glamorous dinners and cocktail parties," Sharon added with a grin. Although it wasn't far from the truth, she avoided the ones she could, but the family and business ones were a must.

"Ha! Can't miss those." Danny ran a hand through his hair. "I suppose Bradley will be taking you?"

Sharon didn't answer right away, creating an awkward silence.

"Honestly, I haven't decided."

"I didn't mean..."

"Yes, you did."

"You're right," Danny conceded.

Sharon's gaze raked over him, trying to determine if his apology was sincere or if he was merely appeasing her because of her client status. "You gave up pretty easily," she challenged.

Danny shrugged. "I know better than to argue with a woman—and a client, to boot."

Sharon laughed. She couldn't help it. His humor was infectious, not to mention him. Something about being around him made her smile and laugh. After so many years of shutting herself away, it felt good to let a little of her out.

Sharon was about to tease him when the front door opened. She stopped, thinking it was the crew arriving.

"Sharon?" her father's voice bellowed.

Oh, crap! Her glance shifted to Danny. "It's my father," she whispered. Sharon straightened her frame and adjusted her clothing just as Mark rounded the hallway.

Mark stopped short, and his gaze shifted between her and Danny.

"This is Daniel Stanley. My new contractor," Sharon stated. "Mr. Stanley, this is my father, Mark Donovan."

Daniel extended his hand. "Nice to meet you, Mr. Donovan."

Mark ignored his hand and snorted. "Why are you alone together?"

Sharon rolled her eyes. "It's morning, I'm a grown woman, and the rest of his crew are due to arrive any moment."

"He could've stayed the night." Mark stared at him as if Danny had assaulted her.

"If he had, it would be none of your business."

"I'll not have your fraternizing, ruining our business reputation."

"Really? Then maybe you should speak with the men in the office. They're no angels and aren't afraid to share their stories in the office."

Mark snorted. "They're men."

Sharon fisted her hand. The last thing she wanted to do was get into an argument with her father in front of Danny. The topic alone was embarrassing enough. "Why are you here?"

"I'll get started working. Nice to meet you, Mr. Donovan," Danny said before leaving.

Mark didn't acknowledge him. She apologized to Danny with her eyes. He nodded in understanding.

"I wanted to know see how the date went with Bradley."

"It wasn't a date, Father." There was no business talk, but that was only because of Danny and his date.

"He's a perfectly good candidate."

Sharon locked her arms. "Bradley can be an obnoxious snob." She wasn't about to tell her father she was considering him. She wanted their relationship to unfold naturally, and not be tampered with by an impatient father trying to ram his get-married-now message down their throats.

"Bradley comes from a good family and is financially stable."

"I'm financially stable on my own."

"Not if I have anything to say about it."

Sharon gritted her teeth. It was a threat her father made whenever things weren't going his way. Remove her from the will and her chair on the board she was struggling to obtain among the good old boys' club.

"That line is getting very old. Would you honestly leave the family business to someone who's not family?" Deep down she suspected the threat was his way of getting her settled and married.

"Yes," Mark said after a long pause.

The stern set of his face told Sharon he was serious. Her heart sank to her toes as the realization of his words slammed into her like a wrecking ball. "You don't mean it." Her voice cracked as she searched his face for a glimmer he wasn't serious. She was wrong. His uncompromising face glared back, unrelenting.

"I think it's for the best."

Sharon grabbed onto the coldness that had settled into her bones the day she realized Mark saw her as merely a marriage commodity and not someone to run their family business. Even though she was the CEO, it was just a small portion of the business. No. Any sons she bore would have the opportunity to run the company from the board, but not her. She would have to lock away any childish dreams and girlish fantasies and be a coldhearted bitch to get what she wanted from her father. It was the only way to protect herself from him and the other men who'd tried to stop her. "I'm sorry you feel that way."

Mark sighed deeply. "If you don't like Bradley, then find someone else you like better. The sooner you're married, the sooner you'll get your seat on the board, and your inheritance."

Sharon glared at him, not caring if the hatred she felt in the moment was reflected in her eyes. "I'm tired of you dangling that prize!" She stormed to the doorway leading to the front door. "I want you to leave now."

"I'll leave when I'm done talking," he bellowed, coming up behind her.

"You're done talking."

"You don't speak to me that way."

"I'm not a child you can intimidate, Father! I'm a grown woman, and at this moment, an employee with a contract and you're trespassing in my family's home," Sharon finished with conviction.

Mark's nostrils flared and he opened his mouth to speak, but changed his mind.

Sharon let out the breath she was holding when she heard the front door slam shut. Moments later the two men from Danny crew peeked around the corner.

"Is everything okay, Ms. Donovan? That was one angry man."

"Yes, he was, but I'm fine. Thanks for asking," she said with a polite smile.

Sharon urged them to have the coffee, grabbed her handbag, and strolled out the front door as fast as her legs could carry her. The tears didn't fall until she reached the highway. She wiped them away, cursing that she'd have to reapply her makeup before she got into the office.

She squeezed the steering wheel as her father's words rang in her ears. *Stupid. Naïve. Woman.* Phrases she'd heard several times over the years. Sometimes directly to her face, and sometimes overheard when they thought she wasn't listening. That's how her father made her feel.

If she were born with a penis, her life would be different. Instead of every door of her father's business slamming shut, those doors would've been held opened with pats on the back as she sauntered in. Regardless of how she tried to maneuver with and around her father, he wasn't going to budge. *Damn him!*

Danny heard the front door close for a second time and knew Sharon and her father were gone. Although he hadn't heard the whole conversation, what he had heard was shocking. Because of her fancy office and CEO status, he assumed Sharon had her father's full support. The conversation said the opposite.

Mark snubbing his handshake didn't surprise him. He was used to it with his high-end clients. Not all of them, but most. They took one look at his clothing and assumed he was the foreman, or one of the workers, instead of the owner. He could make himself more presentable, but being a small-business owner meant getting his hands dirty regularly, and he wasn't getting spruced up just to make his clients think more of him.

Sharon came across like his other clients when they first met, but after their conversations and the interaction he'd overheard, he was beginning to understand why she was unapproachable. She donated her time, along with money and belongings, to worthy charities. That alone changed his mind about her. His mother always said people with a charitable heart were worth getting to know.

Danny raked a hand through his hair. How sad for Sharon. From an early age he realized how blessed he was to have parents who loved him, each other, and who supported his life decisions. The relationship was hardly perfect, but he couldn't imagine his parents snubbing his desire to be a part of their business, and from the sounds of it, just because she was a woman. What would he say when he saw Sharon again? He didn't want her to know he overheard such a personal conversation, but he didn't want to lie or pretend he hadn't heard anything if she asked. Danny wasn't going to bring it up and Sharon wasn't about to ask him, so he was probably stressing for nothing.

Part of him wished he hadn't seen this side of her life. The vulnerable tremble of her voice brought out his protective side, one that hadn't surfaced toward a woman in a long time. The last time had ended badly for him. While Sharon wasn't Teri, the similarities were close enough to make Danny wary.

Those similarities screamed at him to create distance.

Chapter 11

Sharon was beginning to think lunch with Bradley was a bad idea. He'd spent most of it on the phone. If she'd wanted to eat lunch alone, she wouldn't have accepted his invitation. The occasional emergency call was necessary to put out fires, but based on the conversation she had overheard, the phone calls could've waited until he returned to the office. As a courtesy, she'd turned off her own phone as she was confident Ryan could handle things for an hour.

Sharon took a sip of her water and gazed out the window of the restaurant at the people rushing past. Everyone was in a hurry to go somewhere, or talking on their phones. She understood that life was busy better than anyone, but one lesson her mother had taught her was she had to take care of herself before she could give her best. While her mother didn't have a job per se, she was on the board of several charities and ran their busy household, which included organizing business and family events. There were days she spent more time with her nanny than her mother, but her mother always made up for it with girls' spa days. She still went to the spa on her own, but it wasn't the same without her mother.

"Sorry about that," Bradley interrupted with a charming smile.

Sharon didn't respond, hoping he'd take the hint and not answer another call during their lunch. She accepted his invitation because she wanted to get to know him on a personal level outside of the digging Ryan was doing, especially if she was considering him for marriage. The word left a bitter taste in her mouth, making her wish she hadn't gone on such a long hiatus after her relationship with Patrick fell apart. Maybe then she wouldn't feel the pressure of the short time frame.

"Have you decided what you're having?" Sharon was certain the waiter had given up on them after checking their table three times and they still weren't ready to order.

Bradley picked up the menu again, glanced over it quickly, and set it down. He waved the waiter over. So much for seeing if she was ready. She'd made her choice almost thirty minutes ago, but he didn't know that.

Bradley proceeded to order for them both.

"Change the last part of the order." She gave the waiter her order and handed him the menu.

Bradley's cheeks were pink. "I thought women liked men ordering for them."

"Only if they're asked first."

"Understood."

"Good." All the men her father connected her with could well be the same man. Everything about their thoughts, beliefs, and values were the same. The only difference between them was how they treated her at the end of the date. She'd either be pawed at or given a chaste kiss on the cheek. While she didn't mind being kissed—you could learn a lot from a man's kiss—being mauled was another story.

Their actions no doubt came because of their perception of her or Mark.

So far, Bradley had been a gentleman. Not once had he asked to come inside or give her more than a simple kiss on the lips. If she hadn't caught him staring at her breasts on occasion, she might've suspected he was gay. Being gay might have worked in both their favors. They'd both get the covers they needed without the personal obligations that came with being married.

"Are you gay?" Sharon blurted.

Bradley raised an eyebrow.

"I wouldn't tell anyone or hold it against you," she added quickly.

A rakish smile tugged at his lips. "No, I'm not gay."

"I didn't think so, but I thought I'd ask."

"Why would you ask?"

"Well for one, you didn't invite yourself in for a nightcap or try to kiss me."

"I was trying to be a gentleman. We do exist, you know."

Sharon smiled. "I know." She thought of Danny, although the way he watched her mouth wasn't very gentlemanly. "I suppose I'm used to being mauled by men who think I'm available, no thanks to my father."

"I can arrange to maul you if you like," he teased. "By the way, you really should smile more." He took her hand. "You're even more beautiful when you do."

"Thank you." The warmth of his hands felt nice. "I mean about my smiling, not the mauling."

Bradley laughed. "I figured."

The waiter brought their food.

"It's not that mauling you hasn't crossed my mind." Bradley set his silverware on the edge of the plate. "You don't seem the type of woman who likes to be rushed."

"I'm not." She wasn't against a heated tryst every now and then, but only with someone she was dating. She noticed his heated gaze settled on her lips. *I'm kissing him after lunch.*

The attraction was there on his end, but she wished there were more chills on her skin as he stroked her hand with this thumb. Just being around Danny shot sparks through her, even without touching. Sharon pulled her hand away, feeling guilty that she was thinking about another man when Bradley had made every effort to not make her feel rushed. So, he needed to work on his lunch phone etiquette. No man was perfect, especially those in her circle.

As they walked back to her car after lunch, Sharon contemplated how she'd either kiss Bradley or hint that she was open. He beat her to it by holding her hand as they strolled through the parking lot. His arm went around her waist, and he lowered his head. Sharon closed her eyes, but when nothing happened, she opened them again. Bradley was squinting, making her wonder if she had something on her face.

"What's wrong?"

"There's something on your car."

"What?" Sharon twirled around, her heart in her throat. Nothing else had shown up after the dead flowers, but the dread that had settled in her stomach when she opened the box attacked her as she read the paper stuck to her car window.

"I'm coming for you," was glued on with letters clipped from a magazine.

"What the hell?" Bradley asked, ripping the paper off the window.

"It's nothing." Sharon grabbed it and crumpled it up.

"Doesn't seem like nothing."

"It's just another prank," she said with a light smile, hoping Bradley would take the hint and not press her about it.

"That's one hell of a nasty prank. Scaring you like that."

She managed a casual shrug. "Boys will be boys." Sharon used the words her father loved to throw at her, but cringed inwardly.

"You sure you're, okay?" Bradley asked, hands on her shoulders. "Why don't you let me drive?"

Sharon nodded and handed him the keys.

Bradley talked the entire ride back to the office, and she smiled and responded when she had to. Inside, numbness engulfed her. Her mind raced with names and faces of who could've left the note. The flowers could be brushed off as a prank, but the note was not as easy to push aside as she'd tried to convince Bradley. The note wasn't left at her workplace, which meant someone was following her. Terror shot through her at the thought. Who was coming for her? Why were they coming? When?

Did it have to do with her seat on the board she would claim when she married, or just some crazy stalker she didn't know? Whoever they were, they obviously weren't going away. Calling the police should be the first thing she did when she got back to her office, but the last thing she wanted was to bring attention to herself right now. This kind of trouble would be another reason for her father, and possibly the board, to reject her seat. No. She had to deal with this herself. Hopefully before things escalated.

Bradley opened the car door for her, making her realize she'd been sitting in the car even after they arrived.

"Thank you," Sharon mumbled, taking his hand.

"So much for my idea of stealing a kiss in the parking lot before we got back."

Sharon pulled him against her and pressed her lips to his. Bradley took her face in his hand and kissed her back, this time using his tongue. She returned the deepness of the kiss and even put her arms around his neck when he pulled her closer.

Bradley was grinning when he broke the kiss after hearing voices approaching them.

She quickly wiped the edges of her lips, hoping they weren't smudged with more lipstick than she could remove.

Thankfully the people who passed them weren't from their office, and Sharon quickly refreshed her lipstick when they got to the elevator.

"I had a nice time."

"Me too." Sharon adjusted the strap of her handbag before Bradley held her hand and kissed it, forcing her to look at him. The lines of his face were strong and appealing, and Sharon wished right down to her toes that she felt something when they kissed.

The elevator stopped on the floor before her stop and Robert joined them. Bradley visibly stiffened. He didn't like Robert either. Not that she blamed him. Robert had wanted to hire a different lawyer and never missed the opportunity to mention it.

"Sharon. Bradley."

"Robert," they said in unison.

"I didn't know you two were together."

His probing was painfully obvious. "Just lunch, Robert."

"Too bad. Your time is running out."

"Thank you, but I'm well aware."

Bradley's expression was curious, but he remained silent, for which she was grateful. The last thing she wanted was to have that conversation in an elevator with a man she was contemplating making a marriage proposal to before she could properly explain the situation. *Your father or Carlton probably told him already, Sharon.*

"I'm just trying to help, but you might want to consider another choice."

Robert didn't say Bradley's name, but he did glance in his direction. He was nothing if not tactless, like Aunt Virginia. What did he care about who she married? They were no threat to him unless he knew something she didn't. Did he?

Sharon studied Robert's features and he found her watching him. He then glanced at Bradley, and the hatred in his eyes shocked her. Bradley wasn't the easiest person to like, but Robert couldn't have known Bradley long enough to develop the kind of rage reflected in his eyes. The kind a father had for someone who'd tried to destroy his family or caused him to lose his livelihood or business. Bradley didn't have that kind of power, did he?

Sharon suddenly saw Bradley and Robert in a new light, and wished she could read minds. Bradley looked terrified of Robert and the heat from Robert's hatred seemed to turn the elevator into a furnace. Neither man would tell her if she asked, of that she was certain, but Sharon couldn't help but wonder. *What the hell?*

Chapter 12

T he neighborhood wasn't how Sharon remembered the last time she came with her mother years ago. This was the first homeless shelter she and her mother visited. The white-painted brick building was showing heavy wear. The sun reflected off the windows, exposing the peeling blue paint framing them. The space around the building was covered with graffiti, some with artistic flares and others just a jumble of paint and inappropriate words.

The surrounding buildings were showing an equal amount of wear, or were completely dilapidated. It broke her heart when her father decided to withdraw his funding after her mother died. No amount of begging had convinced him. Mark felt other charities would provide better political and business benefits.

Memories of her holding her mother's hands flooded her thoughts as she opened the front door and strolled inside. A lump caught in her throat, remembering how scared she'd been seeing the scruffy men and women for the first time. It wasn't until she saw the kids her own age that she released her mother's hand and ventured around the room. That first experience had been an eye-opener for Sharon, one that had stayed with her each time she wanted to complain about her life. Even with the strained relationship between her and her father, her life was a dream compared to many people. Her mother had been pleased the experience stuck and Sharon retained her mother's charitable spirit despite her father's attempt to warp it for business and political purposes.

The room was buzzing with music and excitement, and Sharon couldn't help but smile. Despite everything life had dealt these people, they still found reasons to celebrate and things to appreciate in life—something many people in her circle hadn't grasped.

Sharon spotted Danny right away, since he was the tallest person in the room. He stood next to an older woman, their resemblance close enough for Sharon to assume she was his mother. Laughter passed between them as they sorted through the clothing spread out on the tables.

As if sensing her, Danny glanced up. His eyes narrowed, as if trying to determine it was her and she waved. Dressed in jeans and a polo shirt, it was attire she didn't wear often.

Danny smiled and gestured for her to join them. It was then that Sharon remembered the clothing in her hands and placed the box in an empty space before approaching Danny and his mother. "Hello." Sharon smiled at them both.

"Mom, this is Sharon Donovan. Sharon, this is my mother, Rose."

Rose gripped Sharon's hand with both of her small ones and gave her the warmest smile Sharon had experienced in a long time. "So nice to meet you."

"Nice to meet you also."

"Are you Danny's new client?"

Sharon noticed Danny roll his eyes before she answered. "Yes, I am."

Rose's face lit up. "Wonderful!"

"Mom." Danny's tone held a hint of a warning.

"I wasn't going to say anything." Rose grinned. "Wait. Are you related to Juliet Donovan?"

"Yes. She was my mother."

"Was?"

"She died last year."

"Oh, I'm so sorry to hear that. She was a lovely woman who did so much for this shelter."

"I didn't know," Danny whispered.

Sharon gave a small smile. "How can I help?"

"You can start by helping my son organize these clothes by sizes, and separate them for men, women, and children. If you're still here and have use of your arms, we'll need you to place all these toiletries in the backpacks for men, women, and children. People are most generous around the holidays, and we like to make sure we meet their everyday needs besides just clothing. It's not much, but they appreciate it."

Sharon nodded. "Are Christmas toys being arranged for the kids this year? I haven't been in the shelter for a while." She blushed.

"A few, but it's not enough. Each year, the number of people on the streets, especially kids, is increasing."

"What do you need?" Sharon asked without hesitation.

Rose graced her with another warm smile. "I knew I was going to like you."

Sharon laughed. "Thank you. The feeling is mutual."

"There are about fifty kids who come through here daily, but with our Thanksgiving and Christmas dinners, I imagine it'll be lots more. The ages range from as young as two to as old as nineteen."

"I'll see what I can put together for you by the second week in December." Sharon felt Danny's eyes on her, but she couldn't muster the courage to glance at him, especially with his mother watching them both.

"Anything you give will be much appreciated." Rose's gaze shifted from her to Danny and then back to her before smiling brightly. "Well, I have other things to attend to. My son, here, knows the drill and will take good care of you."

Sharon sensed Rose's words had a double meaning, but she didn't dare entertain them, and gave Rose a polite smile before she left her alone with Danny. Sharon's gaze darted around, realizing the other two volunteers were on the far side of the room, essentially leaving her and Danny alone.

Heat crept up Sharon's cheeks as she remembered their intimate moment in her kitchen. She had not felt so comfortable with a man since Patrick—at ease enough to talk about her mother. Unlike Patrick, Danny made her smile.

"So do you think this is me?" Danny picked up a Hawaiian-style shirt with an awful pattern.

"Definitely. I could see you wearing that with a pair of Bermuda shorts, white socks pulled up to your knees, and flip-flops." Sharon laughed.

Danny pulled the shirt away from his chest, examining it closely. "A chick magnet for sure." His eyes gleamed.

"I'd totally go for that look."

"Really?"

"Absolutely! Add a fanny pack." She faked a sexy growl.

Danny chuckled and placed the shirt in the right pile. "I'd better put this baby away before I start a stampede." His chin nudged toward a group of elderly women sitting in a corner sorting through the toiletries.

"Better to be safe than sorry, but maybe I should escort you to your car when you leave. Just to be on the safe side."

Sharon gave him a knowing wink. "I agree." They glanced at the women, back at each other, and broke out in laughter.

The rest of their sorting time contained the same humor whenever they came across a piece of clothing that was from another era, or was just plain ugly. It was only when the elderly women in the corner started giving them stern looks that they lowered their voices and the laughter.

Three hours later, everything was sorted and ready for sale. The money from the sale would go toward the Thanksgiving and Christmas dinners.

"Thank you so much for your help," Rose said.

"It was my pleasure. I enjoyed it."

Rose smiled. "So did Danny."

Sharon's heartbeat tripped over itself at Rose's words.

"I'd love to thank you with an invitation to our house for Sunday brunch next week."

Sharon was about to say it wasn't necessary, but somehow, she suspected Rose wouldn't take no for an answer. Besides, she was curious to know more about Danny, since he was privy to so much of her life recently. "Thank you. I'd be honored."

"Wonderful. We eat at 1:00. Danny will give you the address." Rose reached out and hugged her. The woman's warmth engulfed her, and Sharon couldn't help hugging her back. Her joy was infectious.

"I can't wait for my husband to meet you," Rose said before releasing her.

Sharon smiled. She had already said her goodbyes to Danny, but waved for good measure. He waved back and jogged over.

"I thought you were escorting me to the parking lot?" he teased.

"I think they've simmered down now, so you're safe."

"How about a ride home?" Danny's gaze shifted to his mother. "She was my ride but it looks like she's going to be here longer than planned, and I have work I need to take care of."

"At my place?" Sharon's voice quivered.

"No. At home. Those bills don't pay themselves unfortunately."

Sharon grinned. "Sure they do, if you set up autopayments."

"Ah. You're one of those people?"

"What? Organized?"

"No. Those who have an endless supply of money in their bank account to set up autopayments. We small-business owners don't have those privileges."

"Oh." *Next time keep quiet, Sharon.*

"It's not as bad as it seems." Danny laughed. "I just don't like having an overdraft, so I monitor my bills closely."

A million questions ran through her mind to ask him, but she refrained. "I'd be happy to drop you home."

"Great. Let's get out of here before we're talked into another hour. I don't think my eyeballs or arms could handle another minute." Danny placed his hand on her back to guide her toward the door. Sharon laughed and let Danny lead her outside.

"Your mom is nice." Sharon started the car.

"She is, and she liked you."

"I really liked her."

Danny gave his home address and Sharon maneuvered the car to head in that direction.

Orange and red hues danced across the car windows and the buildings and townhomes outside as they drove out of the city. The skyline grew shorter as the sun set behind the brownstones with staggered elm trees and decorative black picket fences.

"So, how are things going with you and Bradley?" Danny asked, breaking the silence.

Sharon's gaze jerked to his before returning to the road. "Okay, I guess."

"Okay, huh? He was a bit obnoxious."

"Just a bit?" she said with a sideways grin.

Danny laughed. "Okay, a lot."

"My father thinks we'd make a good couple."

Danny's breath hitched at the personal information she'd shared. "Not so ridiculous. All my dates this year were setups, compliments of my mother." He chuckled.

"I guess I got off easy then?" She relaxed in the car seat. "I thought going out with Bradley would make the holidays easier. I wouldn't have to find a date for all those family and business gatherings."

"One of the benefits of being a small-business owner. No big parties. I take my guys to lunch.

"What about family?"

Danny pointed to his chest. "Only child with a small family."

"Lucky you. Only child with an extended business family."

"Good thing you've got Bradley." Danny directed her to make a left turn.

"I suppose." Sharon gnawed on her bottom lip.

"I could be your date." Danny couldn't hide the surprise of his offer but laughed it off and added, "Your father and business associates might go ballistic."

Sharon chuckled. "Yes, they would. It'd be worth it to see the looks on their faces when I told them who you are."

Danny laughed and pointed to his driveway.

Sharon's gaze took in his single–story home with large trees that shaded most of the home and the small lawn at the front. There was no distaste or even a hint of it in her eyes.

Danny's heart skipped a beat that she appreciated his home. "Would you like to come in for a drink?" slipped from his lips before he could stop the words. "If you have time," he mumbled.

Sharon's gaze studied his face for several moments. She checked her watch before answering. "All right, but just one."

Danny's breath hitched. She was coming into his home. They were going to be alone. *Get real, Danny! You've been alone together before.* But at his home, there would be no workers interrupting them to start work for the day or rude controlling fathers. They would be totally alone.

Sharon turned off the car and opened her door. Danny followed suit, his heart in his throat as they strolled to the front door.

Shit! Please don't let there be clothes in the living room. He could hide the mess in the kitchen but scattered clothing in the living room was another matter. Sharon's place was always meticulous. *When did you start caring about a few discarded clothes? I don't!*

Danny opened his front door open and turned on the light, quickly scanning the room.

"All safe?" Sharon asked with a hint of humor.

"What were you expecting?"

Sharon's gaze moved around the room. "I don't know. Beer cans, empty pizza or Chinese takeout boxes. Maybe even an article of clothing or two."

Danny laughed. "Clothing, maybe, but I drink wine, not beer, and I cook to save money, so my kitchen is usually the messy room."

"What's your specialty?"

"Mac and cheese."

Sharon laughed. "Straight from the box?"

"Actually, it's homemade. Baked in the oven and everything."

Surprise lit Sharon's eyes. "I'd love to try it sometime." She sat on the large brown leather couch. "What kind of wine do you drink?"

"The good kind." Danny teased. "I've got red and white. I can tell you the names, but don't ask me the year."

"I'll take whatever red you have."

"You got it."

Danny headed to the kitchen and poured two glasses of wine. When he returned to the living room, he found Sharon standing by his fireplace mantel looking at his pictures.

"You've known Josie a long time."

Danny handed her the wine. "Yeah. Since she was in college. She was interning with the company I was working with. We struck up a conversation and became friends, and later business associates. She sends business my way and I return the favor when I can."

"That must've come as a surprise to you. A woman in construction?" Sharon's gaze didn't meet his, and her body was stiff as she waited for his response.

"Sure, but it wasn't that unusual. Most were only interior designers, but Josie knew her stuff and worked as hard as the rest of the crew. That's all that mattered to me." From her question, Danny suspected the men in her circle, including her father, weren't as accommodating.

Sharon's frame relaxed as she checked out the rest of the photos. "You were a cute kid."

He sidestepped her comment about his looks. Dangerous territory. Sharon returned to the couch, sitting as though she were at a business meeting.

"You can take off your shoes and relax if you want. I promise not to tell anyone." Danny winked.

No smile passed her lips, indicating he'd hit a nerve. "I'm sorry," she whispered.

Danny sat next to her. "Hey. I was just kidding."

Ice blue eyes rested on him. "It's never been easy for me to relax. Even as a child. I was always told how to act, what to do, where to go, and even what to wear." She took a sip of wine. "It comes with the territory when you're the only child of a rich, politically connected family. Trying to get your foot into the door of a family business where the only role women have is either to marry a man to run the business or marry into it is not easy." Sharon finished with a forlorn smile.

"That must suck."

Sharon grinned. "You have no idea. Every time I think I've taken a step forward, I'm reminded of how much further I must go."

"I had similar issues when I tried to break into high-end clients. They only saw my appearance and not my experience or skill."

"How did you get past it?"

Danny leaned back onto the couch. "I decided not to change myself for anyone. The good clients would appreciate my work." His eyes twinkled. "And Josie pulled me in kicking and screaming."

Sharon laughed. "I could see that." She shifted her position on the couch so she faced him.

"I've been thinking about what you said about being my date for holiday parties."

"And?" Even though he offered, he didn't think she'd take it seriously. Truthfully, he wasn't sure why he mentioned it. The last thing he wanted was to hang out with a bunch of rich snobs, but he'd seen the expression on Sharon's face at the prospect of her father setting her up on another unwanted date, or having to sit alone at all those parties. He also liked trying to make her smile, which was getting easier with each passing day.

"I'm taking you up on your offer. I'm tired of being around people who have no real sense of humor and talk about nothing but their portfolios, boats, and cars, or how much money they made last year." She rested her hand on his arm. "I want to be around people who appreciate life and what they have, and who make me laugh."

"You should laugh more. Your face lights up when you do." Truth was, she was stunning, but when she smiled or laughed, there was girlish charm about it. Her entire body relaxed, and she genuinely seemed to enjoy herself. Danny wanted to see more of that woman, even if it wasn't a good idea. She removed her hand from his arm, but the heat of her touch still warmed his skin.

"I want to laugh more." She leaned her face against his arm resting on the back of the couch. "There are so many things I want to do." Sharon started to say more, but straightened and remained silent, making Danny wonder about her next words.

"You have plenty of time."

"You're right. I do." Sharon shifted on the couch. "So, about being my date. You do realize you'll need suits and a tuxedo."

"I know. I've got it covered." Clothing he'd purchased to impress and accompany Teri to events. Clothing that was now gathering dust in his closet. At least he'd get his money's worth attending events with Sharon, and because they weren't involved, he wouldn't have to worry about being dumped at the end of it. He was doing a favor for a friend. Danny resisted the urge to laugh. *Friend* wasn't the word he would use to describe how he thought or felt about Sharon, but it was the only word he could entertain.

"Really? You've got a tux in your closet? Is it a rental you decided to keep?" she teased.

Danny's attempt at a smile faltered. "No. A while back I dated someone who needed me to dress spiffy."

Surprise lit Sharon's face. "I hope that's not the word she used."

Her attempt to make him laugh was appreciated, but it didn't help crush the sting of hurt he felt remembering Teri and how things ended. He cleared his throat and checked his watch.

Sharon did the same. "It's getting late, and I have work to finish." She drank the remaining wine, stood, and headed to the door. Danny followed.

"Thanks for the drink and agreeing to be my date."

"My pleasure." The doorway space compressed, making him painfully aware of how good she smelled and how soft her skin looked. Danny's gaze settled on her lips before jerking to her face.

"See you on Monday." Sharon left abruptly, making him wonder what she was thinking and if her rushed departure was because of how he reacted when mentioning Teri. He hadn't said her name, but his reaction spoke volumes. It didn't matter. Teri wasn't coming back, and Sharon wasn't a relationship interest, so mentioning Teri shouldn't make a difference.

He felt like a fraud thinking those words when, truthfully, what he wanted was to pull Sharon against him and kiss her until she was whispering his name hotly in his ear. Those might be his thoughts, but they weren't possible or welcome. He didn't want to make another mistake.

Chapter 13

S haron was bombarded by the commotion in the office when she stepped out of the elevator. Coworkers cluttered the hallway, even the secretaries, their voices a range of soft whispers to loud, indecipherable conversations.

"What's going on?" she asked the first person she encountered.

"Mr. Polk is dead."

Uncle Robert? The words hit her like a lightning bolt. *Dead?* "What happened?"

"He shot himself," the woman whispered, as if it were a dirty secret.

"What!" Not the reason she expected. Remorse stabbed her that she'd been cold and distant on the elevator during their conversation. The man was her uncle, and when she was a kid, he always gave her the best gifts. It was disappointing that their relationship changed due to him trying to play nice because of Mark.

"In his office, at his desk."

Was it suicide? Sharon didn't have time to process anything more because the police and an EMT team came out of the elevator and headed toward Robert's office. Dazed, Sharon walked to her office. Ryan was standing at his desk, waiting for her.

"Are you okay?"

Sharon nodded, too stunned to speak.

"Should I cancel your meetings for today?"

"No," Sharon whispered. "But move all afternoon meetings to tomorrow. I will be taking the afternoon off."

"Of course. Is there anything I can get for you?" Ryan asked.

Sharon shook her head. What could he get? Before she could enter her office, a police officer appeared.

"We're asking everyone to stay behind and not leave the building until we've taken their statements and gotten their information," the tall dark policeman stated. "Stay put until an officer comes to take your statement."

"Of course," Ryan answered. "What do you think happened?" he asked when the man left.

"Someone said he was shot."

"Suicide?"

"I don't know. I don't think anyone knows."

"Let's hope that's it."

"Why?"

"Can you imagine if someone killed him? Someone in this office?" Ryan said with a shiver.

Sharon hadn't considered that. To her, suicide seemed worse. Had life gotten so bad that he wanted to leave his wife and the life they'd built together? What about poor Carlton? She thought about her own life and how focused she was on work and her charities, and while they were fulfilling, especially her charities, they were still work. The only real times she was actively involved were during the holidays, but if she were honest, it was only to keep busy, to keep loneliness at bay. Her involvement with the other charities was mostly signing checks and planning fundraising events. Her efforts suddenly felt small and meaningless. Her own uncle had taken his life, or possibly been killed, and she was so involved in her own life she hadn't noticed he was at risk. Robert wasn't just killed on the street, or in a freak accident, or even from a heart attack. He was killed in his own office. A personal space. As much as she ached at the thought of it being suicide, part of her was beginning to hope it was and not the other possibility...because that meant there might be a killer in the office.

The shock of Robert's death, and the possibility of it being a murder, pressed down on her until she couldn't breathe. She rushed to her office and closed the door, putting the lock in place. After plunking down on the couch, she placed her head on her knees, trying to calm her breaths, which were as erratic as her heartbeat, and thoughts of all the events leading to Robert's death, including her threats. Were they related? If they were, why was he killed, while she was just threatened? Fear coursed through her blood like the chill of a winter day. Was his death another threat? Why not just kill her? Was she next? If it wasn't suicide—which she was beginning to think it wasn't—was she going to receive a message about his death? Another note on her car, or maybe worse? What could be worse?

A soft knock came from the door. "Are you okay, Ms. Donovan? Can I get you some water, or something stronger?"

"I just need a moment, Ryan." Saying she was fine would be stupid.

"Of course. Take all the time you need. I doubt any meetings will be happening today anyway, given the police are taking statements."

"Thank you, Ryan."

She'd talk to the police and tell them about the threats, especially now that Robert was dead. As much as she didn't want to bring attention to herself and the company in the middle of such a big deal, Robert's death threw that option out the window. She needed to find someone other than an officer. She needed a detective or someone higher up the chain. Someone who'd be discreet. As much as it pained her, she needed to reach out to Mark. He had connections and might know someone. Maybe she could speak with Patrick. He'd be a better choice than her father. Patrick was a corporate lawyer, but with his connections he'd know someone who could help her. She loathed the thought of asking Bradley, even though he'd witnessed a threat against her firsthand, and no matter the small progress their relationship had made, Patrick was the best choice.

With the choice made, Sharon's heartbeat returned to a more normal rhythm, and she walked to her desk to review her calendar to see what clients needed to be contacted. After sending a few emails, she leaned back in her chair and looked around her office in a new light. This place had always been a sanctuary for her when alone, or after a difficult meeting, the way it was now, but somehow different. Today, it felt like a prison, like she was waiting for someone to come and shoot her like they did Robert. She didn't handle her business dealings in the same shrewd way Robert and her father did, but not by much. She could be ruthless if she needed, a switch she turned on. Being herself wouldn't cut it in her world, or so she thought. But if it could get you shot in your office, then maybe it was time for a change. Not to mention that being cold and detached was taking its toll—wearing her down and stripping away what little of herself was hidden under layers of hurt, disappointment, and humiliation. The only problem was she had been someone else for most of her life. How did she go about being or becoming her true self? She had no clue.

Chapter 14

S haron waited in her kitchen for Danny, staring at
the invitation to Patrick and Lola's engagement party.
Sadness settled in the pit of her stomach. She and Patrick
hadn't reached the engagement party stage, but she was
in the middle of planning it when Patrick called off their
wedding. Between the invitation and the turmoil of Robert's
death, her nerves were on end.

The day of his death and the ones that followed were rife
with even more uncertainty about her role in the business
and family. Mark had been his same stoic self, although
a little more than usual. Sharon wished she'd seen his
expression when he learned of Robert's death. Virginia and
Carlton had been inconsolable when she saw them the
day it happened. Sharon had tried to comfort them, but
Virginia had rejected her—the way she always did—and
Carlton was too preoccupied with consoling his mother to
notice her. They hadn't returned to the office since, no doubt
planning his funeral and what would happen next. What
would happen next?

The doorbell rang.

"Morning," she greeted him after opening the door. She
hadn't mentioned the death to Danny, afraid she might
break down and cry since her nerves were a frazzled mess.

"Morning." Danny followed her to the kitchen. His gaze settled on the invitation on the counter. "You going?"

"Of course. Patrick is one of my oldest and dearest friends."

"I'm sure they'd understand if you didn't go."

Sharon smiled. "I'm sure they would, especially with Uncle Robert's death. Are you going?" The question was redundant.

"Yes. Wanna be my date?" Danny asked, a teasing hint in his voice.

"Yes." Sharon laughed. "That should get a few tongues wagging."

"That's putting it mildly. Josie is going to grill me." Danny ran a hand through his hair.

"Second thoughts already? I'm sure a big, strong man like you can handle Josie."

Danny snorted. "Wait. You think I'm a big strong man?"

Sharon rolled her eyes. "That's what you took from my statement? Sounds like you're avoiding the real question."

"Josie can be persistent."

"Not so persistent that you changed the way you dressed."

"That's because of T—" Danny stopped himself before saying someone's name. The dart of his eyes anywhere but on her told her it was a touchy subject.

"I'm sure you can handle Josie's inquiries," Sharon added.

"But can you?"

"If I can divert my father's questions, I'm sure I can handle Josie," she answered confidently.

Danny laughed. "You don't know Josie very well, do you?"

Sharon laughed with him before their laughter died and her eyes settled on the invitation once again.

"Did you and Patrick have an engagement party?"

"No. Patrick called off the wedding before it happened."

"Must've been difficult. Being rejected by a friend."

The concern in Danny's eyes warmed her. "Honestly, I was relieved. I loved Paddy, but not the way one should love their future husband." The regret was for the mess it left with the marriage clause and no suitable replacement. Sharon poured another cup of coffee and slid it on the counter toward Danny. "Patrick and I were childhood friends, and it was assumed we'd get married."

"Assumed or arranged?"

Sharon grinned. "There was never a contract, if that's what you mean, but both our families encouraged it, especially mine."

"Even your mother?"

There was no judgment in Danny's voice, but Sharon's heart still felt a twinge. "Yes. She thought Patrick would give me the freedom I wanted that another man wouldn't."

"Freedom?"

"The seat on the Board of Directors. Patrick knew what it meant to me, and he had no interest in it himself."

Danny took a sip of coffee. "Just as well Josie scooped him up then, huh?"

"Yes," Sharon answered, but silently wished she had loved Paddy as more than a friend then she wouldn't find herself in the predicament she was in now. Although she was entertaining Bradley as a candidate, she wasn't giving up her idea of taking her seat without getting married. Bradley was too ambitious to either give up his seat or he'd expect a hefty payment to give it up. While he wasn't as lecherous as she first thought, she was going to keep her options open.

Danny wasn't a candidate her father would entertain, but at the end of the day, it was her choice. Danny wouldn't care about her seat and would probably be cheaper than Bradley. Sharon stopped her thoughts, feeling slimier than a salesman. Dragging Danny into her situation wasn't a good idea, especially given how he felt about her kind of people.

Not every rich person was like the ones in her circle, but Danny would have to deal with them if she went this route. Given their conversation at his house, he hadn't come away from relationships unscathed. Putting him through that would be cruel. Being her date for a short time was one thing, being part of her life long-term was another.

"Are you sure you're okay with our date?"

"Which one?"

"The engagement party."

"I'm sure," Danny said without hesitation.

"I'll understand if you don't want to be around those people." Sharon cringed. She was one of them.

Danny's hand rested on hers. "Hey. If I didn't think I could handle it, I wouldn't have offered."

"You don't have to be nice on my account." The heat of his hand on hers sent tingles up her arm. Tingles she wished she'd felt when Bradley kissed her.

Danny chuckled, sending a flutter of excitement to her stomach. "I'm not that nice."

Sharon gaze met his. "Yes, you are."

His thumb caressed her fingers and sparks shot between them. Danny's gaze settled on her mouth as hers did with his.

The temperature in the room rose as they stepped toward each other. Danny's hand touched her cheek. Her thoughts screamed, *Kiss me!* as her hands rested on his chest. The heat of his skin under the shirt warmed her, and his muscles twitched as her hand traveled up his chest to his shoulders.

Danny's hot gaze scorched her as his head lowered.

The front door opened, and voices pierced their moment like popping balloon. They stepped away from each other. Danny put the counter space between them. Sharon opened the fridge door to grab a bottle of water to cool her heated skin and clear her head of their near kiss.

Laura was the first person they saw. The other guys in the crew headed straight to her bedroom, the sounds of their work boots stomping up the staircase.

"Morning," Laura greeted them, her gaze shifting between their faces.

"Morning," they said in unison.

"I should be going," Sharon stammered, avoiding everyone's gaze as she raced to leave.

In the short time she'd gotten to know Laura, Sharon knew they'd be talking about her, and she longed to be a fly on the wall. Laura liked Danny more than a friend. Sharon saw it in her eyes, and although no dirty look passed, Sharon couldn't help but wonder if Laura saw her as competition, or someone to warn Danny about.

Sharon walked out of the house and got into her car. She started the car and turned up the volume of the radio to block out the noise of the overthinking percolating in her head, especially explaining to her father why Danny is her date instead of Bradley.

"I thought you didn't get involved with clients," Laura said after the front door closed.

Damn! This is the problem with hiring a smart—and nosy—person. "We're not involved." He wasn't exactly lying. Attraction didn't mean involvement.

"You looked involved in something when I got here." Skepticism underlined her tone.

"We were just talking."

"Talking?"

"Yes. It is required with clients." Danny grinned, trying to distract her with humor.

"Hmm. True, but what you were doing wasn't talking."

Danny snorted. "You're reading too much into it."

Laura adjusted the tightness of her ponytail and eyed him. "You're a nice guy, Danny, and you deserve someone who's just as nice."

"What makes you think Sharon's not?"

She shrugged. "Nothing really. She's not like other rich clients, but when this job is over, you go back to your world, Danny, and she's staying in hers. A world where people like us aren't welcome."

Laura's statement made Danny wonder if she knew about his relationship with Teri. "Are you talking from personal experience?"

Laura yanked on her gloves. "People from her world aren't like us. I'm just trying to save you the trouble. You have simple tastes and need a woman to match."

After filling up her coffee mug, she took a long sip. "Besides, she looks high maintenance, and you don't have the time or the money for a woman like her." A smile tugged at her lips.

The conversation was directed back to humor, and Danny was grateful. "Maybe she's looking to be a sugar mama."

Laura snorted. "You're past your prime to be someone's boy toy."

Danny flexed his arm muscle. "What? There's still muscle in there somewhere. Besides, it's not my looks she'll be wanting." His eyebrows wiggled.

"You're disgusting." She punched him playfully in the arm and pushed him out of the kitchen.

As they worked on Sharon's renovations the rest of the day, Danny realized he had to keep his distance from Sharon when Laura was around. He was looking forward to their date and getting to know more about her. Sharon, she wasn't like Teri, but they did come from different worlds. While he joked about it, the last thing he wanted was Sharon thinking of him as a boy toy, or worse, someone to annoy her father.

Having a bit of fun together was one thing, but how far did she intend to take their relationship, if that was her intention? Danny liked the idea of Sharon in his bed, but not if the reason why was her father. That left a sour taste in his mouth. *Easy, Danny! You're jumping the gun. You haven't even had your first date and you're already talking about sleeping with her?* Could he even call it a date? She was looking for someone to hang out with. Danny's stomach turned at the thought that the attraction was one-sided, even with their almost-kiss, and Sharon only saw him as a friend. If he was a friend, what was Bradley?

Chapter 15

S haron pulled into the Stanley driveway. The quaint home that greeted her was unexpected, along with the beautiful landscaping. It was the homemade kind that screamed Rose had a hand in making it happen. The two-story brick home had a small front patio with two rocking chairs outside with colorful, autumn-themed cushions. What stuck out the most to Sharon were the autumn decorations slathered from the top of the roof and scattered about the lawn. She grinned, imaging Danny putting the decorations up, with his mother dishing out instructions of where exactly to put each decoration and having him move them around before deciding.

Sharon opened the car door and headed up the driveway and knocked on the front door.

Danny answered the door wearing a sweater with a pumpkin on the front. "Tell anyone you saw me in this, and you can kiss your deadline date goodbye."

She smothered a laugh. "My lips are sealed."

"Sharon. Come in!" Rose pushed Danny aside. "Don't leave her standing outside, Danny. Where are your manners?"

Rose led Sharon inside, took her coat and threw it at Danny.

"Is that for me?" Rose pointed to the box in her hand.

"Yes, but it looks like you don't need it." Sharon glanced at the kitchen counter stocked full of food, including a pumpkin pie.

"Nonsense." Rose plucked the box from her hand and placed it on an empty spot on the counter. "There's always room for more pumpkin pie."

An attractive older version of Danny peeked his head out from the kitchen. "Perfect timing. We're just about to carve the turkey." The man wiped his hand on a dish towel before extending it to Sharon. "Hi. I'm John."

"I'm Sharon. Nice to meet you." *Now I see where Danny gets his good looks.* "Isn't Danny a little young to carve the turkey?" she joked.

"You're never too young to carve," Danny stated.

Danny placed a hand on his father's shoulder, a gesture that caused Sharon a smidgen of jealousy. Her relationship with her father wasn't the same.

Sharon shifted her position when she realized she was staring at Danny with goo–goo eyes. Rose and John exchanged glances and smiles. *Great.* The last thing she needed was the added pressure of his parents trying to set them up. Had Danny told them about their arrangement?

Rose undid her apron and placed it around Danny's neck. The lettering on the apron said, "Kiss the cook."

Danny gave his mother a *Not very smooth, Mom* glance. "Don't get any ideas," Danny teased.

"You have nothing to worry about."

"Ouch," Rose and John said in unison. "You're going to fit right in, Sharon," John said.

Danny and Sharon gazed at each other before looking away.

"You boys carve the bird and we'll set the table," Rose said, pushing Danny aside and grabbing Sharon's hand.

"Happy to help," Sharon said with a smile.

"So, Danny's renovating your home?" Rose asked as she laid out the placemats.

"Not the whole house, just my closet and bathroom."

"How did you hear about Danny's company?"

"Josie recommended him."

"Ah, you know Josie?"

Sharon chuckled, thinking about her first encounter with Josie. "Not exactly. Patrick introduced us, sort of."

"Oh, so you know her fiancé, Patrick?"

"Yes. Our families are old friends." Sharon left off being engaged to Patrick. Not a conversation she wanted to have with Danny's mother.

"And he was once your fiancé." Rose gave her a knowing look as if saying her son told her everything.

So much for discretion. "Yes."

"Don't worry, honey. You just weren't meant for each other. I was engaged when I met John, but I knew minutes after meeting him he was the man for me. I broke off my engagement soon after."

The words were so matter-of-fact, Sharon almost felt sorry for the poor man whose heart she broke.

"He's happily married with a ton of kids and grandkids," Rose added, as if reading her mind.

Like Patrick was after their broken engagement. While he didn't have tons of kids, he'd found love and was getting married while she was still floundering with a looming deadline.

"You'll find someone new." Rose touched her shoulder and graced her with a warm smile that made Sharon miss her mother.

They finished setting the table and stood back to admire their handiwork.

"I like to serve buffet style, leaving the dishes on the kitchen counter," Rose said with a smile.

"Especially since they won't all fit on the dining table," John added.

Danny grinned. "You just gave away her secret, Dad."

A hand went to Rose's hip. "You're always giving away my secrets."

"Not all, sweetheart." John winked and Rose blushed.

"Behave. We've got a guest." She slapped his arm playfully.

Sharon grinned and Danny rolled his eyes like only an embarrassed kid could.

"Grab your plates and help yourself," Rose encouraged.

They all took a seat once their plates were filled.

"Before we get started, let's share what we're thankful for," John said.

"It's a family tradition," Danny added. "Each person shares one thing they're grateful for before we eat."

"Since you're the guest, you get to go first, Sharon."

Great! Sharon thought on it for a moment. Saying money or her lifestyle seemed petty, but she couldn't think of anything else. "I'm thankful I can help those who aren't as blessed."

They all nodded in agreement.

"I'm also thankful for a contractor who'll keep his deadline and won't go over budget," she added quickly.

Everyone laughed, including Danny.

"I'm thankful for a loving and healthy family," Rose said when it was her turn.

"I'm thankful for finding a partner to spend my life with. Someone who's supported me through the good, bad, and ugly years. Someone who loves me as I am but pushes me to be a better man. I love you sweetheart." John raised his glass toward his wife on the other end of the table. She blew him a kiss and sent a knowing look.

A look shared between two people who'd experienced a life of love, happiness, and difficult times, but had stuck together through it. Their look was one Sharon had never seen on her parents' faces in all the years they were married, or on Robert's or Virginia's. There was always mutual respect, and caring, but she'd seen nothing more. Maybe if there'd been, things with her family would be different. Their business might be different. Maybe Robert would still be alive.

"I'm thankful for parents who set an example for me of love, trust, and support, both for me and each other. I love you guys."

Everyone raised their glasses to toast.

"And I'm thankful for clients who pay their bills on time," Danny added, giving Sharon a playful wink.

She laughed with his parents.

An hour later, the kitchen was a mess—dirty plates and dishes littered the space. Sharon hadn't laughed so hard in years and was grateful for the evening. She needed it more than she realized, especially with all the craziness in her life. Rose and John were wonderful hosts, but her heart ached a little, thinking about her mother and the times they'd never share again. Those moments weren't of them in the kitchen, but of decorating rooms in the house in preparation for parties. The interaction between Rose and John made her long for the same camaraderie, and obvious love and respect they had for each other. If she chose a partner solely for a seat on the board and her inheritance, she'd be turning her back on the chance of finding love.

Love is already a slim possibility, Sharon. Especially in your circle.

She and Danny started washing the dishes while Rose and John packed away the leftovers.

"Why don't we get a fire started on the back patio, John?" Rose suggested.

"But it's cold as hell out there! Colder than it usually is this time of year."

Rose tugged on his arm. "That's why we're going to build a fire."

John rolled his eyes and followed his wife outside.

"That was subtle." Danny laughed.

"Very," Sharon agreed, handing him another dish to rinse.

"I didn't think you knew how to wash dishes," Danny teased.

"I learned working in homeless shelters with my mom. Not my favorite pastime."

"I suppose you're used to making sure a cleaning crew handles it after a party?"

"Yes."

"I'm surprised your mother never taught you to cook."

"She did. I just wasn't very good at it." Sharon laughed, remembering the times she'd burned most of the foods she tried to make. "These days, it's easier to have premade meals. Healthier and safer."

Danny chuckled. "I bet."

Their hands brushed when she handed him another dish to rinse. Sharon returned her gaze to the dishes in the sink instead of thinking about Danny standing so close to her, and his watchful eyes.

"Did you have family traditions this time of year?" Danny changed the topic.

"Sort of. Everything was geared around fundraising and business parties. We rarely ate alone as a family. There was always a business associate or political connection at the table."

"That must've made family time difficult."

"With my father, yes. My mother used planning parties and decorating rooms as a chance to spend time together. We also had spa days once a month." Sharon's voice trailed off, remembering how she canceled on her mother twice before her death. While her mother tried to spend time with her, she'd put work first...just like her father.

"I'm sorry. It must still be painful to talk about her."

"Sometimes, but it's good to remember her. My father avoids it, as if she was never a part of our lives." Her voice trailed off to a whisper. *Stop sharing such personal information, Sharon.* She didn't care. Talking with Danny came so easily. It was like talking to a friend—something she didn't have a lot of. Most of her time was spent trying to prove herself to her father, or to the board. Sure, she had acquaintances from her circle, but she didn't feel like sharing part of her personal life with any of them. A lump filled with embarrassment and sadness stuck in her throat.

She was hard at work finding a husband and didn't even have one friend. Sharon cleared her throat and attacked the dishes, this time drying.

"Must be difficult for him."

"My parent's relationship wasn't like your parents. They didn't marry for love. Their families arranged their marriage."

"Really?" Danny's voice held a hint of surprise and fascination.

"In all their years together, I never saw them joke like your parents, or share affection. I knew they cared and respected each other, but love?" Sharon laughed. "Did you know I thought all married couples were like my parents?"

"That must've skewed your perspective of relationships," Danny said quietly.

"You have no idea," Sharon whispered.

Danny touched her shoulder, pulling her from her melancholy thoughts about her mother and her parents' relationship, and her own over the years.

"You get to choose something different."

Sharon gave him a thin smile. If only he knew. Choosing differently meant giving up everything she wanted since she was a teenager, and walking away from everything and everyone she knew. *Would that be so bad, Sharon?*

"You two finished up?" John's voice broke their moment.

Sharon was grateful. She'd never shared such personal information about herself, but it surprisingly felt good. *Probably the combination of the comfort of his family and their home,* Sharon reasoned. *Keep telling yourself that.*

"Yup. All done." Danny closed the cupboard. "What's our payment?"

"Hot chocolate and pumpkin pies on the patio next to a roaring fire?" Rose offered.

"A fire I froze my ass off to make," John added.

"With or without marshmallows, Sharon?" Rose asked, ignoring her husband's complaint.

"With, of course."

"Of course," John chuckled.

Danny grabbed their coats and led Sharon through the double patio doors to the patio lit with hovering twinkly lights.

Sharon gasped. The backyard itself wasn't large, but was so beautifully decked out in autumn, Marth Stewart herself would be proud to show it on the pages of her magazine. A white wicker patio set anchored the space, along with a firepit set in the middle. Autumn décor accented the sides of the furniture and the end tables. Sharon did a 360, taking in the entire scene. The small fire was cozy, and the chairs were close enough to it to feel its warmth.

She sat on the loveseat.

Danny took a blanket from the back of the large couch and placed it on her lap. He sat on one of the single chairs.

"Your parents are great."

Danny nodded. "They are. I didn't really appreciate them until I visited other friends' homes."

"Never forget to tell them how much they mean to you. You never know when they'll be gone." A sharp pain pinched her heart, remembering when she received the news that her mother had had a heart attack and was gone. Her death devastated Sharon, especially since her already-distant father withdrew even more.

"My parents are one of the main reasons I stayed in Chicago and started my business close to them. We have dinner together at least once a week, and spend our holidays together."

Sharon smiled. Danny was a wonderful son. There was no doubt about it. A wonderful man who'd never be hers, who couldn't be hers. Being around Danny and his family made it easy to believe she was a friend enjoying their company without the worries of her job and her looming deadline, Robert's death, or her threats. Being with them made it easy to wish her life was different, getting to sit next to him on the couch on his parents' patio and snuggle under a blanket covering their legs, the warmth of his body pressed against the side of her, his arm around her shoulder. Not miles away on another piece of furniture. It was easy to imagine their drive home, holding hands and the steamy kiss good night on her front porch. *You don't know if the kiss would be hot, Sharon.*

She glanced over at Danny, who was watching her. The soft glow of the firepit cast shadows over him, highlighting the gold streaks in his hair. Sparks shot through her when her gaze settled on his face and saw the heat of his stare. Yes, their kiss would be hot with Danny pressing her back against the door and running his hands over the layers of her clothes before slipping them inside the folds. Would he ask to come in, or just open the door and lead them inside? There'd be no waiting until they reached the bedroom. They'd make it there eventually, but not before enjoying each other on every surface on the way.

"Well, this is cozy."

John's voice broke through her fantasy and Sharon's gaze snapped away from Danny when she realized their eyes were still locked.

"Danny. Sit next to Sharon so she doesn't freeze," Rose suggested. "We've only got two blankets. Your father and I will share the other one."

Sharon almost laughed out loud when Danny rolled his eyes at another of his mother's attempts for them to be close. Between the thrill of Danny's skin brushing against hers while washing dishes, and Rose and John making her feel so welcome in their home, it was no wonder she was feeling so lightheaded and in a fantasy world. A world she was escaping into from the stress of her own life. No wonder she was having delirious ideas about being a part of Danny's life.

Sharon remained quiet for the remainder of the night, observing the interaction between Danny and his parents, and ignored the occasional twinge of envy because her family lacked the same warmth, even as a child. She bet Danny's parents never missed his school events because of business, or only attended events that provided some political or business gain. They invested time with Danny because he was their son, and not for keeping up appearances.

An hour later, Sharon was driving home and trying not to think about the way Danny's gaze raked over her lips when he walked her to the car. What she needed was for time to jump to when she'd have her seat on the board, and the deal signed. A time when her home was renovated, and Danny was no longer a temptation she couldn't have. That meant she'd be either married or engaged to someone. That person would likely be Bradley.

Her time with Bradley was proving him to be nicer than she originally thought, but a coldness still settled in her stomach at the thought of marrying him. They'd both have freedom to live the life they wanted, but even business agreements had better odds than having the kind of marriage her father was forcing her into. *What century am I living in?*

Sharon suddenly understood how women hundreds of years ago felt about their future, uncertain and out of their control. She didn't like that feeling and knew for a fact, several women throughout history didn't settle for what was handed to them, and neither would she.

There was a missed call on her phone, along with a message. She'd turned it off while she was at Danny's parents. She didn't recognize the number, so she listened to the message.

"I'm coming for you bitch!" was left in a garbled, disguised tone.

Sharon's heartbeat jerked and the hairs on the back of her neck sprang to life. She called back the number, but it said the number didn't exist. Her fingers trembled as she ended the call. First the flowers, the note on her car, Robert's death, and now this message. Someone was trying to scare her. The question of why didn't give her comfort because she had no clue what the hell was going on, and why this person was after her. Sharon suddenly remembered the awkwardness between Robert and Bradley in the elevator before he died. Did he have something to do with what was happening?

Bradley was many things, but she couldn't imagine him killing someone, and for what? Warning her about him?

When she pulled into the driveway, she had the thought of calling Danny, but changed her mind and headed inside the house. She went about checking all the doors and windows first and making sure the alarm was set. She'd give Danny the code tomorrow just to be safe. What would she tell Danny? Sharon longed to tell him the truth, but then what? Attention was the last thing she wanted, especially with the business deal in the works with a new client and trying to navigate her family contract. She'd been putting off calling Patrick, hoping things would blow over, or the police would uncover who killed Robert, and maybe the person who was stalking her. Not to mention he was in the middle of planning his wedding.

Sharon headed upstairs, locked the bedroom door, put on pajamas, and climbed into bed. She lay wide-eyed hours later, the sound of the harsh words and tone of voice echoing in her mind. She disliked guns, but maybe it was time she considered purchasing one.

Chapter 16

S haron opened the door for Danny the next morning when he rang the doorbell. She usually did once she got downstairs and started brewing the coffee.

"Late start?" Danny asked with a grin.

"Not exactly." Her expression must've given her away because Danny asked. "What's wrong?"

Filling her travel mug and a cup for him, she contemplated what to tell him. "I—" she stammered.

"Something happened last night?" Danny offered.

Sharon nodded. She opened her mouth to talk, but the sounds of Laura and the guys coming in the front door stopped her.

"Do you want to cancel going to Patrick and Lola's engagement party tonight?"

She'd completely forgotten. Part of her didn't feel like socializing, but she wanted to support Patrick. Not to mention she wasn't sure she wanted to be alone.

"No. We should go."

"We'll talk then."

Sharon didn't answer, not sure what to say and if she'd be ready to talk. Grabbing her handbag and coffee mug, she headed out the door, saying a quick good morning to Laura. When she reached her office, Ryan reminded her of her meetings for the day, along with a hair appointment.

"I scheduled it for you when I received your invitation for Patrick's engagement party. I figured you could cancel it if you decided not to attend."

Sharon longed to give him a kiss on the cheek for his thoughtfulness, but it'd be out of character for her. Instead, she graced him with words. "Thank you. I don't know what I'd do without you." Ryan blushed under her praise before his fingers returned to the keyboard.

Sharon collected her messages and headed to her office. Moments later, she called Ryan. He picked up on the first ring.

"Can you please research guns shops nearby?"

There was a long silence on the other end before he replied. "Yes, Ms. Donovan." He rang back moments later. "Would you like to know the wait time to get a firearm?"

Sharon hadn't considered that. Her father only hunted if it was required for a business meeting or connection; maybe she should consider asking him. *What would you say, Sharon?* His disapproving expression and words burned in her mind's eye. She'd have to explain why she needed a gun, and that wouldn't do.

"Yes, please."

Sharon spent the rest of the day trying to distract herself with work, but the caller's words kept haunting her. Then she had to meet Danny for Patrick and Josie's engagement party later that evening. Not to mention Danny's expectations that they'd talk. What could she say? Danny would pressure her to contact the police.

Ryan came to her office at the end of the day with the details about guns she asked for. "Is everything okay, Ms. Donovan?"

"Yes, Ryan." She managed a slight smile.

"Would you like me to walk you to your car?"

Sharon appreciated his offer, but as she gazed over his frame and stature, she couldn't imagine him intimating anyone who might attack her. "Thanks for the offer, Ryan, but I'm not staying late. I have a party, remember?" she said lightly so as not to offend.

"Isn't it strange going to your ex-fiancé's engagement party?" Ryan cleared his throat, realizing how personal his question was. "I'm sorry, Ms. Donovan. It's none of my business."

"It's all right, Ryan. Patrick and I were childhood friends and we're still friends. I'm happy for him." Sharon didn't elaborate.

"Maybe you'll find love too, Sharon."

Sharon smiled. He'd finally called her by her first name. She hadn't pushed, assuming it would take him time to adjust.

"I'm sorry. I did it again." Ryan smiled sheepishly, making her realize how young, yet attractive he was.

"That's all right. Maybe I will." She gave him a smile to match his. "Maybe we both will."

Ryan's face lit up as he nodded in agreement.

Sharon expected him to say he'd already found it, but his face said otherwise, making her wonder again about his sexuality.

"Have a nice evening, Sharon."

"You too, Ryan."

Twenty minutes later, she shut off her computer and headed to the elevator.

Bradley was already inside and held the door for her.

"Thank you."

"You're welcome."

The elevator music filled their time, but Sharon felt his gaze. Her heartbeat quickened, imagining him being her stalker, or worse, the person who shot Robert. His arrogant and expressive suit negated her suspicions about him. Bradley wasn't the type to get his hands dirty.

"Are you going to Patrick's engagement party tonight?"

"Yes. You?"

"Yes." His hands were shoved into his pants pocket. "I thought about asking you, but I didn't think you'd want to go."

"A lot of people didn't, but we're friends and I'm happy for him."

"Really?"

"Does that surprise you?"

"Yes. Especially since he broke off the engagement and is engaged to—"

Sharon's gaze dared him to say something derogatory about Josie.

"Someone outside our circle." He chose carefully.

"He's happy. That's all that matters."

"But how much can they have in common? Not a good foundation."

Sharon faced him. "Yes. Marrying for common interests and business interest is a much better foundation."

He winced at her sarcastic tone. "There's mutual respect, and social community," he added.

"Are you trying to convince me or yourself?"

His jawline jumped. "I didn't mean to upset you."

"I'm not upset. I just find it fascinating that people are questioning Patrick and Josie's marriage when families in our circle have married for equally bogus reasons."

"I suppose you're right."

The elevator *dinged,* indicating they'd reached the garage. She didn't object when he offered to walk her to her car. Thankfully there was nothing on her car and she thanked Bradley before getting in.

"See you tonight."

"Tonight."

Sharon started her car and headed to the beauty salon, wondering about Bradley's reaction when she arrived with Danny as her date. Danny was friends with Josie, so his being there wouldn't be unusual, but when he saw them walk in together, it would be interesting to see. *You should be more worried about Father's reaction, Sharon.*

With everything that had happened over the past few days, Sharon hadn't had time to think about him, or his reaction. She suddenly felt sick to her stomach.

Chapter 17

───────◆───────

*T*his was a bad idea. Sharon held onto Danny's arm as they headed up the staircase to the ballroom, where the engagement party was being held. When they reached the top of the stairs, they were greeted by elegantly dressed men on either side of the stairs, one with a tray filled with glasses of champagne and the other with a clipboard.

"Welcome." They spoke in unison.

Danny handed the man with the clipboard their invitations while Sharon grabbed two glasses of champagne. She gave one to Danny as they headed toward large, white and gold trimmed double doors. Sharon's hand trembled and she gripped Danny's arm tighter.

"I'm going to need to use my arm by the end of the night," Danny teased.

She loosened her grip. "I'm sorry. I'm petrified."

"Maybe we should've done shots at your house before coming?"

Sharon laughed. "Maybe next time." If there was a next time. After her father saw them together, neither of them might live to see tomorrow.

"You'll be fine. We're just two friends supporting our friends on their special day."

Sharon took a deep breath and another sip of champagne. "You're right. We should've done shots."

Danny chuckled.

The ballroom was enormous and filled with more people than she had imagined, but Patrick's mother Elsa was the reason. From what Sharon knew about Josie, she didn't have any living family and very few friends, other than Danny and the men on his crew. Glancing around, the people were business and political connections, and friends and family from Patrick's and her family.

"I think I'm the only person here Josie knows—other than Patrick's family and you," Danny whispered.

"I think you're right."

Danny led her to where Josie and Patrick stood, putting their now-empty champagne glasses on a passing tray. "Open bar?" He nodded toward the area at the back of the room.

"Of course."

"Good. I have a feeling we're going to need it."

Both Patrick and Josie were surrounded by people and didn't notice them at first. Josie did and tugged Patrick's arm to bring them to his attention.

Josie rushed forward, hugging Danny tightly. "I'm SO glad you came. I'm dying over here. If I have to nod in agreement or refrain from sharing my political opinion another minute, I'm going to scream, or open fire."

Danny squeezed her against him and laughed. "Looks like I got here in time. And since when do you hold back sharing your opinion?" The question was rhetorical. Sharon knew why all too well.

"When your future father- and son-in-law are running for office and you don't want to offend anyone because your beliefs contradict their way of life."

"And she promised me to be nice," Patrick added. "Hands off my future wife, Danny. You had your chance and you lost."

Sharon glanced at Danny, who was grinning. "Just trying to make you jealous and step up."

Patrick snorted. "I was already rounding the bases and heading home."

Josie blushed and hit Patrick's arm playfully. "Behave, you two. You'll give Sharon the wrong impression." Josie clasped her hand. "Nice to see you again, Sharon. I'm so glad you came."

"I wouldn't miss it for the world."

"You two came together?" Josie asked, glancing between her and Danny.

"Yes," Danny answered and held his hand up to keep Josie from asking more questions. "I'm being nice and escorting her here, Josie. Don't read too much into it."

"But it's a date, right?" Josie pressed Sharon.

"I second what Danny said."

Josie pouted, making them laugh.

Patrick put his arm around her waist. "Don't worry, honey. You can corner them another time when they can't escape."

Josie bumped him with her hip, but the wheels were turning. Sharon was certain both she and Danny would be getting a visit from her very soon.

"How are you holding up since Robert's death?" Patrick asked, his eyes filled with worry.

Danny's gaze snapped in her direction, but he remained silent, waiting for her answer. "As good as can be expected."

"Sharon."

She turned at the sound of her name. Carlton and Bradley stood behind her. This was the first time she'd seen Carlton since his father's death.

"How are you, Carlton?" Sharon asked, genuinely concerned about him. The death of a parent was difficult. "How's your mother?"

"Who's this?" Carlton asked, ignoring her questions, his gaze raking over Danny as if trying to place him.

"Danny Stanley. He's doing renovations at Sharon's house," Bradley answered.

Leave it to Bradley to mention that tidbit.

"Nice to meet you." Danny offered his hand to Carlton, who looked at it for several seconds before deciding to shake it and offer his own name.

"Bradley."

"Danny."

The friction in the air between Danny and Bradley caused everyone close to them to stare.

"How's Denise?" Bradley asked, breaking the moment.

"Who?"

"Isn't she your girlfriend?"

"No, she was a blind date, and we went out once," Danny clarified.

Sharon felt like a spectator waiting for an argument to break into a brawl.

"You should understand... You were out with Sharon, and you two aren't dating."

Bradley's jawline jumped, and she was certain if they weren't at an engagement party, Danny would've gotten a fist to the face.

"Sharon. Would you care to dance?" Bradley didn't wait for an answer but took her hand and led her to the dance floor.

She sensed the lecture coming.

"What are you doing with here with him? I could've brought you."

"You didn't ask," Sharon replied. Not that him asking would've mattered. While she'd enjoyed their lunch together, her distrust of him was growing, especially after the encounter in the elevator with Robert. Uncle Robert wasn't always the best judge of character, but it was still suspicious. Besides, she preferred Danny's company.

"I didn't think you wanted to attend, given the circumstances." He pulled her closer to him. "I'm sorry."

"Don't be. I came with the right person."

"Is there something going on between you two?"

Sharon shrugged. "We're friends. He makes me laugh." That wasn't a lie, but she wouldn't classify the attraction between her and Danny as friendship, but what else could she say? *I like that he makes me feel alive whenever I'm around him.* Those were words Bradley wouldn't want to hear.

"I thought we had a moment at lunch." Bradley's tight grip of her hand softened. "I enjoyed our kiss."

She didn't want to lie to him, but she didn't want to scare him away when she hadn't decided about him as a future husband candidate. "I enjoyed our lunch, too. It was nice getting to know each other in a less formal setting," she said, avoiding his comment about the kiss.

"I'd like to do it again sometime."

"Another lunch would be nice."

He wasn't talking about lunch, but she didn't want to encourage him. Not until she had no other alternatives, and Ryan diving into Bradley's live was done. The first kiss was to see if there was any chemistry between them. There wasn't. It was bad enough that she might have to marry someone she didn't love, but no sexual attraction would make the marriage less bearable until it was in name only. Bradley didn't seem like the type not to expect the perks of married life.

"I meant our kiss, but I'll start with lunch," Bradley teased.

Sharon let her silence answer for her.

"Are you sure there's nothing between you two?"

"Why do you ask?"

"Because of the nasty looks he's giving me from across the room." He laughed.

Danny was standing by the bar, and he did indeed have a sour face.

"No man wants another one taking away his date for the night."

"I can agree with you on that one, but it'd be so much fun to annoy him."

Danny would agree with Bradley. Sharon thought about pointing that out, but didn't think he'd appreciate any similarity to Danny, and neither would Danny. The song ended and Bradley escorted her back to Danny.

Bradley kissed her hand. "Thank you for the dance, Sharon."

"Thank you."

"Perhaps you'll save me another?"

"Don't bet on it, pal." Danny took her hand from Bradley's.

Bradley grinned and winked at Sharon.

She rolled her eyes. *Men.*

"Can you believe that guy?"

"What? Asking me to dance?"

"Yes. You're my date."

"So I'm not allowed to dance with other men?" She thought Danny was less chauvinistic, but he was proving her wrong.

"Well, no, but..."

"Do I need your permission? Is that it?"

"No, I just..."

"You think I should stand here and decorate your arm the whole night?" She crossed her arms.

"I thought that's what I was doing," Danny shot back. "I just don't like that guy. I don't care who you dance with. Just not him."

"Why not?"

Danny raked a hand through his hair. "I just don't like him, okay?"

"I get it, but you can't dictate who I spend my time with."

"You're right. We're just friends, right? I'm here to make you laugh, right?"

"You're not a dancing monkey, Danny." Sharon touched his shoulder, knowing he wasn't really annoyed at her, just digging up old wounds. "You made the offer to come."

Danny's gaze found hers. "I know. Sorry for reacting like an ass, but I really don't like that guy."

"He's not so bad once you get to know him." Sharon raised an eyebrow.

"Like me?"

She grinned. "Yes."

"How about some fresh air? I think there's a balcony through those doors." Danny pointed with his chin.

"Let's get more champagne," Sharon suggested. "We'll need reinforcements to get through the rest of the night." *Especially if Father arrives.*

"You got it." Danny grabbed two glasses from the bar and followed her to the French doors on the other side of the room, weaving through the crowd.

A few people stopped them on the way and Sharon introduced him as Danny, but didn't elaborate. They left a few eyebrows raised and confused faces behind, as people who knew Sharon scrambled to place his face or ask the people his identity.

They were both laughing when they reached outside. The wind was chilly, and Danny removed his jacket and placed it around her shoulders. The warmth and smell of him engulfed her. The tingles it evoked were nice.

"We could've had more fun if you told them who I really was."

Sharon grinned. "Maybe, but I didn't want them to snub you."

"I'm tough. I can handle it."

"Maybe." Sharon watched him over the rim of her glass as she took a sip.

"What? You saying I'm not manly enough to handle a bunch of rich people?"

He was deflecting with humor. Sharon knew the trick well, but she didn't use humor.

"How they treat you has everything to do with them and nothing to do with you," she assured him.

"I know." His expression was reflective, as if he had peeked into the past.

Sharon touched his cheek. "I mean it, Danny. You're a wonderful person, and they'd be lucky to call you friend."

His hand covered hers. Her head was spinning, and it wasn't just the three glasses of champagne she'd consumed.

"Just friends?" He kissed the palm of her hand and sparks raced up her arm, spreading like a bushfire across her body.

"Well, I don't think Mr. Bitter would appreciate you offering his wife your friendship." He was an older gentleman whose young wife hadn't hidden her appreciation at meeting Danny with her eyes.

Danny grinned. "I meant us."

"I think our relationship is complicated enough." He had no idea what she was contemplating offering him. If he did, he'd likely jump over the balcony and run for his life.

"You're not going to be my client forever, Sharon."

"It's not just that."

"You mean your money? Don't worry. I don't want any, other than for my bill, of course." A rakish grin tugged at his mouth and her stomach flip-flopped.

"Normal relationships aren't an option for me." What else could she say? He might think she was crazy.

Danny raised an eyebrow. "What kind of relationship can you have?"

"It complicated."

"How complicated could it be? I ask you out, and you say yes."

"That's the champagne talking." She pulled her hand from his face. "You'll change your mind tomorrow."

Danny's arm went around her waist. "It's not the champagne, Sharon." The deep, sexy tone of his voice made her pulse race, as did the intensity of his gaze on her mouth.

The cold air around them heated, and the jacket around her shoulder felt like a heavy blanket. His amber eyes grew dark as his head lowered toward her. His lips captured hers, soft yet firm. Once, twice, before he nibbled her bottom lip. The balcony spun around her, and she gripped his shoulders. His hands fisted against her back before squeezing her closer.

Someone clearing their throat sliced through their moment and they stepped away from each other. Patrick was gawking at them, as if an alien ship had landed and little green men trotted out.

"Shall we head back inside?" Danny asked.

"Give us a minute," Patrick replied.

Danny searched her for an answer. "I'll see you inside."

Patrick's gaze burned her face. He didn't speak until the door closed.

"Danny's a nice guy, Sharon. Not some toy for you to play with."

Sharon sliced him with a stare. "I know that!"

"Do you? Then what're you doing out here kissing him?"

"That's none of your business," she shot back.

"He's my future wife's best friend. You bet it's my business."

"It was just too much champagne." That was a nasty lie. Well, not on her part, but she was certain she wouldn't need alcohol as an excuse to kiss Danny. And what a kiss! Her body was still humming.

"What's really going on, Sharon? Why is he here with you? And don't say *as a* friend, like you told Bradley. I saw the way Danny watched you when you were dancing. No friend watches another one that way."

"I like him..." she mumbled.

"Does your father know?

"No. You know how he'd react, especially with the contract deadline looming."

"What contract deadline?"

Patrick knew part of the story but not the entirety of it. He raked a hand through his hair when she finished.

"You can't be serious! Is that why your parents wanted us to get married?"

"Partly. I wanted you because I know you'd give me the power I wanted."

"Surely there's a way to get out of it?"

"Not that I've found."

"What does this have to do with Danny?"

"Nothing. I like him. He makes me laugh." Sharon nibbled on her bottom lip in contemplation. Now was the perfect opportunity to tell Patrick about the threats.

Patrick studied her for what seemed like an eternity before he spoke. "Stop by my office next week. Maybe I can help."

"I will. There's another important topic to discuss when we meet." *That was an understatement.*

He nodded. "In the meantime, I suggest you avoid things going any further with Danny."

Sharon knew what that meant and blushed, thinking about her and Danny. Definitely not a good idea, but after that kiss? It wasn't going to be so easy keeping her hands off him. Did he feel the same? *Don't go there, Sharon.*

What the hell are you doing? You shouldn't have kissed her. He should've asked her about her uncle's death, but a party didn't seem like the best time, given how she reacted to Patrick asking. He didn't regret the kiss. It was a bad idea, given their relationship, but he was right. Things would change once he finished renovating her home.

"Normal relationships aren't an option for me right now." *What the hell did she mean? Did she mean serious, or casual?* Sharon didn't strike him as the "friends with benefits" type, but anything was possible. He liked the idea of Sharon in his bed, but he didn't do casual.

Danny watched Patrick and Sharon on the balcony talking, wishing he was a piece of furniture out there so he could hear what they were saying. It was about him. That much he knew, but was Patrick warning her to stay away from him, or the other way around? Patrick knew them both, but he'd been friends with Sharon longer.

"Penny for your thoughts?" Josie studied him with wary eyes.

"They're worth more than that."

She grinned. "You can say that again."

"Are you allowed to talk to me?" Danny teased.

"I begged for five minutes from being on duty, but I have a feeling I'll need more time to unravel this mystery."

Danny took a sip of champagne.

"Want to talk about it?"

"There's nothing to talk about."

"Really? You show up to my engagement party with Patrick's old fiancé, your current client, and there's nothing to talk about?"

He shrugged. "She needed a date."

"She could've come with Bradley."

He snorted. "He's an ass."

"What do you care?"

"I think she can do better."

"Better as in you?"

"Stop trying to get into my head, Josie." Danny graced her with a firm *Stop now* stare.

"I'm just trying to help."

"There's nothing to help."

"I saw you kiss her."

Danny cursed under his breath. "So? This is a date.

"Is that how things are, then?"

"No," he said, a little too quickly. He didn't want Josie to think he had a physical relationship with Sharon, even though he wanted one.

"I confess, I hoped you two would hit it off when I recommended you to her. I know you like blondes." Josie grinned.

"Ah. It was all part of your plan. So what's the problem?"

"No problem. I just wanted to make sure you had good intentions."

"Whose friend are you anyway?" he asked with a hint of teasing.

"Yours, but Sharon is a childhood friend of my future husband. He cares about her and wouldn't want her to be another notch in your belt."

He raised an eyebrow. "There are no notches in my belt."

"I remember a time when there were," she whispered tentatively.

Danny met her with a sharp gaze. Josie had met Teri once and told him what she thought. He didn't listen and ended up nursing a bruised heart and ego. He went through a few women after Teri, but he'd been honest with them—unlike Teri.

"I'm not that man anymore."

"I know." She touched his shoulder. "I'm concerned for both of you. Sharon isn't known for her warm and loving nature. You are."

He opened his mouth to argue that he'd seen a different side of her, but he honestly didn't know enough about Sharon. There was heat beneath her icy gaze, but was it just sexual attraction, or something more? It felt like something more to him, and he wanted to find out if it was.

"I appreciate your concern, Josie, but we're adults and we'll be fine."

Josie studied him for several moments, and he expected another lecture, but she remained silent. When he saw Patrick strolling toward them, he understood why. Was he going to lecture or threaten him? With Patrick, it could go either way.

"Go easy, Danny. Sharon may come across as tough, but she's not," Patrick said.

That was unexpected. Danny nodded with understanding.

Sharon joined them moments later, but Josie and Patrick were called away by Elsa, Patrick's mother.

"So, did you get the speech too?" Danny joked.

"Not exactly, but pretty close." She grinned.

The music changed to a softer tune and the noise of the room dimmed as he took her hand and led her to the dance floor.

"I didn't peg you for a dancer."

He grinned. "My father told me it would help with the ladies."

Her laughter shot straight through his chest. She had a wonderful laugh. He pulled her closer and moved them about. The heat of her skin warmed his hand, and he ran a thumb along the base of her neck. *Soft.* Just as he'd imagined.

The crowd around them provided a shield he was grateful for. As the song played, their movement slowed and she was so close to him, she could've rested her head on his chest. The memory of their kiss from earlier popped into his head, causing the already-intimate moment to escalate. If they weren't on the balcony of a hotel with hordes of people around, Danny would've dug his fingers into her hair and kissed her deeply. He lied about the alcohol affecting him—it tore down his resistance to keeping her at arms length.

Being around her tonight was nice. Every moment was more enjoyable than the last. The sooner he finished renovating her home, the better. He wanted more than a business relationship. He wanted to take her to dinner, share the stories of their lives, hold hands on the table, and kiss her at the end of the night. Not a chaste kiss, but a push-her-against-the-door and hands–all–over–each–other kind of kiss. The kind that led to roaming hands, sweaty bodies, and deep moans and sighs.

To make that happen, he needed to know why she couldn't have a normal relationship. What the hell could be going on in her life to prevent it? Was it work? Bradley? Her father? The song ended, but his mind still raced with questions he'd have to wait to ask until he drove her home.

Danny led them off the dance floor. Keeping her body this close to him any longer was a bad idea in public, especially this public.

"Sharon. How lovely for you to join us." A woman greeted them.

"Elsa, thank you for inviting me."

Elsa was Patrick's mother. Danny had never met her before, but he'd heard stories from Josie. She'd retained her youthful attractiveness, and he wondered it if was good genes or upkeep. The stiffness of her posture and the tight line of her face revealed she was related to Patrick. He'd become familiar with that stiffness when he worked with Josie to renovate Patrick's home.

"Elsa, this is Danny Stanley."

"Ah, yes. The contractor friend of Josie's." Her judging gaze raked over him. "How did you two cross paths?"

"I'm renovating a room for Sharon."

"I see." Elsa's gaze shifted to Sharon. "Does your father know?"

"No."

"He should."

Danny's gaze shifted between both women, realizing he wasn't getting whatever they were talking about.

"It's not the right time."

"There will never be a right time with your father." Elsa placed a hand on Sharon's arm. "Don't be afraid to follow your heart."

Surprise raced across Sharon's face before she hugged Elsa. Elsa then disappeared as quickly as she'd appeared.

"What was that all about?" Danny inquired. It had something to do with Sharon's father, but besides that, he had no clue. Their families had known each other for years, so it must be an inside thing.

"Girl talk," she replied cryptically.

Sharon's face grew solemn, and he followed the direction of her gaze. It landed on Mark Donovan.

Ah, hell. Danny suspected they might run into him tonight, but he'd hoped they wouldn't.

Mark's expression darkened when he saw them, and he strolled toward them like a man on a mission. Sharon tensed. Danny grabbed another glass of champagne and handed it to her. He didn't take one for himself. A clear head was necessary for a man like Mark.

Danny tried to relax, but every muscle in his body flexed, ready for attack, whether it came verbally or physically. Mark wouldn't make a public scene, would he? Danny didn't know enough to say, but suspected he wouldn't. Not with Elsa around, ready to swoop in and stop him.

"What the hell is he doing here?" Mark hissed. "And why aren't you here with Bradley?"

"I decided to come with Danny. He makes me laugh."

Mark stared at her as if she'd grown a second head. "Are you mad? You think you have time for laughter? You're wasting time, Sharon."

"What does it matter, Father? You don't want me at that table anyway. You've said as much. I'll be damned if I'm going to be with someone who'd take away everything I'm working for."

"You don't know that. Have you spoken to Bradley?"

"No, but I don't see him giving up the power or the money."

"And he will?" Mark's chin nudged toward him.

What the hell are they talking about? Danny felt like someone who'd walked into a conversation where no one was speaking English.

Sharon didn't answer.

"I will what?" Danny asked.

"This isn't the time or place for this conversation, Father."

Mark glanced around and his expression softened, as if remembering they were at a party. "If you'd remained with Patrick, you wouldn't be in this predicament."

Her jawline clenched. "Patrick broke off the engagement, not me. Besides, at least one of us is happy. I'm in this predicament because of stupid family traditions you're unwilling to change." Sharon took a sip of champagne.

"If it was good enough for me and your mother, it's good enough for you."

"Times have changed, Father. We need to change with them."

The band started up again, breaking into the words Mark was about to say. He strolled away, not bothering to address either of them with a goodbye.

"What was that about?" Danny asked.

"It's complicated."

"Like your comment about relationships."

Sharon gave him a sad smile. "Yes."

Danny longed to start a conversation about it, but was interrupted by Elsa speaking on stage.

The rest of the evening was a blur, with congratulatory toasts for the couple. Danny was grateful when Sharon asked to leave right after. He said his goodbyes to Patrick, Josie, and Elsa while Sharon said goodbye to them and everyone else she knew. Most people they met tonight were nicer than Danny thought they'd be, but probably because they didn't know him, only that he wasn't part of the usual circle.

As they made their way out, Danny realized how hungry he was and snagged hors d'oeuvres off every tray he passed, whether it appealed to him or not. He'd kill for a giant steak with a huge helping of steamed vegetables, and a baked potato with the works.

"I'm starving," Sharon said when they reached outside.

"Music to my ears. Me too." He opened the car door for her. "What did you have in mind?" he asked when inside the car.

They'd driven her car because it was much cleaner than his work truck. He resisted the urge to gun it with her in the car, but it was one sweet, smooth ride.

"I don't care. Anything that'll fill me up. That finger food just wasn't cutting it."

He chuckled. "I couldn't agree more, especially with all that champagne you drank."

"Yes. My head will be paying me back tomorrow."

"Drink lots of water so you stay hydrated, and food will help," he offered.

"Learned from personal experience?"

"It comes with the territory when you work in the construction industry. Work hard, play harder."

"Hmm." She adjusted the seat.

"How about a steak, veggies, and potato?"

"Yes, but let's get it to go. I've had enough of people and socializing."

"Agreed." He dialed a number and placed their food order.

Danny turned on the radio and smooth jazz flowed. "You have that in common with Josie."

"What? My taste in music or men?"

He laughed. "Music. I'm nothing like Patrick."

"You are in the good ways."

"The money part would be nice," he joked.

"More money isn't always better, Danny." Sharon's gaze shifted to the passing scenery outside the window.

"I know, but a lot of it is nice when you have a business." He grinned.

"I suppose."

"Spoken like someone who's never had to worry about it."

"You're right. I don't know what it's like, but I know what it's like for things to be out of your control," Sharon whispered.

"Your conversation with your father?"

She nodded.

"Want to talk about it?"

"Not particularly."

Of course not, Danny. "What about the relationship comment?"

"That's just as complicated."

"I'm a good listener, Sharon, and talking about it helps."

He pulled into the parking lot of the restaurant, parked the car, and checked his watch. The restaurant was one he ordered from occasionally when his budget allowed. "Food should be ready." He got out and headed inside.

There was still another ten minutes before the food was ready, but he sensed Sharon wanted to be alone with her thoughts. His questions made her uncomfortable. She'd been grilled enough by her father. The last thing she needed was another person pressing her for answers. As much as he wanted to know, he didn't want to make her uncomfortable. She did that enough on her own.

Sharon watched Danny head inside, relieved to have a minute to herself and pleased that he sensed it. Her father didn't make a scene, but a talk was coming about Danny, and there was no avoiding it. Mark was trying to help her in his own way, but he'd help her more if he were open to her suggestions to change the contract.

Patrick offered to look over the contract. She planned to take him up on it. Maybe he'd see an option she and the other lawyers had missed, or offer an alternative her father would be open to. Nothing she'd come up with had worked. How was she going to break the news about her stalker? Sharon still wasn't sure. Robert's death made the situation worse. Was his death suicide or murder? There'd been nothing around the office except rumors and speculations. Virginia hadn't shown up and Carlton avoided answering how she was doing, which could mean bad, or she was plotting something big. When it came to Virginia, you never knew.

Bradley wasn't off the table, but she wished she had other options. Danny's face popped into her mind. She pushed it back. He'd be insulted by any offer she made. He wasn't from their world, and wouldn't understand. She cringed, thinking about the disappointment in his eyes if she did make him an offer of marriage in exchange for money. No, she wouldn't drag him into her mess. It occurred to her for a second when he mentioned his business, but he wasn't in dire enough straits, and again, would be insulted by such an offer.

Danny would end up with a woman like Laura or Josie. Someone who'd love and support him, and they'd have a relationship like his parents. Jealousy stabbed her, thinking of him with another woman and enjoying everything she wanted for herself but couldn't have.

Tears pooled in her eyes, making her wish she was someone different, someone who could choose their own path. Sharon brushed the tears aside when Danny came out of the restaurant with their food. While she couldn't have a relationship with Danny, she'd enjoy the way he made her feel while she could. Laugh while she could. Be herself while she could.

"Hot food coming through," Danny said as he got in the car.

"Yay! Let's get home so we can eat. I meant, back to my place," she quickly corrected. His gaze was on her, but she didn't dare look, especially since she was crying earlier.

"Yes, ma'am."

"Ma'am? Women my age do not want to be called *ma'am,* Danny."

"Of course." He saluted. "I'm at your service and will drive you home."

Sharon chuckled.

The drive to her house was filled with music and quiet stillness as she watched the passing cars and buildings outside the window. Danny handled her car like a pro, considering it was a stick shift. She'd expected him to balk, like most men did. Few people drove stick anymore, especially in populated areas, but she loved it. It reminded her of the few times she spent with her father. He taught her to drive. He believed learning to drive a stick shift was an important skill, although he never said why.

Sharon's stomach was rumbling by the time they pulled into her driveway, and she jumped out and headed inside. She turned on the lights leading them to the kitchen, and sat at the counter. While she had a formal dining room, she only used it when entertaining. She usually ate perched on a stool at the kitchen counter.

Danny set the bag of food down and tore it open and pushed a container toward her, along with plastic silverware. Sharon stood and fetched real silverware instead. "Eating steak with a plastic knife is never a good idea."

"Agreed. I didn't peg you for a meat eater."

"I don't indulge often, but I enjoy it to the fullest when I do." She popped a bite in her mouth, closed her eyes, and savored the juicy flavor of the steak.

"Well, I indulge as often as I can. And believe me, it's often." He cut into the large steak.

"I bet you'd eat meat and potatoes everyday if you could. Or do you?"

"I throw in an occasional vegetable now and then, along with a healthy helping of mac and cheese."

"Ah, yes. The famous baked mac and cheese. I have yet to see if it'll live up to its name."

"It will!" he said with a wink.

"That remains to be seen." Sharon hoped she would.

Chapter 18

⸺⸻⸻◆⸻⸻⸺

T he chill in the air and the light rainfall reflected the mood of everyone standing in the cemetery. Sharon shifted her umbrella to her other hand. People dressed in black surrounded the priest, who stood before the coffin and open grave below. Virginia and Carlton were closest, their backs to most of the crowd.

Sharon recognized people from the office but was surprised how few attended, considering how popular Robert was compared to her father. They were both ambitious, but unlike her father, Robert didn't trample on people to gain his power. Pushed and threatened, sure, but not trampled. Sharon realized how ridiculous that statement sounded the moment it entered her mind. *And I want to be a part of this?* She didn't aspire to get closer to what the people were, just what she'd worked hard for and deserved as her birthright.

There hadn't been a clue to the cause of Robert's death. There was very little on the news except to say that he died, which meant the truth could be either he was killed or it was suicide. Either truth was not what the company or his family wanted leaked, as it would be damaging either way.

Sharon wished she knew the story, but Virginia would never tell her. Carlton might, but she couldn't trust anything he told her. What were their expressions? Were they sad he was gone, or plotting what would happen to his seat? Sharon would guess the latter.

Moments later, the ceremony was over and a small crowd went to offer their condolences, while others left the cemetery. The rain had stopped, so Sharon closed her umbrella and went to stand behind the line of people in front of Virginia and Carlton, waiting for her turn. She wanted to be last, since her words wouldn't be for other's ears.

"I'm so sorry for your loss, Virginia, Carlton."

Virginia's already thin lips pursed in response. "Thank you," Carlton offered.

"This is all your fault! If you'd given up your seat, then this wouldn't have happened!"

What the hell is she talking about? Did she just blame me for Robert's death? How was giving up her board seat going to make a difference? "I earned that seat and deserve it as much as your son does." Carlton visibly stiffened.

"Your family has had too much power for too long. It's time it went to the rest of us," Virginia barked.

"We're all family, Virginia. Some of us were born into it, while others had to marry to get what we want." Sharon regretted the words the moment they left her mouth. This was neither the time nor the place for this conversation. "I'm sorry. You've lost your husband and Carlton, his father."

"You'll have to marry too, dear," Virgina mocked. "Let's hope that you get what you want and not end up like Robert."

Is that a threat? Why would she end up like Robert? Even if she died, the seat wouldn't go to them. *Would it?* Sharon couldn't see her father allowing it.

"Carlton has his own seat, especially with Robert's death. He will inherit the seat, right?" The moment the words left her mouth, a thought hit her. Had they killed Robert to get his seat? Why? They'd gain nothing from killing him except getting Carlton on the board soon. Carlton was far from smart enough to handle the position, and neither was Virgina. Out of the three of them, Robert was without a doubt the smartest.

Virgina laughed snidely. "You have no idea what's going on, do you?" She linked her arms into Carlton's extended one. "You'll find out soon enough. Then you'll be dead."

"Mother, that's enough." Carlton tugged on her arm, pulling her away from the grave and toward the limo waiting for them.

"What is she talking about?" Sharon asked Carlton, who hadn't said anything this whole time.

"She's just in shock from my father's death. She doesn't know what she's saying," Carlton offered, his eyes filled with sadness. A sadness she hadn't seen before in his usual arrogant gaze.

Robert's death had impacted him. Until today, she wasn't sure. They didn't have the best relationship, much like her and her father, but Robert had cared enough to fight for a seat for him, even if it was hers. Sharon watched them leave and then threw a single red rose on the coffin with the others.

What the hell was going on with the board? And why did Virgina think someone would try to kill her for her seat? Did she know about the stalker and their threats? Was she or Carlton behind them? Although the words weren't said, Sharon was beginning to think that Robert's death wasn't a suicide, but something more sinister. The real question was, *Why?* Everyone had their own seat, and that seat was handed down to their children. That was the way it always worked. Robert had tried to get her seat for Carlton. What would that have meant if he had? He'd have more power for sure, but maybe there was more to it than she originally thought, and why her father was so adamantly against it at the last board meeting she attended. Did her father have to give up his seat on the board for her to gain hers? She'd never thought about it before, since she was too focused on getting the seat. There was certainly nothing in her contract that she remembered. Is that why her father didn't want her to get the seat? Because he'd have to give up his and his power? Did he kill Robert so he wouldn't have to?

Sharon rejected the thoughts the moment they entered her mind. No, her father was many things, but a killer?

Chapter 19

H eat flared in Sharon's cheeks as Patrick read her father's contract. She'd told him some of the details during his engagement party, but he was finding out every sordid detail with each sentence he read. Would some of the conditions upset him, since they would've applied to him if they'd married? She couldn't tell from his stoic expression. She'd read through the contract again to see if there was anything about her father giving up his seat when she took hers, but she found nothing.

"This is more ironclad that I thought." Patrick flipped another page.

"It's had a few generations to be perfected. Daughters must marry, and their seats go to their husbands, but they are able to sit on the boards of the charities of the company. I was able to convince my father to let me take the seat, but that means finding a husband willing to give it up."

"You'd think they'd modernize it."

"Not when it's the men updating it." Sharon grinned. "Sorry."

"No apologies necessary. You're right. I'm surprised your mother didn't push to make her own changes, since your father married into it."

"Grandfather was painfully old fashioned, so she didn't stand a chance."

"It seems your father is too. Strange, since you've more than proven yourself capable of the responsibilities."

"I agree, but he doesn't see it that way." Sharon adjusted her position in the chair. "He's fearful I won't marry, and the family name will die with me."

"There's always your cousin Carlton."

"Bite your tongue!" The response was an automatic one that she felt guilty about. Carlton was not a bad guy, but she loathed to think what direction he'd take the company if he had any kind of control. She doubted he even wanted the control, just the money and status that came with it so he could live a carefree lifestyle.

Patrick grinned. He also knew Carlton wasn't the sharpest tool in the shed.

"Although, he has had more business opportunities without having to scrape for them."

"I'm sorry, Sharon. I know how much this means to you."

"I'm sorry, too, that I didn't tell you about these conditions while we were engaged. I was afraid you'd back out. You broke things off anyway."

"We both knew it wasn't the right thing to do."

"You're right, but it would certainly have made things easier. You knew what that seat means to me."

"True, but are you sure you're ready for this kind of sacrifice?"

"I don't want to make it. I'm hoping you can find an alternative solution my father and the board will agree to."

"What about Bradley?"

"My father thinks he's the best candidate, but I haven't decided. He's not as big of an ass as I first thought, but I'm not completely sold on him. I don't think he'd be willing to give up his chance for a seat at the table. I'm looking into his background before I decide for sure. In the meantime, I need to focus on the contract."

"I can put some suggestions together, but they should be what you really want, Sharon."

"My father will never agree to what I really want." That wasn't likely to change anytime soon. With Robert's death and her encounter with Virginia, her thoughts of her father went in more directions than she cared for them to go.

"You're right. Is that why you've started seeing Danny?"

The question was the elephant in the room, and one she was surprised he didn't start with. "No. Any offer would insult him, and there's not enough time for mutual affection to form for the kind of commitment I'd need from him."

"Oh, the attraction is there, but you're right about the time, and Danny's character. Give me a few days to get back to you and if you think of anything new, let me know."

"Thanks, Patrick." *Now is the perfect time to tell him about the warnings.* Sharon didn't move from where she sat, waiting to find the courage. "I've been getting threats."

Patrick eyebrows knotted. "What kind? You must tell the police, Sharon, before something serious happens. A similar thing happened with Josie, and she almost died!"

His answer took her by surprise, as did the story about Josie. She had no idea.

"The merger I'm working on is already hanging by a thread. I need someone who'll be discreet. With Robert's death, the company is already under speculation. I can't risk word getting out."

"Is a deal worth your life, Sharon?"

Sharon didn't answer. She hoped the transaction would convince her father and the board that she deserved her seat.

Patrick raked a hand through his hair. "How are the renovations coming along?" he asked, knowing she wouldn't budge.

"They'll be finished in time for my annual party. I'm thinking of inviting Josie. I'm sure the doors haven't been flung open for her with the other women."

"She'll appreciate it. No, but my mother's working on prying them open."

Sharon grinned. Elsa was nothing if not determined, and woe to anyone who tried to get in her way. "How's Josie holding up?"

"She's been a trooper, but I can tell the stress is beginning to get to her."

"Does she know it'll just get worse after the wedding?"

"I haven't had the heart to tell her, but I think she suspects, based on hints from my mother. She could use a friend—someone other than Danny," he added with a grin.

She could use one too. While she was social because of family obligations, she found most of the women in the circle had their own agendas and were quick to stab you in the back if it'd help them or their husband. Finding real friendships was tricky. Josie was genuine and had no ulterior motives, except maybe to grill her about Danny. Not a topic she wanted to discuss, but she'd take it over backstabbing. "I'll give her a call."

"I gave her your number. She planned to invite you to her bachelorette party, so..."

"Bachelorette party?" *Heaven forbid.* The thought of bar hopping in a ridiculous outfit did not appeal to her. Josie was certain to feel the same.

"I'll wait for her call, but I'll send an invitation in the meantime." She stood. "Thanks again, Paddy." She kissed his cheek.

"I'll speak with my connection at the police station, but meanwhile be careful, and don't take any crazy risks." He didn't add *Like Josie did*, but it was implied.

"I won't."

As she opened the office door, Sharon stopped to add, "And good luck to you with your bachelor party. Isn't Noel your best man?" Noel, his younger brother, although running for office, was a rebel when it came to parties. This gave him the chance to cut loose—something he'd been unable to do recently.

The horror on Patrick's face almost made her feel sorry for him.

"Be sure to invite Danny. He's levelheaded and will make sure things don't get out of hand," she added before closing the door. She hoped those words wouldn't come back to bite her.

Chapter 20

Danny rolled his eyes at Josie, who stood in his doorway. It'd been a week since she saw him with Sharon, and he was surprised she waited this long. There were no phone calls the next day, but things must be serious if she was at his house. The last thing he wanted was to talk about Sharon, but Josie could be relentless. Now that she'd found happiness, she was determined for everyone else to find it too...whether they wanted it or not.

Josie strolled in and glanced around as if she expected Sharon would be there from the night before. If she were, Danny wouldn't have answered the door.

"How's it going?" Josie made a beeline for the couch and plopped herself down.

"It's going."

"Got any coffee?"

"Yeah. I just made a fresh pot."

Josie headed to the kitchen and poured herself a cup. "So, how did things go with Sharon?" She blew on the coffee before taking a sip.

Danny crossed his arms. "Fine. Since when do you care about my dates?"

"I do when it's my best friend."

"I'm you're only friend," Danny corrected.

"I saw the way Sharon looked at you."

Danny's mouth opened to speak, but changed his mind when he saw the glint in Josie's eyes. *Damn it! She's trying to bait me for information.* "I don't know what you're talking about."

"Yes, you do. I saw you together. You don't do that with clients."

He did with Teri, but not until the job was finished. "You don't know what I do with clients."

"I'd lecture you about clients, but..." She couldn't because Patrick had been a client when they became involved.

"You'd be a hypocrite?" Danny offered.

Josie pouted. "Maybe, but Patrick was the one and only."

"The only one you told me about."

Josie shot daggers over the rim of her cup. "You're avoiding talking about Sharon."

"No." Danny headed to the couch and sat.

"Yes." Josie set her mug on the wood table. "You are. Like her that much, huh?"

It was Danny's turn to shoot daggers.

Josie threw her hands up in defeat. "All right! Am I going to see you at any other parties? I want to know so Patrick and I aren't surprised. Not to mention, I'd hate for us to be poaching each other's prospective clients."

"You know damn well our clients wouldn't be the same, and if they were, we'd be working together, not competing." She wasn't going to let up. Danny had known Josie for almost fifteen years, and she was more stubborn than his mother. That was saying a lot.

"She just wants to keep her father off her back during the holidays."

"I see. And what do you get out of it?"

"I get free food and a chance to connect with high-end clients. Just like you did with Patrick."

Josie studied him for so long, Danny could feel his skin begin to itch. "I think it's great you're trying to help Sharon out, but I saw the way you two looked at each other. I just want to make sure you're okay and that this relationship doesn't turn into another Teri situation. I know how easy it is to get swept up in that world. I don't want you to end up like last time."

"I know. I'm fine." *Liar.*

He really wasn't fine. Sharon was withdrawn after their steak dinner at his place, and it was killing him. He didn't know if she was doing it to protect herself or if that night was a mistake. Talking about it with a team of workers at her house wasn't an option, and she'd been working so late that their paths didn't cross in the evenings. In the mornings, she remained in her room until she heard the crew come in. Danny thought about knocking on her door with a lame excuse about the renovations, but he didn't want to be that guy, so he gave her space. They'd have time to talk at their next dinner party, unless Sharon changed her mind.

"She likes you. Just be careful."

The silence stretched out before them as they sipped their coffee.

"Oh, I've got a job for you," Josie said, breaking the silence.

"About time. I was beginning to think this was just a social call. When does the job start?"

Josie laughed. "In January. I'm still working through the details with the client, but it's a pretty big job and I'll need you and your team."

"Of course you need me."

Josie rolled her eyes. "There are other construction companies."

"True, but none as professional or fantastic as mine."

Josie shook her head. It was a phrase she used when talking to clients. "No need to get a big head, Danny."

"Me?"

"Yes, you, hotshot."

"Wow. Now I'm a hotshot? This list of compliments is just getting better and longer. Next you'll be telling me I'm the best friend and business partner you've ever had."

Josie threw a cushion at his head. "Cool it before I change my mind."

Danny caught the cushion. "You won't. You love me too much."

"Would you quit it so we can talk business?"

"I thought you came to talk about my love life and how wonderful I am?" Danny said with a fake hurt expression.

Josie shook her head. "When does your job for Sharon end?"

"Two days before Christmas."

The rest of their time was spent talking about the new job and what they needed to iron out with the client before construction started in the new year. Danny was grateful for Josie stopping by. She took his mind off Sharon for a while, and the confusion he felt about their relationship. When Josie left, he was alone again with his thoughts.

Danny raked a hand through his hair. Tomorrow was Monday and they were scheduled to do a walk-through and go over some design decisions. Would she put off their meeting? She couldn't if she wanted to meet her Christmas deadline.

Danny was overreacting. She was a successful businesswoman. Of course she was too busy to talk with him over coffee. Not to mention, she was dealing with a death in the family. He was tempted to ask her about it after they ate dinner, but she looked so tired that he didn't have the heart to press her. The pain from her mother's death still lingered, and Danny didn't know about her relationship with her uncle.

She had a lot going on. He knew he shouldn't take her reaction personally, but he couldn't help feeling she'd changed her mind about him. Had he gotten too familiar? No. He wasn't the only one sharing that night. Maybe that was the problem: she wasn't used to revealing intimate facts about herself. Was she worried he'd take it as more? Maybe if she'd been the only one disclosing details, but she wasn't.

He grabbed the remote next to him and pushed the On button. The sound of news filled his living room, pushing aside thoughts of Sharon.

Chapter 21

The team was wrapping up for the day when Sharon peeked her head into the room. "Have you got a minute?"

Danny smiled. "Sure. See you tomorrow, guys."

Laura cleared her throat.

"I meant you too."

"Do I look like a guy?"

He rolled his eyes. "And lady," he added.

"Drinks at Arnold's later?" Laura asked. "A couple of the guys are going." Her gaze shifted between him and Sharon.

"Maybe next time."

The lines by her mouth crinkled, but she managed to smile. A smile Sharon suspected was for her sake.

"Don't work too late." The words were meant for Danny, but Laura's eyes pierced her.

Sharon wasn't sure if Laura was jealous of her or if she was being protective of Danny. Laura liked him, but her interactions jumped around too much to know for sure.

"Have a nice evening, Laura. Thanks for all your hard work," she complimented. Laura reminded her of Josie, and Sharon wanted them to remain on good terms.

"Thanks. You too. Night, boss." Laura left the room.

Sharon walked around the room. "It's looking great!" The bathroom was small, but the closet space was bigger and was coming together just as she imagined. While she'd enjoyed her luxuriously large bathroom, having a larger closet was going to be more fun, especially when she filled it with new outfits, shoes, and other accessories.

"I'm glad you like it. Have you got some time tomorrow to pick out some items?"

"Sure. How much time do you need?"

"Just a couple hours, if you can spare it."

She pulled out her phone. Only one meeting was scheduled for tomorrow, and it was one she could reschedule. She typed Ryan a message. "Done."

"Perfect. It'll be free sailing after that, and you can start putting up your Christmas decorations. Or is someone coming to decorate for you?"

"A bit of both, but it really depends on how much time I have. This time of year is pretty hectic. Between charity and business events, hiring someone makes it easier."

"That must suck. The best part of Christmas is putting up the decorations, baking, and decorating cookies."

"You bake?"

"No, but I'm a decorating fiend."

"I bet you are." An image of Danny in one of his mother's aprons and the tools in his hand, making a mess, made her grin.

"What about you? Do you bake, or do Christmas cookies?"

"My mother and I used to make a gingerbread house, but not from scratch. We'd get a blank house and decorate it together. My mother didn't cook."

"Sounds like she did a lot of other amazing things. Spent quality time with her daughter and taught her the value of charity."

There were a lot more lessons her mother taught, and she hadn't realized how many until she died. Sharon swallowed the giant lump of grief in her throat.

"I didn't mean to bring up painful memories."

"You didn't. I just miss her." She smiled sadly. "Especially this time of year. I try to keep myself busy with the charities that were important to her."

Danny's amber gaze caressed her face, and the room closed in around them, reminding her they were alone. The memory of him nibbling her lip burst into her mind, making her wish she hadn't fallen asleep on the couch the night of Patrick and Josie's engagement party. She'd woken up in her guest bedroom and in her pajamas. Her bra and panties were on, for which she was thankful, despite the painful marks left behind from wearing a bra overnight.

It had warmed her knowing he'd been nice enough to put her in bed instead of leaving her on the very uncomfortable couch in the living room. She'd been too embarrassed to mention it the next morning, and thankfully he hadn't teased her about it, although his eyes twinkled with mischief more than once.

"So, we're on schedule?"

"Yeah." He cleared his throat.

"Good."

"I keep my promises."

I know. Sadness washed over her from remembering her mother and remembering Danny's kiss and all the intimate moments they'd shared. She'd miss them, and miss him. His question about relationships implied he was open to one with her, and her heart ached, knowing she couldn't encourage it.

She'd gone out of her way to come home late the last couple of weeks and asked to reschedule their check-ins. Work was busy, especially with the deal only days away from closing, but she was avoiding Danny, and he knew it. His patience was amazing. He hadn't pushed her or been offended, which was another way he was perfect. *No one is perfect, Sharon.*

True, but in her mind, Danny came damn close. "Would you like to stay for dinner?" she blurted out.

He started to say yes, but his expression changed before he answered. "I can't. Promised my parents I'd help them put Santa on the roof tonight. Mom doesn't want my dad up there anymore."

"It's okay. I've got work to do anyway," she mumbled.

His hand touched her cheek. "I'd love to take you out to dinner this weekend."

The butterflies in her stomach went crazy. "I wish I could."

"Busy schedule?"

"Yes. No."

"Still not ready to talk about it?"

Sharon shook her head. *I wish I could.* Maybe when this deal was over, she could confide in him. That was in two days. What would confiding do? There wasn't anything they could do about it. Telling him wouldn't make things easier between them. If anything, it might make things awkward, since Danny was interested in changing their relationship. She hadn't lied, saying she wished she could have dinner with him.

"Last time I checked, you were a grown woman, Sharon. Free to make her own choices."

Danny thought it was because of her father. Although he wasn't far off, there was more to it than he could imagine.

"Another time."

"Don't lie." His tone wasn't harsh, but it was firm.

"I can't." Her pained voice was barely audible.

"Can't or won't?" he pressed.

"It's complicated."

"Doesn't seem complicated to me. Just tell your father to go to hell." A smile tugged at the edge of his mouth.

"This isn't just about him."

Danny crossed his arms. "Really. Is it because of me?"

"In a way, yes, but not in the way you think."

"Really? Then what other way is there?" Annoyance and hurt lined his tone.

"It's not something you'd understand or agree with."

"I understand more than you know. It's one thing to go out on one date, but what if someone thought things were more serious? You don't want Daddy and the others to think you're slumming. Is that it?"

"That's not it." His words spoke volumes, and why he felt the way he did about people with money. A woman with money must have done a number on him. She'd suspected as much for a while, but he just confirmed it. She touched his arm, but he pulled away. "I have a contract."

"Contract? I don't understand."

"I know you don't, and why there can never be more between us."

Puzzlement danced across his face.

Sharon left and headed to the kitchen before he asked more questions. She'd already said too much. His footsteps followed behind her.

"What kind of contract?"

"I don't want to talk about it." Tears pooled in her eyes. "I wish that I was free to go to dinner with you, Danny. I thought about telling you why and asking for your help, but you're too nice a man for me to drag you into this. And I care about you too much for you to become a pawn...or a casualty." She did care about him, but wished to hell she didn't. It would've made things easier.

"What the hell is going on, Sharon?" Despite the strong words, his tone reflected genuine concern.

"I..." she started to say, but stopped. "I think it's best you leave, and we keep our relationship professional from now on."

"Sharon."

"Please! Don't make this harder than it must be."

A series of emotions crawled across his face before he responded. "So... Going together to Patrick's and Josie's engagement party. What was that all about? A ploy to make Bradley jealous? Upset your father? A game?" he gritted out the last word.

Sharon was about to refute his claims but changed her mind. Better for him to hate her than try to peel away the reasons they couldn't be together and get dragged in, or to see the look of pity and disgust on his face if he found out the truth.

Danny's jawline jumped. "Good night, Sharon." He stormed out the door, leaving her alone with her thoughts and the decision she'd made.

Tears spilled out and pain clutched her throat. She shoved aside the emotions and hurt trying to crawl their way up her neck. This was why she'd closed herself off. The coldness and no emotions were better than facing the truth. The love she desperately wanted in her life would never be.

Danny punched the dashboard when he got in his truck. His hand gripped the door handle to prevent himself from going back inside and demanding that Sharon tell him everything. There was more to the story than she was sharing, but the determined glint in her eyes was proof she wouldn't budge. What kind of contract prevented her from seeing him? It didn't make sense. Would her father cut her off?

Danny raked his hand through his hair. Sharon didn't strike him as the type of woman who'd bend to her father. Surely, she made enough money in her position. *A position in her father's company, Danny.* Sharon was being held by the short and curly, as his father would say. *The price of being part of a rich family. You want the money and privilege that comes with it? You have to play the game.*

Maybe Patrick knew what was going on. They were friends, and involved. Was the contract the reason Patrick broke off their engagement? Josie never said, but then maybe she didn't know either. He turned his vehicle toward Patrick and Josie's home. The only way to find out was to ask someone who might know.

Danny ran through all of their interactions and what he knew so far. She liked him. He was no expert when it came to women, but the way she responded to him, physically and in their intimate conversations, told him there was something between them. An attraction that at times she seemed ready to explore, while at other moments she pulled away. Was the contract the reason?

Sharon was a smart woman. She knew he had history with someone from her world. Was that another reason she backed off? She came across as cold and harsh, but there was more to her underneath all that. Based on what he knew about her father, and the people in her world, it was no wonder she closed herself off.

Why had she agreed to go with him to Josie and Patrick's party? Was it merely curiosity, or had she tried to make waves? Her interaction with Bradley screamed that she didn't want to be with him. Was he wrong? The talk with her father was strained, but Sharon wasn't some spoiled child trying to get back at Daddy—the way Teri was. She was a professional and had made a place for herself in her father's world. According to her, she had fought to get it. No, there was more to the story, and Bradley and her father were involved somehow. He just had to figure it out. He'd have to try and pry it out of Patrick. *If he knew.*

Danny was relieved when he saw Patrick's car in the driveway. Josie's car wasn't there. *Perfect.* He jumped out of the car and headed to the house.

Patrick's surprised face greeted him.

"Danny. Come in."

"Thanks."

"You want something to drink?" he asked as Danny followed him into the living room.

The house had changed since he and Josie did the renovations. Josie had added her own special touches, but hadn't removed anything of Patrick's. It was a good combination that fit them.

Jealousy stabbed him. They'd found their happy ending. Two unlikely people from different worlds he wouldn't have put together under any circumstances. Josie had rounded off his rough edges and Patrick had brought out the best of her that had remained hidden for years, and she'd become more confident because of it. They complemented each other. Danny hoped the people in Patrick and his family's world wouldn't change that.

"Just some water. Thanks." Danny took a seat on the leather couch while Patrick headed to the kitchen.

"So, what brings you here?" Patrick handed him a glass of water.

"Sharon."

Patrick raised an eyebrow and took a seat on the single recliner. His gaze studied Danny for several moments before speaking. "What about Sharon?"

"I asked her on a date, but she turned me down."

"I thought you were already dating."

"No. Your party was the first time we went out."

"Your exchange at the party, specifically on the patio, said otherwise."

"We're not dating. That moment was too much champagne."

"I see."

You don't see, Patrick, but I don't blame you. "The champagne just made it easier for both of us to say and do what we really wanted."

The words were hard for him to say, but they needed saying if he was going to get answers.

"I thought you didn't date clients."

"The renovations are almost done, and I was hoping to get to know her better in the meantime, but she shut me down when I tried to ask her out to dinner. Something about a contract?"

"She told you?"

"No. If she had, I wouldn't be here." He took a sip of his water. "Do you know anything about it?"

Patrick relaxed in the recliner.

Oh, great. He wasn't going to say *crap.* Maybe he should speak to Josie instead, although he didn't think she knew Sharon well enough.

"It's personal, and not for me to say."

"Look, I'm not digging for military secrets here. I just want to date the woman I care about."

"You care about her?"

"Of course. Do you think I'd be here if I didn't?"

Patrick sighed and straightened. "I understand where you're coming from, but she's asked me to examine the contract, so I can't tell you without her permission."

"What the hell is going on, Patrick? I just want to date her. She can't date anyone like me?"

"It has nothing to do with you, and more to do with her."

"She's not allowed to date someone like me. That doesn't make sense!"

"It does if you knew the whole story."

Danny set the glass on the side table. "I came here hoping to get some answers, but all you're giving me is more questions. She's your client now?"

"She hasn't officially hired me, but she did ask me to read the contract and find solutions."

Patrick was trying to drop hints, but unfortunately for him, they weren't enough for him to get answers. "To what? Being able to date me?"

"It's more complicated that than."

"*That* is a saying I'm more familiar with than I'd like."

"She cares about you, Danny, and that's why she isn't pulling you into her situation."

"Like what?" Patrick wouldn't answer his rhetorical question, but he still had to ask it.

"The one she's trying to free herself from, and live her life."

"She an adult!"

"She is, but there's a lot at stake for her."

"Money." He wanted to spit the word. It always came back to money with people like her.

"She's got more than money at stake, Danny."

"Her job? She's a smart woman. She could easily get another job."

"Could she?"

Mark was a powerful man with powerful connections. Sharon had clawed her way inside his company. How would he react if she left?

Danny raked a hand through his hair. Her job meant the world to her. She hadn't said the words, but he'd picked up on it. So did the respect of her father and the men in his company, and Mark knew that. Danny bet the bastard was using it against her.

"Can you help her? Can I?"

"I'm trying. I don't think you would understand if you knew the whole story. Or would want to get involved."

"You don't know that!"

"I know you, Danny. Your life is important to you. Being drawn in would change it forever. Sharon knows that. You two don't know each other well enough for you to ask or understand her world. She's trying to spare you."

"And herself."

"Yes. She's afraid of what you'd think of her."

What I'd think of her? What the hell is in that contract? His gut was telling him to drop it and walk out, but curiosity and his heart were saying something else. "I wouldn't feel different."

"Are you certain?"

He wasn't, and Patrick was right. He and Sharon didn't know each other well enough to take the risk of changing his life the way Patrick implied.

"Give her time, Danny. This is a difficult time for her."

"Will that really change things?"

"Probably not, but it might make her ready to tell you, so you'll understand. Only she can explain it."

Danny stood. Patrick was right. Maybe in time, Sharon might confide in him. "Thanks for listening and telling me what you did." Even though he hadn't given him exactly what he wanted.

"She cares about you, Danny. You should know that," Patrick said at the front door.

"Thanks."

Patrick nodded and closed the door.

He hadn't found answers. Instead, he'd gotten more to think about and decipher. His next step was to convince Sharon she could trust him and confide in him.

Chapter 22

S haron glanced across the table at Bradley, wishing she'd heard what he said.

"You're distracted today. Is it the merger?"

"Yes...and no."

"You've got nothing to worry about. You've covered everything. The deal will close without a hitch."

"I know."

After the way things ended between her and Danny, she went out of her way to ask Bradley to dinner and a couple of lunches to get to know him better. Her thoughts about him changed from one minute to the next, like a seesaw. One instance she enjoyed his company and knew he was the best candidate, and the next she hated what being with him represented. Plus she couldn't stop thinking about Danny and the way he made her feel.

"Your father told me about the contract," Bradley blurted out. "Is that what's been on your mind?"

"Did he tell you all the details?" It wasn't like her father to show his hand, but he did want Bradley, and wanted her to decide.

"Not everything, I'm sure. Care to tell me about it?" He adjusted the napkin in his lap.

"Not really, but I suppose that's best since it's you he wants me to choose." She waited for his expression to change, indicating he didn't know her father's plan. It didn't. He knew. The question was, *What else does he know and, more importantly, what is he willing to give up?*

"I like you, Sharon. I'm open to an agreement."

I'll bet you are. What man wouldn't consider all the benefits that came along with it? "I'm more interested in what you're open to sacrificing."

Her comment got his attention. "What do you mean?"

"You don't think I'd give up my seat on the board, do you?"

"I figured—"

"You figured wrong, Bradley," she interjected, knowing what he thought: That the seat would go to who she married because she was required to surrender it. Her firm gaze held his as he contemplated her words, and Sharon suspected what he'd say in response. Bradley was a smart man and wanted the same thing she did. Would he relinquish it for the money?

"I would, of course, make it worth your while, and there are other perks of being part of my family. Business opportunities are one. You could start your own firm," Sharon offered. Bradley was ambitious... Maybe having his own firm would be enough.

"Perks like you?" His hand caressed her hand on the table.

She jerked it away. *Damn.* While she suspected it would be on the table, she'd hoped to convince him otherwise. "Your personal life wouldn't have to change. Just be discreet."

"What if I wanted it to change?"

"Name your figure, Bradley."

Her answer surprised him, and he contemplated for a few moments before answering. "I'm open to an offer, but I want it to include you in every way." His gaze moved over her face, settling on her lips for emphasize.

Her skin didn't crawl...exactly. Bradley wasn't unattractive, and probably knew his way around a woman's body, but the problem was, he wasn't the one she wanted around her body. The thought of giving herself to him, even if it'd be for a short time, didn't appeal to her. Bradley wanted what he couldn't have and when he got it, he would lose interest, but Sharon knew it wouldn't be soon enough for her.

"Let me be clear, Bradley. If I agree to look at you as a candidate, it will be on my terms. The only consideration you'll get is the money and the other perks. Not me."

"And if I don't agree?"

Sharon gritted her teeth. He knew about the deadline. *Damn you, Father.*

"Then I find someone else."

"Like Danny Stanley?" A smirk tugged his lips. "I don't see your father agreeing to him."

Sharon returned with a smirk of her own. "My father doesn't get to choose who. Only ensure that I choose."

Bradley tried to hide that he'd lost ground, but failed. "A man like Danny doesn't belong in your world."

"Maybe not, but he wouldn't care about my seat, or the perks that come along with being part of my family and world."

"I'm guessing he'd want the same perk I would. You." Sharon blushed.

"But I'm assuming from your exchange at the party, you wouldn't mind." Anger stained his voice.

Was it because she'd rejected him, or because it was for Danny?

"I don't see a man like Danny being happy with such an arrangement, even with you as a perk."

Bradley hit a nerve, and she couldn't hide it.

"I wonder what Danny-boy would think of you if you offered?" Bradley laughed. "Is that why you haven't? You care what he thinks of you?"

"Stop it!" Sharon hissed. In a restaurant was the last place she wanted to make a scene. "Keep speaking and you'll talk your way right out of being offered a contract." She was beginning to reconsider already.

"I don't like losing. And losing to someone like Danny doesn't appeal to me. I want you, Sharon. If you need more time, I can wait. I'm not a patient man, but I'd wait for you. I've wanted you for a long time."

"Wanted me...or my money?"

"Money I've got, Sharon."

"You don't have a seat on the board."

"I'd hoped to have a seat, but it obviously means a lot more to you than I thought. I'd be happy with my own firm, and you as my wife. If that's what it takes."

Again, the seesaw reactions about Bradley. Sharon thought of her own emotions when it came to Danny and began to sympathize. Bradley was used to getting what he wanted—without sacrifices. She knew a lot about sacrifices, but her seat wasn't one she was willing to make. She'd worked too damn hard to get it into her contract.

"You'll get my offer soon."

His stiff frame relaxed. "All I want is an opportunity, Sharon."

That was what he'd get, but on her terms.

Chapter 23

"A Josie Fagan is here to see you," Ryan announced.

Sharon's fingers paused over the keyboard. "Send her in."

Josie strolled in with a strained smile on her face.

Sharon straightened. "What's wrong? Did something happen to Patrick? To Danny?"

Josie's eyebrows knotted. "No, no. They're both fine." She slumped into the loveseat across from Sharon's desk. "It's my future mother-in-law. She's driving me crazy with the wedding planning."

Sharon grinned. "Welcome to high society—" She joined Josie on the loveseat "—with a side of political connection."

"Thanks," Josie said sarcastically. "The wedding count is up to 300 people. I have twelve bridesmaids. I don't even have one girlfriend." Josie frowned. "That sounded pathetic."

Sharon rested her hand on Josie's arm. "Not at all. I don't have one girlfriend either. Not a real friend."

They smiled knowingly at each other. Josie ran her own business and took care of her mother most of her young life, and hadn't had time for partying and friends.

"Please come to my bachelorette party this weekend. I don't want to be with a bunch of strangers," Josie begged.

They barely knew each other—only met on a couple of occasions—but Sharon had liked her instantly, especially the way Patrick lit up when he was around her. Despite their relationship not working out, Patrick was a good friend, and she was delighted to see him with someone who brought him joy. Mostly she was happy to have her friend back.

"I'm surprised Elsa didn't invite you as a last-minute attempt to break up the wedding." Josie rested her face against her hand.

"She's not that mean. Besides, she invited me to the wedding, just not the bachelorette party. She probably did that for your sake."

"Really?" Josie straightened. "I don't mean to sound ungrateful, but 300 people?"

"You have to understand that the Pullmans are a very prominent family and people will be insulted if they're not invited, especially if they have political and business ties."

"I hadn't thought of it that way."

"Unfortunately, it's the world you're marrying into."

"I'd hope that not being from that world would keep the guest list small."

"It still might, but you'd be surprised how people will try to work everything to their advantage." Sharon took Josie's hand in hers. "While you want to accommodate a lot of Elsa's decisions—especially those that impact the family politically, and their business—don't let yourself be a doormat. Fight for what's important to you. If you don't assert yourself starting now, you'll end up in a wedding and life that is not what you want," Sharon finished quietly.

"Is that what happened with you and Patrick?"

"Yes. I loved Paddy, but..."

"You weren't in love with him."

Sharon gave a weak smile. "No. I wasn't capable of giving him the love he wanted."

Josie squeezed Sharon's hand. "It's amazing how our lives can change when the right person steps into it. How we can change."

Josie's expression made Sharon wonder if she was talking about herself and Patrick or her. But there was no her and Danny. Not the way everyone thought. Knowing that saddened her.

Sharon cleared her throat and pulled her hand away. "I'd love to come to your bachelorette party. Are there going to be male strippers or a cop coming to break up the noise?" Sharon teased.

The horrified look on Josie's face made Sharon want to laugh. "I hope not!"

"You've never been to a bachelorette party, have you?"

Josie shook her head.

"Send Ryan the itinerary and I'll make sure I'm there to help you through it." Sharon checked her watch and stood. Her next meeting was starting in ten minutes. "Word of advice. Make sure you eat and pace yourself. Drink less if there's lot of shots."

"Shots?" Josie asked, shocked, as she headed for the door.

"Lots of shots."

Josie's eyes were as wide as saucers when she finally closed the door. Sharon couldn't help grinning. It was going to be an interesting night. She'd make sure her calendar was clear. Bachelorette parties weren't really her thing, usually only attending when it was unavoidable, and dodging much of the drinking and activities if she could, but Josie needed her help. Elsa wouldn't be completely in charge of this party, and Sharon wanted to make sure whoever Elsa assigned as maid of honor wouldn't embarrass Josie.

Humiliating Josie wouldn't be Elsa's plan, but Sharon wouldn't put it past the other women. Josie was a kind, good-hearted person, and Sharon hoped that she wouldn't be crushed under the weight of the pressure from being connected to Patrick's family.

Ryan strolled into the office, a wave of cologne in his wake. He placed files she'd need for her meeting on the desk. "Should I order your usual lunch?"

From his mannerisms, Sharon had assumed he was gay, but changed her mind his first week working there when she caught him gazing at her in a way men usually do. While she'd never heard him speaking to a girlfriend, he had brought female dates to the Christmas parties.

"Yes, please, Ryan. Order something for yourself, too, if you don't have lunch plans."

Ryan's gaze shot at her in surprise. She'd never offered to buy him lunch before. His expression softened. "Thank you."

"You're a great assistant, Ryan, and I don't tell you that enough."

His posture straightened as he beamed under her praise. Brown eyes grazed her face before he caught himself. "Do you need anything else, Sharon?" He handed her a handful of papers with missed calls.

Sharon sifted through them until she saw Danny's name. A wave of heat hit her chest. She'd been keeping her distance, trying to keep things as impersonal as possible, but she missed him. His jokes, his quirky smile, and their conversations. Most of all, the way she felt around him, relaxed but on edge because she wanted to kiss him. Also, happy because he made her laugh, but sad, too, because she couldn't pursue a relationship.

"Are you all right, Sharon?"

Ryan's question pulled her back. "I'm fine."

"Your meeting starts in five minutes," he reminded her.

"Thanks, Ryan." She directed her attention to the files on her desk and focused on what she'd need.

An hour later, Sharon dialed Danny's number, not wanting to wait until they were home alone in case it was a private conversation.

"Hi, Sharon."

The sound of his voice sent a shiver through her. "Hi. You called?"

"My mother wanted to make sure you're still coming to the house for lunch on Sunday."

Sharon paused, knowing she should say no, but saying she was too busy seemed lame, and she didn't want to lie. Rose was a sweet lady and Sharon didn't want to disappoint her. "Tell her I'll be there."

"I can skip it," Danny offered.

"No, they're your parents. Besides, I suspect your mother will read into your not being there."

Danny chuckled. "You're right. Want me to pick you up?"

"No," she said too quickly. "I mean, I think it's best I take my own car. So you're not inconvenienced."

"It's no trouble."

Sharon didn't want to be rude, but the last thing she needed was to be alone with him. At least at his parents' house, they wouldn't be alone.

"I don't bite, Sharon," Danny stated when the silence stretched on. "Unless you want me to," he joked.

Sharon grinned. "I'll make my own way."

"You're smiling. I can hear it in your voice."

"I'm a very busy and important person and don't have time for lowly people who work for me," Sharon countered.

"Ouch. Fine, but we both know you're going to laugh when you hang up the phone."

"Goodbye, Mr. Stanley," Sharon said coolly.

"See you Sunday, Sharon."

The low, sexy way he said the words made Sharon fumble as she tried to end the call. *Crap!* So much for laughing when she got off the phone. Laughter would be a darn sight better than the frustration of this sexual tension. In that moment, Sharon wished she were capable of a causal relationship with Danny. *You're perfectly able, Sharon.*

Laughter bubbled inside her, thinking about the expression on Danny's face if she showed up at his front door in a winter coat and nothing else. Would he invite her in, or slam the door in her face? Danny was too nice a guy to slam the door in her face, but he might suggest she go home and sleep off whatever alcohol she'd consumed. He might actually invite her inside and play out the fantasies rolling around in her head since they met. She had enough to keep them in bed for an entire month. *Stop it, Sharon!*

"Carlton here to see you," Ryan's voice interrupted.

Damn. He was the last person she wanted to see, especially after the encounter with Virgina at Robert's funeral. Maybe he'd tell her what Virginia's comments meant. "Send him in."

Carlton sauntered in and plopped himself down on a chair in front of her desk.

"What can I do for you Carlton?"

"Quit."

This was a game they played. One he was too stupid to realize he'd never win if he didn't get his finger out of his ass and do the work. Sharon was a little disappointed to see he'd returned to his old self instead of the mature version she'd gotten a glimpse of at the funeral. "And who'll do my job? You?"

"I could."

"You couldn't handle my job for a day. Besides, you'll have another job soon—your father's. And there's a lot to learn."

Carlton snorted. "I'm a glorified secretary."

There was no hint of grief in his eyes at the mention of his father, like there'd been at the funeral, but she was never privy to much of their relationship except what she saw at dinner parties. Not a true reflection.

"You'd have more responsibility if you could handle this one first. That's the way it works, Carlton."

"I shouldn't have to handle anything menial first. I deserve more. My name allows it!"

She leaned back in her chair. "Will you listen to yourself? It's no wonder you haven't progressed in the company. Both of our fathers believe you should prove you deserve the responsibility instead of handing it to you on a silver platter!"

"You didn't have to work hard to get where you are."

Was he serious? "I didn't start in this job, Carlton. And the only reason why I started above an entry level position was because I hustled and brought in two high-end clients and demanded a higher position."

Her statement surprised him. "I thought—"

"I know you did." *You and everyone in this company.* Her father took the credit, of course, but she'd demanded the high position as compensation, along with the salary to go with it.

"What about your seat on the board? It should be mine!"

Arrogant bastard! He'd obviously been getting this fed to him by his mother. "You'll get your seat when you turn twenty-five, maybe sooner now that he's gone." Unwelcome thoughts rushed into her mind...that Carlton killed his father to get the seat soon. No. Shooting someone was messy and personal. She couldn't see him getting his hands dirty.

"Have you spoken to your mother and Uncle Mark about it?" she probed. Given her last encounter with Virginia, she didn't know what to think about what was going on. She certainly couldn't talk to her father.

"Uncle Mark will just want me to wait, and my mother is going off her rocker since Father died," Carlton whined.

Sharon clenched her fist to avoid grabbing him by his collar and punching him. "I don't make the rules of the contract, Carlton. If I did, I wouldn't have to jump through hoops to get my seat."

"You mean marrying?"

"Among other things."

"Have you made a decision yet?"

She was still hoping Patrick would find a loophole, or a suggestion that her father would agree to, but she wasn't about to share her plans with Carlton. He was known for having loose lips. "Not yet."

"Bradley seems like the logical choice."

"You sound like my father. I thought you didn't like him?"

Carlton shrugged. "I don't hate him, but he'd a better choice than that construction guy. You weren't seriously considering him, were you?"

"He was just a date. Nothing more."

"That's good. Uncle Mark would've blown a blood vessel if you chose him."

"What do you care who I choose?" Was he hoping her time ran out so he could swoop in and take her seat?

"I don't, but we don't need someone like him diluting the family gene pool."

Smug, snobbish bastard! Sharon gripped the arms of the chair. "Danny is a kind and decent man and we'd be fortunate to have a man like him added to our gene pool."

"Whatever. He just doesn't blend in."

"He fit in fine at the party."

Carlton snorted. "A party is one thing, but being part of our family is something else completely. Everyone thought you were either slumming it or trying to make Bradley jealous so he'd make an offer of marriage."

"Say another bad word against Daniel again and I'll kick you out of my office."

Her statement surprised him. "You like him?" He smirked. "Looks like Bradley really does have competition."

"Danny is a nice person and doesn't deserve someone like you talking bad about him."

Carlton's face blistered. "Someone like me?"

"A spoiled, arrogant child who's never done a hard day's work in his life and wouldn't know decency if it bit him in the ass!"

Carlton shot to his feet. "I don't need your insults." He stormed to the door and yanked it open. "And you're nothing but a coldhearted bitch who's going to lose everything." The door slammed behind him.

Ryan came through the door moments later, her lunch in his hand. "Are you okay?"

Sharon took a deep breath to calm her erratic heartbeat. "I'm fine."

"He's a conceited jackass."

"Yes, he is." She pulled the container with her food closer and opened the lid.

"He's wrong about you, Sharon," Ryan assured her.

She gave him a sad smile. "Thanks."

Ryan left and she took a bite of her food, but it refused to go down. In some ways she was or had been a coldhearted bitch, going after and getting what she wanted, not caring if she stepped on a few people along the way. She'd done it to survive in her father's world, becoming someone she hated. She'd hoped to be free to find herself, but the chances were slipping away with each day that took her closer to the time limit. A deadline that meant marrying a man she didn't love or respect, and barely liked.

Tears streamed down Sharon's face as she wished her mother was still alive and able to give her advice. But she wasn't, and she'd have to make the difficult decision to continue to be a version of herself she hated, or worse, to live through what lay ahead.

Chapter 24

Sharon tucked a stray hair behind a hairpin. She took a deep breath to gain the composure she'd lost speaking with Carlton. The reflection on the elevator doors mocked her, and she shifted her handbag from one shoulder to the other and stepped inside when the door opened. The rest of the day was hell, but it wasn't the first time she made it through...and it wouldn't be the last.

She called Patrick before leaving her office, but he was in court. He'd left a message saying he found a loophole in the contract. Sharon smiled, thinking of the shock on her father's face. Life hadn't played out the way she'd hoped, but she'd given her father years to change his mind and to bring his thinking into this century. The waiting was over.

The sound of her heel clicking against concrete echoed in the almost-empty parking lot. Even though the space was well lit, Sharon hated walking through it no matter what time of day or night. The space was a concrete box that isolated anyone unfortunate enough to find themselves alone there. You could be attacked, your body carved into little pieces, and no one would hear you scream. A camera was by the elevator, but heaven forbid you walked too far away and out of camera view, ready to be slaughtered. Nervous laughter sputtered out as Sharon reached her car. *Made it unscathed again.*

A gloved hand covered her mouth. Sharon screamed and bucked her body against the arm that came around her waist holding her tightly. "Did you get my gift, bitch?" A man's hot breath hissed in her ear. Sharon stilled, the hammering of her heart causing her chest to ache. This man left the note on her car and sent her the flowers. Her legs wobbled as she waited for him to tell her more, especially what he wanted from her. Her mouth went bone dry as a multitude of options spilled into her brain.

He arched her neck and pressed his lips against her flesh. "So pretty, but soon you'll be dead."

A sob caught in her throat and her stomach became rock hard. *He's going to kill me!* Tears streaked down her face as she realized she wouldn't find out why. She couldn't ask because his gloved hand covered her mouth. Was it for the same reason as Robert? This man wasn't from her world—that much she knew. Someone had hired him, but who, and why? To get her seat?

In a flash, he released her and rushed off. The sound of the elevator and people walking toward her echoed off the walls. Sharon dropped to her knees and longed to weep, but dreaded the thought of someone seeing her, especially if it was someone from her office. Scrambling to her car, she climbed in and started the engine. She was pulling out of the parking space as two people appeared in her rearview mirror. No one from the office.

Sharon wanted to sob in relief and pull over, but she kept driving until she was out of the parking garage and heading back to her home. She could weep when she got home. Oh, God. Would Danny still be there?

When she left the office, she was excited about Patrick's possible plan to derail her father's plans, but after what just happened, she needed to rethink that strategy. Was it someone on the board? Carlton? Virginia? Bradley? Each had their own agendas, but they didn't strike her as killers, even to keep her from acquiring what they wanted. And what would Bradley gain from killing her? If they were married, she could see it...but before?

Sharon pulled the pins from her hair and opened the windows, letting the cold air blow away the scary event that had iced her blood. A bodyguard was the best option, but the last thing she needed was some six-foot man with a linebacker's body following her around. He was bound to draw attention, and that was the last thing she wanted. While it might deter any future attacks, that wouldn't fix the problem of it botching her business deals. What she needed was someone who could fit in and not cause waves.

Bradley was a choice, given the possibility of their future together, but somehow she couldn't imagine him trying to protect anyone but himself. Without the contract or a ring on her finger, he'd gain nothing other than what he already had—a position in the company. Sharon paused. Maybe that was his plan. Without her in the way, her father would probably choose him over Carlton to fill the seat on the board. Bradley wasn't family, but she was sure her father could convince the board to fill the seat with anyone but Carlton.

Sharon banged the steering wheel. She could be wrong. The frustration was in not knowing and having no way to find out. Whoever was behind the attack hadn't had time to reveal their plan before being interrupted. Did they even know the plan, or were they just hired to scare or kill her? She wasn't about to wait around until she was attacked again.

Danny flashed in her mind.

Sharon couldn't imagine him fighting off an attacker, but he looked intimidating enough to scare away one. He already worked for her and had an excuse for being around. He'd already accompanied her to an event, but the business ones might be a bit trickier to explain, but not impossible, and he was a darn sight better than some hired bodyguard who would stick out like a sore thumb and raise more questions. The real question was if Danny would go for it, especially given how strained things were between them. Sharon contemplated using another reason to keep him around, but she didn't want to lie to him. Not about something this important. Her life might depend on it.

As the skyline grew darker and lined with shorter buildings, Sharon thought of how she'd approach him. Would he insist on calling the police? Would he be offended given how strained things were between them? Several questions and scenarios raced through her mind, until they were silenced by her ringing phone. Danny's name flashed on the display.

"Hello." Sharon hoped her voice sounded steady.

"You okay?"

"Yes. Why?"

"We were supposed to meet almost an hour ago. I was worried."

A lightness filled her chest at his words. "I'm on my way." She sidestepped answering with she was fine. She wasn't fine and was still deciding how to broach the topic with Danny. "I'll see you soon." She hit End after he said, "Okay."

Sharon checked her watch. She'd be home in fifteen minutes. Not much time, but enough to figure out what she'd say to Danny to convince him to be her silent bodyguard and stay close, so no one tried to attack her again.

What would she tell Bradley? Her father? The complications were piling up. She didn't want to alienate Bradley if things fell through with the loophole Patrick found. There were too many unanswered questions and directions her future could go, and she hated the helplessness of it. When she received Patrick's message, she was beginning to see a light at the end of the tunnel, but after tonight, the tunnel was stretching farther away and the light a dim glow in the distance.

Sharon eased her BMW up the driveway next to Danny's truck. The two vehicles were as different as night and day, like her and Danny. Asking him for help was the right decision.

Chapter 25

Sharon's heart was racing and her palms were sweating as she sat in Patrick's waiting area. Last night with Danny was a disaster. She hadn't had the guts to talk to him about what happened, or to tell him the plan. She argued with herself it was because she wanted to hear what Patrick had to say first, that way she knew what to do about Bradley, but when she walked through the door and came face to face with Danny, fear stopped her. Fear of how he'd react to her offer, and withholding news of the attack from the police.

She assured herself that waiting until she heard Patrick's plan was the best option. *Coward!* Well, maybe she was, especially when it came to Danny, but things were complicated enough without adding Danny to the scenario.

Patrick's office door opened and he came out with a man she assumed was a client. They shook hands and the client left.

"Sharon. Come in." Patrick greeted her with a smile.

"Thanks," she mumbled and followed him inside, her legs trembling. "I was excited to get your message."

"It might be nothing, or it could be something useful to you."

"Anything would be appreciated."

Sharon sat.

Patrick sat behind his desk and pulled out her contract from a pile of files on his desk. "I had to read it through carefully several times before it dawned on me."

Sharon regarded him expectantly.

"The contract requires you to get married to a man of your choice by the end of the year, and to be married for at least two years, but there's no stipulation on the contract becoming invalid if the marriage ends. Which is surprising, but given that most people in our world often marry for reasons other than love, perhaps not so surprising."

"My father would never agree to a marriage that I could break off later."

"Who said anything about telling him?" Patrick grinned. "It's not in the contract, and that's to your advantage."

Sharon sat in silence for several seconds, waiting for him to say something more. It sounded too simple. A plan her father would see through and stop before it started, but it was worth a shot.

"I was surprised to see charity boards in the contract."

"Charities have been important to the women in my family, and I believe someone added it over the years to keep them in line. If they don't agree, they can neither sit on the boards nor be in contact with those charities in any form," Sharon paraphrased.

"Harsh."

"One of the many harsh clauses."

"Yes. You would lose everything if you walked away. Your position in the company, seat on all boards, your inheritance, and everything that comes along with being a Donovan."

"Let's not forget the verbal threat from my father that he'll bury any business I try to set up anywhere."

Patrick stared at her in disbelief. That wasn't in the contract, but her father continued to remind her. At first, she'd thought he'd said it out of anger, but he'd proved his threat when she started approaching clients outside the company about going out on her own. Her father had threatened their businesses, and that had stopped those ambitions in their tracks.

"I had no idea your father was so ruthless," Patrick whispered.

"Only the people who cross him know." Sharon straightened. "Is there anything else?"

"Unfortunately, no. I thought about suggesting more time, but I saw a clause where it had already been extended and no more extensions would be given. Have you considered threatening your father with walking away? He'd be left without a family member to take a seat on the board. That might buy you some time."

Sharon smiled knowingly. "If only I could believe that."

Patrick closed the file and handed it to her. "I spoke with my contact at the police station, and he said there are no options right now, especially since there's no suspect or any indication about who it could be. They recommended a bodyguard. I'm inclined to agree with them."

Sharon neglected to tell him about the recent attack, since according to police, there wasn't anything to be done because she didn't see the person's face. "So, until I know who the threats are coming from, there's nothing they can do?"

Patrick nodded. "I'm sorry, Sharon. I agree with them about the bodyguard."

"And for how long?"

"As long as you need to feel and be safe," Patrick added.

"Thanks for taking the time to look through the contract, Patrick. I really appreciate it." She stood, knowing there was nothing more either of them could do at this point. "Please send the bill to Ryan."

He waved his hand. "I told you, it's the least I can do for putting you in this position."

"You didn't put me in this position, Patrick. My family did when they drew up this ridiculous contract."

"Maybe, but I didn't help things by breaking off our engagement and forcing you to start over."

"The only thing I regret about our broken engagement is the time lost to our friendship."

"Same here." Patrick hugged her before walking her to the door.

"Stay in touch. Let me know how things go."

"I will."

"Oh, Josie mentioned you're joining her bachelorette party. Please keep an eye on her for me."

Sharon grinned. "Already on my agenda."

As she walked back to her car, she was plagued with hope and dread at the loophole Patrick had given her. Bradley might be open to a temporary arrangement, but she wasn't sure he could be trusted to keep the secret, or to make conditions of his own with the knowledge of her plan to dupe her family's contract. Sharon was certain he'd use it to his advantage, and being at Bradley's mercy didn't appeal to her. No, she needed someone she could trust. Again, Danny came to her mind.

The phone rang. Patrick. He must've forgotten to tell her something, or maybe he'd thought of another loophole. "Hello?"

"Sharon, I forgot to ask you about Bradley. You mentioned you were considering him as a candidate and were digging into his background."

"Yes. I didn't find anything to raise any red flags."

"Well, when you mentioned you were thinking about him, I decided to do my own digging."

"And?"

"He's in debt up to his eyeballs, and some of the clubs he attends are questionable in the services they offer clients."

"I had no idea. Thanks for telling me, Patrick." That was good news. She could use that to her advantage if she wanted to.

"He's dangerous, Sharon. Stay away from him."

What he mentioned didn't sound dangerous. "What aren't you telling me, Patrick?"

"One of his ex–girlfriends was badly beaten. No official charges were pressed, but you know what that means."

Bradley or his family had paid her to keep quiet. Sharon shuddered, thinking about Bradley. Her instincts had told her something was off with him, and she was right. She had imagined many things, but Bradley hitting women hadn't been it. The money had been a surprise. He'd hidden his debts well, since Ryan hadn't been able to uncover anything, but then he didn't have the connections Patrick had. While she was disappointed about Bradley, she was partly relieved. The thought of being married to him made her stomach turn. The only problem was she was back to square one. *There's always Danny.* She'd happily consider Danny, but would he consider her or her offer?

Chapter 26

———————◆———————

Sharon longed to go home instead of back to the office, but the business deal was closing this afternoon, and she had to speak with her father about Bradley. Maybe she could buy herself more time. More moments with Danny to get to know him without the pressure of the contract date looming over her would be wonderful. Bradley might've been on her father's list as backups for her seat, but with this news about his debts and the abuse, Sharon was certain her father wouldn't want someone like that on the board anymore than the other members.

The contract said there were no more extensions, but she knew her father didn't have another candidate. He didn't want to give the seat to Carlton, so maybe he'd be forced to work with her for other alternatives to the contract. *Or maybe he'll threaten to give the seat to Carlton.* There was only one way to find out. Talk to him. But it wouldn't be until after the business deal was closed. Being distracted or unnerved by a run-in with her father was the last thing she needed.

Lunch was waiting for her when she got back to her office. She thanked Ryan. She hadn't even thought about eating with so much on her mind. After eating, she headed to the meeting and avoided Bradley's gaze as much as possible, afraid it would give away what she'd learned about him. He greeted her with indifference, which she assumed was due to the meeting.

Everyone shook hands and was smiling when the contracts were signed, making Sharon wish the signing of her contract would be as happy. Bradley tried to get her to notice him, but she avoided him and focused on getting her father's attention.

"We need to talk."

"Not now. I have another meeting."

"This can't wait. It's about my contract."

Her father paused and glanced at her and then Bradley.

Damn. She didn't want him to think they were speaking about Bradley.

Mark checked his watch. "Do you want to meet here?"

"No. My office," Sharon countered.

She and Mark walked in silence to her office. Ryan nodded to them as they passed his desk.

"Make it quick, Sharon. I haven't got all day."

Sharon gritted her teeth. *"It's my future, Father. You haven't got time for it?"* Silence was the reply. "I found out some unsavory things about Bradley."

Mark's expression didn't change.

Her heartbeat slowed and coldness settled in her stomach.

"You mean about his debts? I knew."

"Did you also know about him abusing his girlfriend?"

Mark shoved his hands in his pockets. "I hoped you wouldn't find out."

The room spun and Sharon gipped the edge of her desk to keep from falling. *He knew?*

"It was a long time ago," Mark offered.

That makes it okay?! Her voice vanished from the shock of her father being okay with marrying her off to an abusive man. Mark could be cold and calculating to get what he wanted, but somewhere in the back of her mind—and buried deep in her heart— she'd hope he cared enough about her to want someone who'd treat her with the same respect he'd treated his wife. Or had he?

Sharon suddenly wondered if the respect she'd always seen between her parents was a façade. It would explain why he didn't respect her or other women, but appeared to respect her mother. *Perhaps it was written in his contract.*

"Two years isn't a long time ago."

"Look, he needs the money, so you can control the conditions of the contract. That's why I thought he'd make a good candidate. He hadn't had another abuse incident. He comes from a prominent family and has the company's interests at heart."

"He put her in the hospital, Father. It wasn't an accidental slap." *This can't be happening.*

"Bradley would never lay a hand on you. You could put it in the contract," Mark offered.

"Like my mother put, 'Treat me with respect' in hers?"

Knotted brows met her. "What the hell does that mean? I genuinely loved and cared about your mother."

"Did her father pick you? What secrets in your past did she find out about and had to live with?"

"Enough! I'll not be spoken to with such disrespect."

Sharon paced. "How about you extend some of that respect to me and change the conditions of the contract so I don't have to get married to get the seat, or my inheritance. I'll not marry a man like Bradley, even if it means I'd hold the cards because he's broke. Bradley knows my situation too, Father. What's to stop him from holding that over me? He's already made his own demands."

"What demands?"

Sharon's cheeks heated. "I wanted a marriage in name only, but he wants a traditional marriage."

Surprise shot across Mark's face before he mumbled, "Surely you can work something out."

"So, once again, I must compromise? What happened to holding the cards, Father? Besides, I don't want to work things out with him or any other man. I want what's mine. What I would get if I was your son!"

Mark remained silent.

Damn stubborn man!

"Maybe I'll just walk away, and Carlton can have my seat."

"That would never happen. I'd make sure of it!"

"Is that what happened with Uncle Robert?"

"What are you talking about? He killed himself."

"Did he?" She still didn't know what really happened, but her father didn't know that.

"Of course. I saw the police report myself."

"Saw it or made sure it said what you wanted? Virginia insinuated someone had killed him because he wanted more power on the board. More power than you."

"Virginia is a nut who's obsessed with her position in society more than power."

Sharon didn't miss that he neglected to answer the question and, in this moment, she couldn't ask him. She was already heartbroken that her father would marry her off to a man like Bradley. She crossed her arms.

"Maybe walking away is the best choice. You can give Bradley my seat, so you'll have more power. That's what you want anyway."

"You'll lose everything!"

"I'd rather have nothing than be married to a man I don't love or respect for money and a job."

"You won't last five minutes in the real world," he retorted.

"I would if I started my own company." She had broached this warning before.

"I won't allow it!"

"And how will you stop me? Will you really be able to keep the clients I cultivated and nurtured all these years? Especially if they knew I was leaving?" she threatened.

"You know the kind of power I can exert."

And there he was. The man she'd witnessed intimidate and belittle people to get his way.

"Your reach doesn't extend everywhere."

"Do you really want to test that, Sharon? You won't have anything but the clothes on your back. You think anyone will take you in once they know I've put you out?"

"I'd live in a homeless shelter until I got back on my feet." The statement was an empty one—she did have her own money.

Mark laughed. "A homeless shelter? You couldn't survive in a place like that."

"I'd have my freedom."

"But at what cost? You'll never make it out there. I'll make sure of it!"

Pain shot across her body and then coldness before it settled in her stomach. Parents are supposed to love and support you, but her father had done none of those things.

While she was appreciated, she had to strive hard to get what she achieved. Most of the obstacles she encountered were from him and the company she longed to be belong to like other family who came before her.

Sadness beat at the back of her throat and stung her eyes. Fear raced through her as every setback she'd faced flashed before her. The emotions crushed her defiance into submission, and she hated herself for it.

"Please leave. I have a lot to think about." Sharon sat behind her desk and didn't look up until she heard the door close. She wanted to weep but couldn't, not until she got home tonight, and even that wouldn't be an option if Danny was still there.

The office that she'd carefully decorated with her mother seemed like a prison now. The accomplishments hanging on the wall mocked her: *"Look how far you have come, but you're still not good enough."* She missed her mother. Longed to have someone to talk to.

Ryan came in moments later. "Are you all right? Things sounded heated."

"I'm fine."

"You don't seem fine."

He was right, but her relationship with Ryan wasn't close enough for her to share what was troubling her. They were barely on a first name basis after almost five years. That was mostly her fault, but she wasn't ready to spill her secrets and frustrations with him. "Clear my calendar for the day, Ryan."

He recited all her appointments before confirming he'd reschedule.

"Shall I book the spa?"

"Please." A spa day wouldn't solve her problems, but it'd help her relax and waste time until she could go home finally unpack everything bothering her and cry.

He nodded and headed to the door before she stopped him.

"Thank you, Ryan."

He smiled brightly. "It's my pleasure, Ms. Donovan... Sharon."

Ten minutes later she had packed up her office and headed out the door. Hopelessness followed her to the elevator, to her car, and during the drive to the spa. Every possible scenario was explored as her body was poked, prodded, and wrapped until she was putty in her soft white robe.

As she lounged on a couch hours later, sipping cucumber water, she had a clear plan of what she needed to know and who was going to help her. Fear be damned, she wasn't going to let anyone stop her from getting what she deserved. She'd worked her ass off for this, and no one was going to stop her. *Nobody.*

Chapter 27

R elief coursed through Danny once he heard the front door opening. When Sharon hadn't shown up for their meeting, and didn't call or answer his call, he became worried. She was too professional to neglect a meeting, even one with him. This was the second time. Something was wrong. He could tell from the tone of her voice after he spoke with her the other night, and the way she sidestepped his questions. Danny adjusted his spot on the barstool to keep from rushing to her.

To his surprise, she appeared calm and relaxed. As she got closer, he could see the strain in her eyes.

"Everything okay? I got worried when you didn't show up for our meeting and didn't answer my call."

"I'm sorry. I've got a lot on my mind, so I asked Ryan to reschedule all my appointments."

He looked down at this phone and felt stupid because it came from a name he didn't recognize; he'd dismissed the email notifications from earlier, too.

"I missed it. Glad you're okay. Want to talk about it?" he offered, although he knew what the answer would be.

"I was attacked the other night in the parking lot," she whispered.

He shot off the stool and rushed to her. "Are you okay?" He put his arms around her. "What did the police say?"

"I didn't call the police."

The hand stroking her back paused. "Why not?"

"It's...complicated."

How the hell could it be? Someone attacked her, the police needed to know so they could find who hurt her. Wait. Did she know the person? Is that why she didn't call the police? "Was it Bradley?" *I'll rip his heart out.*

"No. I don't know who it was." Her hands rested against his chest. "I asked Patrick about it because there'd been threats before that, but the detective he spoke with said there was nothing the police could do since there wasn't a suspect, and I didn't see their face. I didn't call the police because it would've caused problems with the deal I was working on. We closed today. It was an important deal," she clarified when she saw what she knew was his *Are you insane?* glare.

Sharon stepped out of his embrace and slowly told him everything that had happened, including her conversations with Virginia and Carlton about Robert's death, and all the threats.

"Shit! Isn't that good enough for the police?"

"I don't have any proof. I can't describe the man who attacked me, and there's nothing to go on but a bunch of random incidents—none of which I can tie to anyone."

"What happens when they come after you again?"

Sharon gnawed on her bottom lip. "I have a plan."

"Good." The look on his face said he wasn't going to like her answer.

"I want you to be my bodyguard."

Danny paused, not sure if she was serious or if he'd heard her correctly. When her expression didn't change, he knew she was serious. Him? Her bodyguard?

"I don't know the first thing about being a bodyguard."

"I want someone who'll blend in, not stick out like a sore thumb, the way some burly security guy would. This gives me a chance to poke around and find out who's threatening me."

"I stuck out at the engagement party."

"Which makes you perfect. No one will suspect you're protecting me, since I plan to tell them we're dating."

Say what? Danny was certain he'd misheard her. Surely she wasn't serious. With everything that had gone down between them, this turn of events seemed like they'd taken a U-turn—and not for the right reasons. "No one will believe you."

"They believed it at the engagement party. I think it's possible." She didn't say but no doubt was thinking about their growing attraction. If Laura and his parents saw the sparks between them, it wouldn't be a stretch to convince others.

"What about your father?" Mark was going to blow a gasket when he saw them together, especially given the interaction of their first meeting.

"I'll deal with him," Sharon offered.

"I think you're better off with a real security guard, or at the very least a bodyguard who can blend in."

"Blend in? With my crowd?"

Danny raked a hand through his hair. "It can't be me."

Sharon crossed her arms and glared at him in determination. "I'll pay you."

Annoyance crawled up Danny's back. "It isn't about the money, Sharon."

"What is it about then?"

"You need someone who can protect you. Keep you safe. I'm not the right person."

A range of emotions shifted across her face before she answered. "If I was being shot at, or someone tried to run me off the road, I'd agree with you, but these attempts were meant to scare me, nothing more. I need to remove those opportunities by having you around."

"Can I think about it?"

Sharon's stiff frame relaxed. "Of course." She placed a hand on his shoulder. "I want you to take the money. You can give the workers a cash bonus for Christmas. You might not need or appreciate it, but I'm sure they will."

She was right. It'd be nice to give the guys something extra for Christmas, especially Rodriquez, whose wife was expecting twins. Although he was leaning toward a yes, he'd think about it more. "I'll give you my answer tomorrow."

Sharon smiled, and in that moment, he became agonizingly aware of how close she stood and that her hand still rested on his chest. The softness of her stare, and the way her blue eyes settled on his mouth, shot sparks through his body and filled the air. She sensed it and stepped back. Danny was grateful, but wondered what she'd do if he pulled her against him and kissed her.

She'd slap you, jackass! Danny cleared his throat and shoved his hand in his jeans pocket. "I'll check the doors and windows. You make sure the alarm is active after I leave. Okay?"

Sharon raised an eyebrow. "I've been living alone for some time now, Danny. I know the drill."

"I know you do. That doesn't mean you don't need a reminder now and then."

"Thanks for your concern."

"Do you have a gun?"

Sharon shivered. "No. I don't like them."

"You might not like them, but you should get one."

"Why? I'd probably shoot myself in the foot."

Danny grinned. "You don't have to keep it loaded. The sight of it will give you time to hold someone off long enough for the police to arrive, or scare them off."

"I don't think so."

"Sharon—you were attacked. You need to learn how to protect yourself. What if the next attack is here?"

She glanced down at her hands before meeting his gaze. "All right. I'll think about it."

"Good. I'll lock up and we'll review the renovations tomorrow."

Danny rushed off before Sharon could argue with him. He still couldn't believe she'd been attacked. He wasn't 100 percent convinced it was the individuals she suggested, but people did crazy things when money was involved. Perhaps Carlton and Virginia were better than the alternative: some nutjob who was stalking her. Those kinds were dangerous and unpredictable.

He double-checked all the doors and windows, along with the door to the attic. No one was going to get inside. At least, not tonight. The coldness that settled in his stomach when he first saw her was starting to disappear, along with the searing desire to tear apart the person who'd tried to hurt her. While she didn't break down and cry, a tear brimming in her eyes tugged at his heart. Sharon wasn't the type of woman to show a vulnerable side, which meant the attack shook her up.

Danny wanted to do more than just check the windows for her, and make people think they were dating so she wouldn't be attacked again. But short of him living here or parking outside her home at night, there was little more he could do.

Sharon thought he was thinking about her offer, and he'd have to answer her eventually. He would tomorrow, but tonight would be better so she didn't worry, or come up with an even crazier plan. Saying yes to Sharon meant changing their relationship, which was already strained. Pretending they were dating?

Excitement rushed through Danny thinking about having his arm around Sharon, or having her cheek pressed against his as they chatted intimately, or having to kiss again. The first kiss had been too much champagne. The next time would be for show—not how he imagined. Was Sharon willing to let it go that far?

Sharon calling his name jerked him from his thoughts. Maybe their time together would give him the opportunity to find out more about the contract Patrick had talked about, and to convince her she could confide in him. He wanted to show her how much she meant to him and that their relationship was worth taking a risk for. After speaking with Patrick, Danny couldn't stop thinking about Sharon, and wondering if he cared enough about her to make the life changes that might be required. He didn't know what they were, but he was willing to learn and make that decision if it meant helping Sharon get the life she dreamed of.

Sharon gave herself a lecture after Danny left. She hadn't told him her entire plan. As much as she wanted to, she had the feeling that easing him into it was a better idea than dropping it all on his lap, especially when he didn't give her a definite yes.

No, waiting until he agreed was better. *You're running out of time, Sharon!* All the time in the world wouldn't matter if Danny turned her down solely because she rushed him. Suggesting that they date as a cover was one thing, but marriage? That was a whole different story, especially given the type of marriage his parents had. She suspected he didn't take marriage lightly and would be offended, and probably horrified, by her offer, but she had no choice at this point. Especially after what happened with Bradley and her father. She cared about Danny and didn't want to drag him into the mess that was her life, but then she realized she was taking away his choice completely, mostly because she was afraid of his rejection and what he'd think of her. The company Christmas party was days away, and she needed a response. He said he'd tell her tomorrow. She could only hope his answer was yes.

She still hadn't confronted Bradley about what she found, or let him know that her offer was off the table. A public place was needed for that conversation. Then there was her father. He'd be furious, but at this point she could care less. He was willing to throw her to a wolf.

The real problem would come if Danny said no to her offer. She had no backup. Thankfully, the merger was out of the way. That was something. In retrospect, it suddenly seemed insignificant compared to what she had to tackle next: her future and the possibility of dying.

Chapter 28

◆───────── ◆ ─────────◆

"**B**radley here to see you, Ms. Donovan," Ryan said over the phone.

She couldn't avoid him forever. The office Christmas party was tomorrow night, which was likely what he was here to see her about. Time to nip his expectations of an offer from her in the bud, especially since her father probably told him she knew about his past. The last thing she wanted was to drag it out. She still had to convince Danny to accept her deal. Regardless of his answer, Bradley was not a second choice.

"Send him in." Sharon cleared her desk and took a calming breath.

Bradley swaggered through the door and sat. "What time should I pick you up tomorrow night?"

"I've decided not to move further with our relationship, or your offer."

"What? Why?"

"You know why."

"Okay, so I lied about having money." He shrugged. "I had to keep up appearances for my family's sake."

"That's not the reason I was thinking of."

His jawline jumped. "I knew that girl would cause me trouble. It was nothing."

"Putting her in the hospital is nothing?"

"She fell after I hit her. I didn't hurt her that badly," Bradley argued.

Seriously? His answer cemented that she made the right choice. "I've decided."

"What about your contract? You'll lose everything!"

Her father had obviously shared all the details with Bradley, hoping to convince him he was a shoo-in.

"I have another plan. It doesn't include you." *Both you and Mark can go to hell!* She hoped her spoken words wouldn't come back to haunt her.

His face contorted in anger. "You can't do this! Your father promised me!"

Her father made him promises? She clenched her fists. "He shouldn't have. I mean what I said. It is my choice who I marry, not his."

"But—-"

"You should leave." Sharon punched a button on the phone. "Ryan, can you please escort Bradley out?"

Ryan didn't answer, but moments later he came into her office. He looked ready to grab Bradley by the collar and haul him out.

"I won't be set aside so easily when you're left high and dry, Sharon. You're going to pay, and big, when you come back crawling because you don't have any other choice."

Ryan grabbed him by the arm, but Bradley jerked it from his grasp. "Don't touch me!" Bradley seethed as he stormed toward the door, Ryan following closely behind him.

One down. One more to go. Her father wouldn't be so easily dismissed. She'd need a public place to tell him Bradley was no longer on her list. She'd hoped when he found out about Bradley's past, her father would've changed his mind. Once again, her father proved he was more interested in what was important to him and the company than his daughter's life.

The pain and disappointment should've dulled over the years, but it hadn't. It hurt more now because she had been trying to remove the walls she'd built around herself for protection from him and others over the years. That was a mistake. They should've remained up and fortified.

Memories of her time with Danny and the intimate conversations and moments they shared filled her thoughts, along with the emotions he'd stirred. He'd woken her up with his humor, sexy grins, and caring nature. She felt more alive in the short weeks she'd known him than she'd experienced in years. She wouldn't trade it for anything. The pain was proof she was alive. Dealing with her father was unavoidable, since they worked together, but she didn't have to let him into her life, or into her heart. She could fill the space left behind with other experiences that would satisfy her life. It'd be his loss, not hers.

Tomorrow night she'd walk into the Christmas party with Danny on her arm, and if she was fortunate, he'd become a permanent figure in her life.

Chapter 29

———————◆———————

Danny glanced at Sharon, who stood next to him. She was trembling, and he knew it wasn't from the chill in the air since she was wearing a heavy coat. Her nerves were just as on edge as his. Sharon had seemed her normal calm and confident self when he picked her up half an hour ago, but as they drove up the heavily landscaped brick driveway, the expression on her face became solemn, and she kept clutching the small bag in her hand.

He'd tried to unwind her by making a joke, but it had slid past her. Danny got out of her car and handed the key to the valet as he opened the door for her. A small smile was now on her face, but he suspected it was only for show as her grip on his arm had tightened. "I'm going to need the blood to get to the rest of my arm," he teased.

As if awaking from her trance, she loosened her grip and blushed. "Sorry. I'm a little nervous."

"I gathered that." Danny lifted her chin. "It's going to be fine. We'll just be ourselves, like we were at the engagement party," he assured her, even though this was nothing like the engagement party since he was here as her bodyguard. He'd been around rich people when he dated Teri and knew what was expected, which is how he was able to get through the last party they attended and would get through tonight.

"I know. I just don't want them to insult you."

She's worried about me? "You know they will, but I've got tough skin."

"Yes."

He patted her hand resting in the crook of his arm. "Let's do this!"

They entered a room lit by a giant chandelier and crammed with elegantly dressed men and women, along with a string quartet in the back of the room playing classical music. Danny led her toward the bar and ordered them two glasses of champagne. *We should've had a shot of whisky before leaving her house. A stiff drink would've helped calm our nerves.* Danny sensed every pair of eyes in the room on them before they left the bar. Everyone wasn't staring at them, but it sure as hell felt like it.

Moments later, Mark was strolling toward them. His eyes raked over Sharon before they turned and scrutinized him, and then widened in recognition. "You!"

Danny didn't know whether to be insulted by his tone or surprised that Mark remembered him. Danny decided to focus on the latter. "Nice to see you again, sir."

He didn't bother extending his hand for Mark to shake. He wouldn't make that mistake again.

"I can't say the same," Mark mumbled, then turned to Sharon. "What is he doing here?"

"He's...my date."

Danny put his arm around her waist. "Her date, and more," he clarified, and grinned when Mark's face turned red.

"I thought we'd agreed on Bradley."

"You agreed, not me."

"I'm much more fun to be around than Bradley." Danny pointed a gun-shaped finger in recognition at Bradley, who was eyeing them a few feet away.

"Fun?"

"Yes. Fun! If I'm going to spend my time with someone, I want it to be about more than business."

Mark gritted his teeth and glanced around. "He's not suitable."

"He owns a successful business," Sharon argued.

"He's a glorified construction worker."

"And you're an overpaid salesman," Sharon shot back.

Danny felt like a spectator at a tennis match, but one without a winner. "We came to have a nice time tonight, and starting a fight that'll embarrass you both is definitely not my idea of fun." Danny ushered Sharon away from her father and onto the dance floor.

"That went better than expected." Danny pulled her against him and led her into a waltz.

"I have to disagree."

"Your father could've had me thrown out." He grinned.

"He wouldn't dare make that kind of scene. Maybe if this was a family gathering, but not at a business party."

"I can't wait for the first family gathering." Danny wiggled his eyebrows.

Sharon burst out laughing, nearly losing her step, but Danny caught her.

Her face lit with laughter was breathtaking, and he couldn't help staring. "You should laugh more." Danny noticed he wasn't the only one staring. Bradley and half the men and women were staring at them—at Sharon.

She brushed imaginary fluff from his tux. "It's easier when I'm around you."

"Good thing I'll be around then, huh?" But what about after Christmas when their deal was over and the renovations to her home were done? Then what? Would she continue laughing? As Danny glanced around the room, he couldn't imagine any of the men here making her laugh, especially if they were anything like Bradley.

The song ended and they left the dance floor. They were immediately approached by people who were eager to learn his identity. He and Sharon had convinced Mark, so far, that they were dating, but what about everyone else?

Sharon introduced him as her date to each couple as they approached, and answered the questions about how they met. Most people were friendly, even after finding out he was working for Sharon, but Danny couldn't help but feel like a buck with the way the women assessed him, as if he was nothing more than eye candy or a boy toy for Sharon.

"I didn't expect to see you here."

Danny turned to find Bradley standing behind him. "Same."

"I was speaking to Sharon."

"I could say the same about you, given our last encounter," Sharon said.

"This is a company party, and since I still work for the company, I thought it best to attend." Bradley's cool gaze shifted to Danny. "Mr. Stanley, I didn't think this was your kind of party."

Danny was stunned the man remembered his last name. He hadn't expected Bradley to recall anything about him. "I like all kinds of parties."

"So it would seem." Bradley held his hand out to Sharon. "Shall we dance?"

Sharon was about to decline his invitation. "It's all right, Sharon. I see someone here I know. Dance with your *friend*."

Bradley's jawline jumped as he led Sharon onto the dance floor.

Danny glanced around the room, trying to find someone he could pretend to know. Guilt nipped him for putting Sharon in that predicament. No doubt she'd give him an earful, and he'd deserve it. He'd suggested they danced not for her sake, but his. He wanted Bradley to know that Sharon was with him, and it didn't matter if they danced together. She was going home with him. That wasn't the complete truth, but Bradley didn't know that.

Danny strode toward a man standing by the bar and ordered another glass of champagne. When he turned around, he nearly spilled his glass on the person before him.

"Josie? What are you doing here?" *Shit.* She was the last person he wanted to see, especially in his situation.

"I was about to ask you the same question." Her gaze moved over him from head to toe in appreciation. "I didn't know you owned a tux."

"Well, now you know." Danny glanced at the dance floor, looking for Sharon. "You look lovely as always."

"How do you know? You're not looking at me." Josie's gaze moved in the direction Danny was looking.

"Are you here with Sharon?" The surprise in her voice was very apparent.

"Yeah. So? She needed a date." He wasn't going to elaborate on their agreement.

"And you agreed to get dressed up and come with her to this type of event? For a second time."

Danny gritted his teeth. "Yes. What about it?"

"I didn't think you dated clients..."

"That's your rule, not mine."

"I thought it was our rule."

"What are you doing here? Is Patrick with you?"

"Of course."

Danny's gaze darted about the room, looking for Patrick. "I didn't see you guys when we arrived."

"We just got here. Patrick is talking to Mark Donovan."

Great.

Danny found the two men standing close to the exit doors, and the moment Patrick's gaze found his, he knew the news was out. He couldn't read Patrick's face from this far away, but Danny was certain he wasn't happy with what he heard, because moments later he was striding toward him and Josie.

"Nice to see you, Patrick." Danny extended his hand.

Patrick's shake was brief. He put his arms around Josie's waist. "I heard you and Sharon came together. Are you dating now?"

No beating around the bush or filling the time with polite conversation before getting to the point. That was one of the things he'd admired about Patrick from the first time they met.

"It's a long story," Danny offered, knowing it wasn't his place to tell Patrick about his arrangement with Sharon. Josie's gaze was burning a hole in the side of his face, but he didn't dare glance at her.

"I've got plenty of time," Patrick answered.

"Not now."

"I think it's perfect."

"Drop it, Patrick. It's none of your business."

"Her father thinks you're taking advantage of her."

"Does Sharon strike you as the type of woman to be taken for a ride?"

Patrick's jawline jumped, and he grabbed two glasses of champagne from a passing waiter. "According to her father, you're out for her money."

Danny laughed. "Figures he'd say that. He's a snob who's pissed about his daughter going out with a carpenter."

"You're not a carpenter." Josie defended him.

"You think he cares? I'm not in his circle, so..."

"What's really going on?" Josie asked.

"That's for Sharon to say, not me."

"We're your friends, Danny."

They were right, and it shouldn't be a problem to tell them about his and Sharon's arrangement, but he didn't want to betray her trust. As if sensing his dilemma, Sharon showed up at his side, with Bradley close behind.

"Hi, Patrick, Josie. I didn't know you were coming tonight."

"Your father sent a last- minute invitation," Josie said.

"Really?" Sharon raised an eyebrow.

"I think he's trying to stay on my parents' good side," Patrick said with a chuckle. The Pullmans and Donovans were old friends, with lots of business and political connections.

"It seems our engagement has shaken things up a bit," Josie joked.

"To say the least," Bradley interjected, appearing as if out of thin air.

Everyone's gaze settled on Bradley as if waiting for a deeper explanation, but none came.

"It seems marrying outside your status is frowned upon." Patrick shook his head. "Makes you wonder what century we're living in."

"Status and race," Bradley added, glancing at Josie.

Danny resisted the urge to knock Bradley on his ass.

"Good to know you're still a pompous jerk," Josie responded.

Bradley's face flushed red, but Danny suspected it wasn't from embarrassment.

"Excuse me. I see someone I need to speak with," Bradley said, before leaving abruptly.

"Good riddance," Sharon mumbled.

"So, what's going on with you two?" Josie asked.

Danny glanced at Sharon.

"You didn't tell them?"

Danny shook his head. "I figured you wanted to." He held his breath, waiting to hear how much Sharon was going to share.

"Danny and I are pretending to date, but he's really acting as my bodyguard."

"Bodyguard?" Josie asked, confused. "Why do you need a bodyguard?"

"It's a long story, and one I'll tell you later," Patrick answered. "What happens after the stalker is caught?"

"Then Danny and I aren't dating anymore."

Her statement caused a twinge to race up his chest, especially the casual way she relayed the words.

"And you agreed to this?" Josie's gaze pierced him.

"Why wouldn't I? Sharon needs help and there's nothing the police can do at this point."

Both Josie and Patrick glared at him. They knew he hated dressing up and being around people with more money than they knew what to do with.

"I was very persuasive," Sharon answered, running her hand along his jacket and then winking at him.

"Yes, you were." Danny put his arm around Sharon's waist and drew her closer.

The expressions on Josie's and Patrick's faces were so funny, neither he nor Sharon could keep a straight face for long. They burst out laughing.

"The look on your faces," Danny said.

"Priceless," Sharon added.

Patrick gaped at Sharon as if she were an alien before his glance shifted to Danny and then Josie. "It's great to see you laughing again, Sharon." He rested a hand on her shoulder.

"It's good to laugh again. But it's hard not to with this guy."

"Yes. Danny is a barrel of laughs," Josie smirked.

<u>Oh, damn!</u> Danny could almost see the wheels of matchmaking turning in her head.

"I told you Danny was a miracle worker," Josie said to Sharon.

What? When had she said that?

"Although at the time, I was just trying to distract him because I thought he had feelings for me other than friendship."

"Distract him?" Sharon asked.

"Yes. Danny has a thing for blondes." Josie's eyes twinkled with mischief even as Danny glared at her.

"Why did you think Danny had romantic feelings for you?"

"He was trying to make Patrick jealous enough to ask me out." Josie put her arms around Patrick's waist. "It worked."

Patrick squeezed Josie against him. "Hey. I didn't ask you out because I was jealous. I knew you were already hot for me."

"Haha! You knew no such thing."

"I saw it in your eyes that first morning," Patrick said confidently. Josie and Patrick had a special agreement while she renovated his home.

"That was shock. You were half naked when I came to get coffee."

Patrick snorted. "Shock didn't make you devour me with your eyes."

"I was looking at the coffee machine." Josie grinned.

"No. You were looking at me and thinking about yanking down my pajama bottoms and having your way with me."

"Patrick!" Josie scolded, blushing.

Danny and Sharon glanced at them and grinned.

"You see why I can't take him anywhere?" Josie crossed her arms.

"You love taking me places." He whispered something in Josie's ears that no one else heard and she blushed and grinned.

They had shared this story before, but never in so much detail. More than Danny—and, he was sure, Sharon—wanted to hear.

"Danny?"

Danny turned at the sound of his name and his heart stopped. Teri stood a few feet away, looking as devastatingly gorgeous as ever in a slinky blue dress that not only showed off skin but her curves as well—curves he was very familiar with. His thoughts stopped short when he saw the man standing next to her.

"Teri. Gerald," Danny said coolly. Since they were in public, he couldn't tell them to go to hell, and he didn't want to embarrass Sharon.

"You two know each other?" Sharon glanced between them.

"Yes. Danny renovated my kitchen a few years back," Teri answered.

He did more than renovate her kitchen.

"Danny does great work." Sharon linked her arm in his.

"Yes, he does." Teri's gaze moved over him seductively before settling on Sharon. "What's he doing for you, Sharon?"

"He's helping me redesign my bathroom, my closet, and my bedroom." Sharon emphasized bedroom.

"Hmm. We never made it to the bedroom. Did we Danny?"

"He does his best work there." Sharon stepped closer so her body was pressed against his.

Josie and Patrick were glancing between Sharon and Teri, while Danny felt like a stallion horse being raved about by two perspective buyers. He didn't like it.

"I'm sure he does." Teri grinned, but her lips twitched.

"So nice to see you again, Teri. Danny, sweetheart, they're playing our song." Sharon tugged on his arm and headed to the dance floor.

Teri's face flushed, knowing she was being dismissed and yanked on Gerald's arm, taking them toward the bar.

The tension released from his body when Danny reached the dance floor, but it was replaced with annoyance. He expected to be bombarded with questions from Sharon, but she remained silent as they danced. Unable to stand the silence, Danny spoke. "Aren't you going to grill me about Teri?"

Sharon shrugged. "It's none of my business," she said absently, but the way she nibbled on the edge of her lips told Danny she was itching to ask.

"It was years ago. She hired me to renovate her kitchen and one thing led to another."

"You don't have to explain."

"I know, but I know Teri and how manipulative she is. I don't want her thinking she's holding something over you."

"I know Teri too. She's known for, as she calls it, *slumming* to piss her parents off. It's a game she used to play at college, and apparently hasn't changed her ways."

Danny didn't like being considered *slumming*, but those were the words Teri used, so he couldn't fault Sharon for using them. "I take it you aren't old college buddies?"

"Our families have known each other for years, but we've never been friends. I'm surprised we didn't run into each other when you and Teri dated."

"I wouldn't call it dating. We went out in public a few times, but only to events hosted by her parents and just to satisfy me. I didn't like being someone's booty call."

"I thought men loved those types of relationships?" Sharon gazed up at him.

"Not always," Danny said between gritted teeth. "And especially not with someone I care about and who led me to believe they cared about me. I prefer honesty. That's what annoyed me the most."

The song ended and Danny led Sharon over to the bar for another champagne, now that Teri and her date had moved. Damn, she did look good. Danny glanced at Teri over the rim of his glass. He would've felt better if she had wrinkled or put on weight or something, but she looked even better than he remembered.

Sometime later, Sharon checked her watch. "I think you've suffered enough. My father is sufficiently annoyed, and we've made all the rounds. Let's go."

"You sure?" Danny asked but was grateful to leave.

Sharon took his arm. "Absolutely."

As they waited for the valet to bring her car, Danny could practically feel the tension floating from Sharon. He waited until they were seated in her car and on their way to his house before speaking. "What's on your mind, Sharon?"

"Nothing."

"Don't lie to me."

"I...I'm starting to feel like Teri. Using you," Sharon mumbled.

"You're not. You were honest with what you needed from me. Besides, this is nothing like Teri. I'm trying to protect you and I'd never regret that."

"I'm glad you feel that way. I didn't want you to think I'm like Teri."

"I may think a lot of things about you, but you being like Teri isn't one of them." His gaze settled on her before shifting back on the road.

"Really? Like what?"

Next time keep your mouth shut, Danny. "Well. You weren't wearing provocative clothing when I worked late or bend over to show off your assets whenever you're around me."

"She did that?"

Danny grinned. "Yeah. She wasn't very subtle."

"I'll say, but then, she never was." Sharon shifted in the seat so she faced him. "No wonder you couldn't control yourself."

"Hey. I wasn't that weak!" *Yeah, I was.*

Sharon raised an eyebrow. "Really? I've seen Teri in action. How long did you hold out?"

Not long enough to brag. He'd been single for a long time before Teri came along and when she started hitting on him, Danny thought he'd hit the jackpot. He could've taken a page out of Josie's book about not dating clients. Although these days, she couldn't lecture him. "Longer than you think," he said.

"Two weeks?"

"Longer."

Surprised flashed in Sharon's eyes. "Really? Three weeks?"

Danny shook his head.

"Four weeks?"

"Close. I'm only human."

Sharon laughed. "No wonder she reacted the way she did. Four weeks must be a record for her. Were you dating someone? Is that why it took so long?"

"No. I don't usually date clients, especially in the middle of a renovation."

"But I'm guessing she made it worth your while?"

Danny smiled sheepishly. "You could say that. She realized she had to try a different approach with me."

"A different approach than sexy clothing and throwing herself at you?"

"Yes."

"What approach was that? Buck naked on the bed when you showed up for work?"

Danny laughed. "Not quite."

"Then what?!" Sharon begged.

Danny gave her a sideways glance. "She cooked me dinner and invited me to watch a movie with her."

"What? You're joking."

Danny turned the car down the road toward his house. "I know she didn't cook the food, but I liked the gesture. It was...sweet."

Sharon shook her head. "You're easier than I thought. Dinner and a movie? Really?"

"What?" He pulled into his driveway. "I'm a simple guy with simple needs."

"An offer of sex isn't simple?" Sharon shook her head. "It doesn't get any simpler than that."

Danny put the car in Park. "I'm simply not easy."

Sharon chuckled.

"Want to come in and watch a movie?" Danny wiggled his eyebrows mischievously.

Sharon laughed. "No movie, but how about a glass of wine?"

"That I can do."

They exited the car and headed inside the house.

"Excuse the mess," Danny said, picking up a discarded shirt off the couch.

"How about I get the glasses of wine while you clean up?" Sharon said heading to the kitchen.

"Sounds like a plan." Danny plucked a pair of shorts from the arm of the couch and took the clothing to the laundry basket in his bathroom. When he returned to the living room, he found Sharon sitting on the couch with a glass of wine in her hand.

She smiled in welcome and Danny's stomach lurched. She looked good on his couch. In his home. Her feet were firmly planted on the wood floor, but her back relaxed against the back of the couch. A definite change from the last time.

Danny cleared his throat and sat down. He took the glass of wine Sharon held out.

"How long have you lived in this house?"

"About five years."

Sharon glanced around, as if taking in the atmosphere. "It's nice."

"Thanks. I like it. There's still more I'd like to do but..."

"You're busy renovating other people's homes," Sharon added.

Danny kicked off his shoes. "Yes. That's how it works. What about you?"

"I purchased my house right out of college."

"Really? No high-rise apartment in the city?"

Sharon took a sip of wine. "No. Most of my friends got their inheritances at twenty-one or twenty-five. I went to work with my father. The only money I had was earned working at my father's office. A job I had to worm my way into."

"I would've thought your father would be happy you wanted to be involved in the daily operations of the family business and not out partying and spending your family's money, like Teri."

A forlorn expression crawled across Sharon's face. "I think he'd rather I was like Teri—planning parties, dating every man in sight before she finally settles down with one her father chooses."

"That explains a lot."

"About Teri?"

"Yes."

"Don't be fooled. She might be rebelling, but that's no excuse for the way she treats people."

"I suppose."

Sharon placed her arm on the back of the couch. "You cared about her." It was a statement, not a question.

"I did. I thought she cared about me too." A small ache clutched his chest as he remembered her cruel words and the night things ended.

Sharon touched his arm. "I'm sure she cared about you in her own way." Her gaze shifted to the fireplace. "Caring about people is a luxury when even your own family manipulates your affections."

"It must be hard."

Sharon shrugged. "You get used to it."

"Do you?" Danny asked. The sadness behind her eyes said otherwise. "It must be hard to know where you stand with people when everyone has an agenda you don't know about."

"You learn to play the longer you're in the game."

"Must be exhausting."

Sharon leaned against the couch and pressed a hand against her forehead. "You have no idea. Business. Personal. The lines become so blurred."

"I can't imagine." A part of him almost felt sorry for Teri now that he knew what it was like on the inside. It didn't excuse her behavior, but for someone who grew up in that world and had those experiences? Who's to say he wouldn't have acted the same way, or turned out like Bradley? Danny shivered thinking about it.

"What?" Sharon straightened, sliding the feet she'd tucked under her legs on the couch back to the floor.

"I was imagining I'd grown up in your world and that I turned out like Bradley."

Sharon's head fell back as she started laughing. Her hair curled around the lines of her neck and her breasts shook gently the more she laughed. This wasn't the first time he'd seen her laugh, but it was the first time he'd seen her laugh with her whole body. Tears pooled in her eyes, and she brushed them aside. "You're nothing like Bradley, and I suspect that your parents would've kept you grounded."

With each minute that passed while they sat on the couch talking, he'd notice her relax enough to remove her shoes and tuck her feet under her legs, and she hadn't checked her hair once to make sure no strands had fallen out of place. Her hair lay in messy waves about her face and neck, as if she'd just rolled out of bed. Danny suddenly had the urge to kiss her neck and spread her and her hair across the couch.

As if sensing his thoughts, her gaze locked on his. The air between them sizzled as their glances moved over each other's faces and settled on their lips.

Sharon broke the spell, placing her feet back on the floor and setting her wine glass on the coffee table. "I should go." She slipped on her shoes and headed to the front door. Danny followed behind her, his mind racing with words to say to make her stay longer. *Bad idea, Danny!* He knew, but didn't care. He was enjoying her company, and seeing her on his couch. Her smile and laugh gave him stomach pains—the good kind.

He wanted to pull her against him and kiss her until she didn't want to leave. Ever.

Sharon turned, and the solemn woman he knew too well had returned.

"Thanks for tonight. I had fun."

"Sure. Me too."

The sound of keys jangling filled the silence before she opened the door. "Good night, Danny."

"Good night, Sharon. Call me when you get home so I know you made it safely. And we should talk about temporary arrangements so you're not home alone. I don't want to take any chances."

"Good idea."

Danny stood in the doorway, watching her get inside her car safely and drive away. When he could no longer see her car, he closed the door. Tonight was a glimpse of their nights ahead. Nights filled with champagne, Sharon dressed in scanty gowns, her camaraderie and laughter. Even with the threats looming, the time would be enjoyable. He could get to know Sharon better and have her talk about her contract. He longed to ask her tonight, but she was so relaxed and enjoying herself that he didn't want to ruin the moment. There was always tomorrow.

Lights from the streets and buildings danced inside Sharon's car as she drove home. The heat in Danny's gaze taunted her, along with the way his eyes crinkled in the corners when he smiled, or the way his mouth twisted when he told a joke or tried to make her laugh. There weren't many men in her life who made her laugh, or tried to make her laugh. She could get lost in the warmth of his amber eyes and the curves of his smile.

Her thoughts were dangerous. Thoughts that could lead to a relationship she couldn't act on the way he wanted and deserved. His interest was clear in the heated way he gazed at her mouth, in the gentle way he touched her, and even the way he made her smile. He'd also implied he wanted to pursue a relationship after the renovations ended.

In that moment, she wished she were more like Teri. Then she could have a casual relationship with Danny. But that wasn't her. It was one of the reasons she'd gotten together with Patrick. They were friends, and she trusted him. At the time she thought that would be enough, but it wasn't, and Patrick had wanted more. If she were honest, she wanted more too. Her relationship with Patrick was comfortable—too comfortable. One her father had approved and agreed to.

Her father would never approve of Danny, but it didn't matter because the choice was hers. Danny was the kind of man who wouldn't care if she was more successful than him. Neither would he let her take him nor their time together for granted. There were several parties before Christmas and her dreaded deadline, and tomorrow was another day. The day she'd finally share her plan with him.

Chapter 30

S̲haron pulled into her driveway and turned off the car.
She'd left the lights on so no one could hide in the
shadows, but she checked carefully before going inside. She
checked out the renovations before getting dressed for bed
and calling Danny to let him know she made it home safely.
She'd just turned out the downstairs lights when something
cold pressed against her neck. Ice raced through Sharon's
veins when she realized it was a knife.

"I told you I'd find you," the man's voice rasped in her ear,
sounding like someone who'd smoked for years.

*How had he gotten in? And where was he hiding? I
checked every possible hiding place.* "What do you want? If
it's money, you can have anything in my wallet. I don't have
cash in the house." He wasn't there to rob her, but maybe
keeping him talking would help her to find answers.

"I want you to give up your seat on the board. You're a
woman, not a board member."

Realization sliced through her. *I was right.* The attack
was someone trying to scare her, but this man wasn't
anyone from the board. They wouldn't risk getting their
hands dirty. "Who hired you?"

The knife pricked her skin. "I'm just doing my civic duty.
Women don't belong in companies. They belong at home,

taking care of their family. Working women are ruining the American family."

The man was a nut. Worst of all, he believed those words. That made him dangerous. "What happens if I don't listen? Are you going to kill me?"

A crackly laugh filled her room. "Do you really want to find out? Next time I won't be so nice." The knife grazed over her clothing. Sharon's heartbeat thundered until the knife was gone, and then him. *Is he the same person who killed Robert? Why didn't he kill me?*

Sharon's limbs trembled as she waited for time to pass to make sure he was really gone. How had he gotten inside? She'd set the alarm before she left, and Danny was the only person who knew the code. Did he share it with one of the guys or Laura? Had they forgotten to set it after they left? No. It was the weekend, and she was the last person to leave the house before going to Danny's parents' house for dinner. She set the alarm, so he found another way to get inside, or figured out how to disarm the alarm, but the man who attacked her didn't seem intelligent enough for that. Was she wrong, like she was wrong about everything else? Was it disarmed now? There was only one way to find out.

Danny reached for the phone. *Who the hell was calling this late?* It couldn't be Sharon, she'd already called. He shot up when he saw Sharon's name on the screen. His hand shook as he pressed the accept call button. "Sharon?"

"Someone broke into the house."

He heard the tremble of her voice. "How?"

"I don't know. I turned the alarm back on as soon as I got inside."

"You okay?" A stupid question from the sound of her voice, but he needed to hear it from her lips.

"Not really."

Danny had expected her to lie. He was glad she hadn't. "What did the police say?"

The silence from her end told him that once again she hadn't contacted the police. "Damn it, Sharon. You need to call the police."

"And tell them what, Danny? Someone broke into my home and told me to stop gunning for my seat on the Board of Directors? Do you know what'll happen? They'll start investigating board members and my father's company." Sharon switched the phone to her other ear. "I didn't see his face. It was dark, and I didn't recognize the voice."

"This is your safety we're talking about, Sharon."

"The board holds my future in their hands, Danny. My dad will use this against me—I know he will."

Shit. Shit. Shit. Danny longed to tell her that no type of future was worth her life, but she was right about the police not being able to do anything if she didn't see their face or recognize the voice. Being part of her family's business meant everything to her, and he had no doubt that Mark would use an investigation into the board against his daughter.

"Can you please come over?"

"Give me a few minutes." Danny pushed himself out of bed and grabbed the shirt he'd thrown on the floor earlier.

"Thanks, Danny."

"Sure."

So much for thinking this charade of being Sharon's boyfriend to fend off whoever was trying to scare her was going to be simple. There was nothing simple about this situation he'd gotten into, but there was one thing he could do to keep Sharon safe.

The Sharon he knew had returned by the time he reached her house. Danny reset the alarm. She must've been too shaky to think clearly, not that he could blame her.

"Tell me exactly what happened."

Her voice was shaking when she finished telling him all the details, and he wished he hadn't asked. He didn't want to upset her, but he needed to know everything. "I'm moving in with you. I'd suggest my place, but I think that'll just prolong this playing out. The sooner we catch this guy, the sooner our lives can return to normal. We knew something had to change to keep you safe. This is it. The renovations will be finished in a week, and I'll sleep on the couch until you move back into your bedroom, and then we'll talk about new arrangements."

She opened her mouth to answer.

"This is nonnegotiable, Sharon. I don't care if your father or Bradley doesn't like it."

"I was going to ask what you're going to tell Laura and your crew."

"Nothing, at the moment. I'll keep my stuff hidden for the week."

"I... I don't know what to say," Sharon stammered.

"Say 'yes.'"

"Yes."

"Good. Now that that's settled, where are your blankets and pillows? It's late and we both need some sleep."

Sharon took him to her linen closet and let him choose what he wanted, and then walked him back to the living room.

"This couch is really uncomfortable."

"I slept on a futon in college. I can sleep on anything."

"Tell me that again in a few hours once you've slept on it. It's meant for style, and not comfort."

"I'll be fine," he assured her.

She stood at the end of the couch, and for the first time, he noticed she was wearing a short robe and her hair fell in waves around her face. He'd never seen her so vulnerable and uncertain. She was afraid to be alone.

He patted a spot next to him on the couch. She sat.

"I'll install a new alarm system tomorrow and I'll be here, so even if someone tries to break in, I'll be there before anything bad can happen, okay?"

She nodded.

He put his arm around her shoulders and, to his surprise, she rested her head on his shoulder. He leaned back so they'd be more comfortable, and he stroked her back. Moments later, her body relaxed again him. Danny lost track of the time they lay there, and the next he knew, his phone alarm went off. He had just enough time to get the stuff from his car and take a quick shower before Laura and the guys arrived. He'd already packed a bag before coming over last night, knowing he couldn't leave her alone.

He eased her onto the couch, and thought about taking her to the room, but decided against it. Instead, he got his bag from the car and headed upstairs to take a shower before the crew arrived.

Chapter 31

———— ◆ ————

Danny glanced at Sharon, certain he hadn't heard her correctly. "What?"

"I said, I'd like you to marry me. I'll give you four million dollars. Two once you sign the agreement and the remaining two million at the end of the contract time."

"You can't be serious!" Danny raked a hand through his shaggy hair.

"It's the only way I'll get my full inheritance," she clarified.

"You need to get married to get your inheritance?"

"Yes. That's the reason I couldn't start a relationship with you, as much as I wanted to." Sharon adjusted the plate before her on the counter. "I was scared of what you'd think of me if I told you the truth and asked this question sooner."

"Patrick had said being with you would mean changing my life dramatically. I thought he was talking about having to deal with your father, or people in your circle. I had no idea this is what he meant."

"I know it's a lot to ask, and I understand completely if the answer is no."

"What will happen to you if I do say no?"

"I'll lose everything."

In her world that could mean anything. "What's everything?"

"This house, my inheritance, my seat on the board, including the charities my mother and I setup, and possibly my job."

Shit. That is everything. Everything that was important to her. "Possibly?"

"My father will use it as a last resort to humiliate me."

Who does that to their daughter? Danny could understand if she was a problem child whom her father was trying to steer in the right direction, but that wasn't the case. "There's gotta be a way out of the contract without giving up what you want."

"I've known about this contract since I was eighteen. I managed to get a couple of clauses changed, but not this. Patrick came up with this alternative. I had thought about offering it to Bradley, but that's no longer an option."

"Why not?" He didn't like the guy, but he fit more into Sharon's world than he did. Danny cringed, thinking about Bradley and Sharon together.

"I uncovered some unpleasant things about him."

"Can't say I'm surprised."

Sharon took a sip of wine. "I know it's a lot to ask. I know you don't take marriage lightly. It would be just for a couple of years, Danny. When that time is up, you'll be financially free and can seek the kind of relationship you want."

Danny pushed his frame away from the kitchen counter. She'd said she wanted a relationship with him. Something he'd wanted too, but marriage? The money was tempting as hell, but his parents would never go for it, and he'd hate deceiving them. His family didn't take marriage lightly, and a casual marriage wasn't part of his plan. Danny had a feeling she didn't either, and that's why she didn't make the offer to Bradley, not to mention it was a big step from where they were now. Four million was a lot of money, enough money for him to expand his business the way he'd always dreamed. "Where would we live?"

"We'd have to live together for a short while for people to believe the marriage is real, but we'd have our own lives. Nothing would change, except you'd be richer and I'll have what I want."

It sounded like the perfect arrangement, but if Danny wanted a relationship, it wasn't. Relationship? That seemed crazy since they'd be married.

"Why two years?"

"That's the minimum requirement time for the contract. It was added after the sixties when my great-grandmother married a man for six months before divorcing him and taking his seat on the board." Sharon grinned. "She'd found a loophole in the contract. Her father didn't want a repeat, so he changed the requirements."

"Shrewd."

"She thought so."

"Are there any surprises I should know about?"

Sharon shook her head. "You should have a lawyer look over the contract to make sure you're happy with it, just to make sure you're comfortable with everything."

"What about our families?"

Sharon glanced at him over the edge of the wine glass. "They'll need to believe the marriage is real, but I understand you have a close relationship with your parents, so you're free to tell the truth. But keep in mind it could be a breach of contract if someone from my family finds out the truth, especially before the two years are up."

His parents would appreciate the benefits of the money, but they'd be against the reasons for the marriage. Telling them the truth would break their hearts, even though they adored Sharon, but so would finding out he'd lied to them for two years. "I'll need time to think about it."

"Of course! I'll draw up the contract for you to review and decide, but I need to know quickly, as I must get married before the new year."

"What? That's a few weeks away!"

"I know it's rushed, but those are the conditions of the contract."

"It'll be a stretch for people to believe we fell in love so quickly."

"They'll think it was lust at first sight," Sharon said with a grin.

"We'll have to convince them." Danny leaned over the counter.

"You'll need to kiss me more in public to be convincing." Sharon blushed.

"I'm sure we'll manage it." They'd be fine if the kisses were anything like their first and only.

"Yes. And not everyone marries for love."

"Seems like a waste if you don't," said the man practically agreeing to marry someone he hardly knew.

Sharon shrugged. "Most people in our circle marry for business, and other reasons, but rarely love. Especially when a prenup is involved. Less risky."

"Then why get married? Why not just have a business arrangement?"

"Marriage is a type of contract, Danny, whether people admit it or not."

"My parents' marriage isn't a contract!" Danny insisted.

"Really? Did they promise to love, cherish, and take care of each other in sickness and in health?"

"Of course."

"Contract. Whether it's written or verbal, the intent from both parties is implied and expected."

While he couldn't find fault in her reasoning, it was still a warped way of looking at marriage.

"Look. I understand your need to make it easy on your parents, but wouldn't it be better to tell them the truth?"

"What? That I'm getting married for money? They'd be disappointed. They take marriage seriously. And so do I," Danny added.

"I do too, Danny. This is my last and only option. I know it's not the norm, but please think about it."

"What? Deceiving my parents so you can get your money?" Crap, he hadn't meant it to come out so harshly. He'd wanted time for them to get to know each other and have a normal relationship. A rushed marriage with money would only create problems.

"This isn't just about the money, Danny!" Sharon paced before him. "Do you know what it took for me to get here? To live through the snide, sexist remarks; being told I'm too bossy; or asked why I want to be on the Board of Directors instead of home taking care of my children?" She poured herself a glass of wine. "I deserve that seat and money because I'm my father's child, and I worked hard to get it."

Danny pushed his frame away from the kitchen counter and sat on one of the stools. All this time, he'd assumed it'd been easy for her: the money, the job. All of it handed to her on a silver platter. He thought her only real problem was her father.

Married to Sharon. The words didn't terrify him, but except for the money, he wasn't going to get any benefits that came along with marriage. An image of Sharon lying naked in his bed with her hair spread across his pillow flashed in his mind. Damn, but it was a nice image—one he wished was in his foreseeable future, but it wasn't. Their union would be on paper only, and that didn't sit well with him. *I could add it to the agreement... Don't even think about it, Danny.* "I'll have some requirements of my own."

"What?"

"If we're going to be married for two years, you can't expect me to be celibate, so I want sex. Once a week, minimum."

Sharon raised an eyebrow at his request.

"Does that mean you'll agree to my proposal?"

Damn. That hadn't worked out the way he planned. The serious set of her face said she meant to go through with his demands. Maybe she was bluffing. That had to be it. "Maybe."

Sharon's gaze held his over the rim of her wine glass. "What else do you want?" Her voice was low and seductive.

Shit! Shit! Shit! Either she was calling his bluff, or she was entertaining his offer of sex in their marriage. God help him either way.

"I want to see if that kiss on the balcony was a fluke because of the champagne, or real." *Where did that lame statement come from? A kiss? Seriously, Danny?*

"Right now?" She leaned over the counter so her face was almost touching his.

Oh, she is damn good.

A smile curled on Sharon's lips. "I couldn't agree more. I'd hate to be disappointed on my wedding night," she prodded.

Danny pushed the stool away from the counter and strode toward her. She was facing him when he put an arm around her waist and pulled her against the length of his body. His other hand captured her face, and he lowered his head to kiss her. Sharon's body didn't tense, like he thought it would, but melted against him as his lips touched hers. There were no sparks or shots of excitement racing up his back, but a searing heat. That heat spread like wildfire to the rest of his body when Sharon dug her fingers into his back, bringing them closer, and opened her mouth under his.

There was no shyness or hesitation. Her tongue met his and sucked and stroked with so much boldness, Danny knees trembled. He'd gotten a glimpse of the fire behind her eyes on occasion, but the woman in his arms was a phoenix.

Danny released Sharon abruptly. If he didn't, he might not anytime soon.

Sharon gave him a shrewd smile. "Real enough for you?"

Danny gave a curt nod and wiped his lips with a thumb. "I'll let you know my decision by Monday."

"Good." She shoved the contract toward him. "Have your lawyer look it over and add any other requirements you want."

Danny grabbed the paperwork and headed to the living room. With their new arrangement of him living with her until her stalker was found, he couldn't leave. *Stupid!* The only lawyer he knew to handle something like this was Patrick. Did Patrick go through this when they got engaged?

Was it the reason he broke off the relationship? Danny planned to find out.

He turned on the television to distract himself. What happened a few moments ago still seemed unreal, like a bad dream—or a lucky one, depending on how you looked at it. Four million dollars was a lot of money. Sex with Sharon would be the icing on the cake. The rest of what would come with it was what didn't appeal to him. As much as Sharon thought their lives could continue as before, Danny knew otherwise, especially if they were going to fool both of their parents. His parents might believe he'd fallen for Sharon, but Mark would know the truth. The dinner parties would continue, as well as the snide comments from Sharon's friends and family, probably escalating once they were married. Everyone would know he'd married Sharon for her money, even though he hadn't, and that didn't sit well with him.

There'd be no denying it, since it was the truth. What would his parents say?

He couldn't accept her offer, no matter how enticing it was. He had a new job lined up in January with Josie. He blushed when thinking about the way he'd goaded Sharon into kissing him, and adding sex to their contract. He'd been a complete ass trying to show how ridiculous her offer seemed. The only thing he'd shown Sharon was what a jerk he was.

He punched Patrick's phone number into his phone and asked for a time to see him about a contract. Patrick said he had free time later that afternoon and would be happy to help him out.

Patrick would be surprised that Danny was considering Sharon's offer. Danny would ask Patrick not to tell Josie about the contract, at least until everything was finalized... If it was finalized.

Chapter 32

His parents were going to kill him. They'd be happy he was getting married, but not under the circumstances, and not with it ending. They liked Sharon, but would they still like her when they heard about the arrangement? Danny snorted. If his mother had her say, he and Sharon would remain married and give her a couple of grandchildren. Warmth spread across him when he thought of waking up to Sharon every morning, and then her pregnant with their child. Did Sharon want kids? Somehow, he couldn't imagine her changing dirty diapers or putting their kids to bed. Working at a homeless shelter for a few hours was one thing, but taking care of kids every day? He doubted that fit into her CEO life.

Danny shivered as he thought about Mark being his father-in-law and grandfather to his kids. Over his dead body. Good thing kids weren't part of the plan. Talk about nightmarish Thanksgivings and Christmases.

Maybe speaking to his parents was the way to go. They'd talk some sense into him and give him alternative ideas than this crazy one. Danny changed his mind when his parents' faces appeared in his mind, their eyes filled with disappointment. No. If he decided to accept Sharon's offer, he had no intention of telling his parents the truth. Let them believe he'd found love, even if it was for a short while. It wasn't far from the truth.

Later, Danny pulled into the parking lot of Patrick's office. He set the alarm before leaving and told Sharon he'd be back in a couple of hours. He hated leaving her alone, but this had to be taken care of.

The building was smaller than he expected. He exited the car and went inside. The offices inside were richly decorated, except for Patrick's office. The design in his office had clean, modern lines with no extra frills, and Danny knew instantly that Josie had designed it for him. Patrick's assistant led Danny into his office and offered him something to drink. Danny declined and took the seat Patrick directed him to take.

"Good to see you again, Danny." Patrick shook his hand before sitting down. "What can I do for you?"

Danny pushed the contract across the desk to Patrick before he lost his nerve and left. "You weren't kidding when you said having a relationship with Sharon would mean drastic changes to my life."

"She told you." It was a statement. "I'm glad. You needed to know it wasn't just about you." Patrick pushed a button on his phone. "Cancel my 1:00 appointment, Betty."

"Thanks." Danny shifted his position on the chair. He'd tried reading through the contract himself, and while he understood some of it, there were parts too legalese for him, and why he wanted Patrick to look through. Did Patrick cancel his appointment because of the contract or because it was his contract? Whatever the reason, it couldn't be a good one.

Patrick leaned back in his chair when he finished reading. "Did you want me to read this because of changes you wanted to make, or because you wanted to make sure you weren't getting screwed?"

"Both." Danny hadn't thought about Sharon screwing him over, since the contract seemed straightforward, but better safe than sorry.

"Are you seriously considering this?"

"Yes. No. I'm not sure. My business could really use the money, but..." Danny raked a hand through his hair. He should've waited until he made up his mind before coming to see Patrick. He didn't want to waste his time. "I guess I wanted your advice and whether you thought this was a good idea."

"I can give you my advice, but only you can decide if signing this contract is a good idea."

Danny nodded.

"The contract itself looks good, but I would definitely recommend you adding an escape clause, and one that benefits you financially if things go south."

Spoken like a true lawyer. Danny appreciated it. Patrick and Sharon were friends, and he could've left the contract as is. "Would you add it for me and let me know the charge?"

"Sure, but it's on the house. I insist."

"I couldn't."

"Consider it done. Don't argue. It'll take me less than ten minutes to add it."

Danny was certain the time was an exaggeration, but he'd take it.

"If changes are suggested during the signing. Don't sign until I've looked the new contract over. All right?"

"You got it. So, what do you really think?"

Patrick leaned back in his chair and linked his fingers.

"I know Mark and how difficult it's been for Sharon to get what's she's entitled to, but I also know Sharon, and she can be ruthless when it comes to being a part of her family's business and getting her inheritance. I'm worried those two will go to war and you'll be caught in the crossfire."

Shit! Danny was so worried about the crossfire between him and Sharon, he hadn't thought about her father.

"On a personal note, you and Sharon seem to genuinely care about each other, and the two years could be time to truly get to know each other. You might find that you stay married. However, two years can be a lifetime if you don't like the person. Hence why I suggested the escape clause. She needs you so she won't object to the change, regardless of the money."

Was that a good thing? It sounded like it, but Danny had a feeling he'd need a shower to wash the dirt from his body after the contact was signed.

"I'll speak with Sharon about the contact changes, and I'll review the new contract to make sure all is good before you sign."

Danny stood. "Thanks, Patrick. I really appreciate you doing this."

"Don't thank me yet. Between Sharon and Mark, it's going to be one hell of a ride. One you might not enjoy."

"Tell me about it."

"What are you telling your parents?"

"I haven't decided yet, but whatever I tell them, they have to keep the truth a secret from Sharon's family."

"Good luck with that." Patrick stood and walked with Danny to the door.

"Thanks. I have a feeling I'm going to need it."

Danny and Patrick shook hands and Danny made his way to the exit.

A blast of cold air rushed over Danny, and he pulled his coat closer against his frame before getting in the car. The drive back home didn't give Danny the calm he thought would come after speaking with Patrick. He'd hoped that visit would make the decision easier. It hadn't.

Chapter 33

The contract on Sharon's kitchen counter loomed between them like spoiled food no one wanted to touch. This was what she asked for, but that didn't stop fear and dread from coursing through her veins in a way no other business deal had. Maybe because this wasn't just another business deal. This was her life. She cared about Danny a lot, but this was a huge step. She and Danny hadn't known each other long, and in the short time they'd gotten to know each other, he'd stirred up more emotions in her than any other person had. It was exhilarating and terrifying all at once. When they signed this contract, he'd be a regular part of her life for the next two years. Two years was a long time. A lot could happen in those two years. Sharon smiled when she remembered him wanting to add sex as part of the contract. He was bluffing and trying to point out the ridiculousness of her proposal, but she'd added it anyway.

The call from Patrick about the escape clause had been a surprise, not only that Danny had involved Patrick, but that Patrick hadn't tried to talk Danny out of it, or Josie, for that matter. Maybe they tried. Sharon was happy the money was going to him. "Did you have any questions?" Sharon asked, trying to break the ice of silence that had remained in the room when he saw the contracts.

269

ELKE FEUER

Danny shook his head. "Did you make any changes other than the ones we spoke about?"

"No. I would've told you if I had."

He grabbed one of the contracts and skimmed through it. Danny paused on page five. It was the page with the sex clause.

"You didn't have to put this in." Amber–colored eyes locked on Sharon.

"I know, but I thought it should be there. Just in case." Her voice was a whisper.

"Are you sure it's a good idea? Sex complicates things."

How much more complicated could their relationship get? They were about to sign a contract to be married. "You don't need to ask for it, but it's there if you want it." *OMG! Did those words just come out of my mouth?*

Danny's gaze pierced her, heating the room. "You have the choice to ask yourself."

Heat raced to Sharon's cheeks and other parts of her body as she remembered his mouth and tongue against hers. What the hell was she thinking, including that clause? She managed to nod.

Danny continued reading the contract and picked up the pen to sign. His hand paused. "We must agree to be honest with each other if we're going to do this. And if anything changes between us, good or bad."

"Agreed. The escape clause covers that."

"The escape clause is just words on a page, Sharon."

He was right. In the end, while this contract bound them legally, it was just words. A marriage contract didn't guarantee a happy marriage. "I promise to be honest with you, no matter what happens between us."

Danny signed the contracts and pushed them toward her. She signed both copies. Sharon was still staring at her signature and didn't notice that Danny was standing next to her. When she met his gaze, the heat in his eyes made her gasp. He placed an arm around her waist and pulled her against him. Before she could say a word, his mouth crashed into her, hot and demanding, making her knees melt. Was he claiming his right in the sex clause now? Her mind raced with excitement and dread. He softened the kiss until it was as sweet as the first time they kissed. This kiss was more terrifying. It said he could take what he wanted, but he'd be gentle, passionate. Sharon didn't know whether to wrap her arms around him or run like hell. Her arms made the decision for her, clinging to his shirt, drawing Danny closer. His moan filled her mouth and her knees trembled when his hand dug into her back and he pressed closer, pushing her against the kitchen counter.

As quickly as the kiss started, it ended, leaving Sharon hot and satisfied and unsatisfied all at the same time. *I'm in big trouble.* She met his gaze, her eyes asking why he kissed her.

"I wanted to seal the deal another way," Danny mumbled, answering her question.

Sharon opened her mouth to speak, but what could she say? *Thank you?*

The sound of the guys arriving to start work saved her. She straightened and grabbed the contracts, closing them and stacking them neatly in a pile. "I'm going to work." *Of course you are, Sharon. You can't stick around here.*

"See you later." His heated gaze melted into a friendly one just as two crew members entered the kitchen to get the coffee Sharon always made.

"Happy working, fellas," Sharon said and waved goodbye, the contracts in hand. She grabbed her handbag at the end of the counter and headed out the front door. It was going to be a long day. As Sharon drove to work, she was trying to decide if she wanted Danny waiting for her to return and pick up where they left off. *Icing on the cake.* Those were the wrong words. What happened between them when they kissed wasn't icing, it was a damn volcano. Sharon just prayed she wouldn't get burned.

What the hell was that? Danny scolded himself when he heard the front door close. A kiss to close the deal? *The deal was the last thing on your mind while you were kissing Sharon.* He hadn't been able to stop thinking about the sex clause, and with Sharon standing across from him looking like she'd stepped out of a magazine, he couldn't help himself. He'd wanted his mouth on hers, his hands on her skin, even if it was just her arm. He resisted the urge to run a hand through her hair, knowing doing so would mess it up and make his guys, who were arriving any minute, wonder what they were up to.

Sharon's shock reflected in her eyes, but the way her body responded when their mouths and bodies met made him want to text the guys. Send them to another work site and keep Sharon home for the day. The words of the sex clause were there in black and white, and after he signed his name, it was all he could think about. Danny wished he was at home so he could take a cold shower and clear the memory of Sharon from his head and skin, but he had a full day of work ahead of him that couldn't be avoided.

It was done. The contract was signed, and he'd be tied to Sharon for the next two years, or at least after they were married. *Married.* The clause in the contract was about a simple ceremony with only close friends and family. Danny wondered if Mark would agree to those terms. Mark might not since he was the person his daughter was marrying and not some hotshot from their world.

Danny grinned as he imagined the discomfort on Mark's face when he heard the news. While he wasn't looking forward to Mark as his father-in-law, Danny was going to enjoy watching him squirm. When he was with Teri, he'd gone out of his way to fit into her world, sacrificing parts of himself to make her happy. He wasn't going to do that this time around. He was going to be himself and to hell with what anyone else thought. Sharon liked him the way he was; otherwise, she wouldn't have proposed to him. They'd had fun together, and he planned to keep it that way. Sharon needed fun in her life. She needed him.

Maybe that was another reason why he agreed, other than just keeping her safe. Sharon was a strong woman, but she needed someone to make her smile and forget about the world she lived in, and the people in it, who were cold as ice. She needed him to remind her that life could be fun. Sharon needed someone to pull her out of the office in the middle of the afternoon and screw her against the back of her door or on the kitchen counter. She needed someone to remind her there was more to life than work and the malicious people around her. She needed him.

Okay, he had to admit the sex part was mostly for him, but he'd gotten glimpses of the woman who smiled and laughed, and Danny liked her...a lot. He planned to see more of her over the next two years, with and without clothes on. As to what came after the two-year mark, he'd worry about it when the time came.

Chapter 34

Mark stood outside the front door when Sharon opened it. It had been two days since she and Danny had signed the contracts, and she'd left one on his desk. She'd expected him to come storming to her office after reading it, but he hadn't arrived. Sharon was certain he was planning how to break their contract.

"Is Danny here?"

"Yes. What do you want?"

"Can I come in?"

"Only if you don't plan to insult him."

"I've got thick skin, remember, Sharon?" Danny said.

She stepped away from the entrance so he could come inside. Mark followed them to the living room.

"I've read through the contract, and while I'm not happy with the arrangement, given Danny is not someone from our world, the choice is yours to make."

Sharon let out the breath she was holding. "I'm glad we agree on that." She'd expected him to storm in with fire and spit, but he was being reasonable. While she was relieved, something in the back of her mind remained on alert.

"The two years came as no surprise either, but the sex clause was."

They both blushed.

"Why are you here?"

His gaze shifted between them before settling on Sharon. "I've made an amendment to the contract, as is my right as your parent."

Her heartbeat slowed and her skin tingled, threatening to break out in a sweat.

"I've added a baby clause."

The word *baby* was a bomb exploding in the room as the silence stretched on for several moments.

"If there's no baby at the end of two years, Sharon, you forfeit your seat on all company boards, including your charities; the rest of your inheritance; and any property you've obtained. Danny gets to keep the deposit, but forfeits the balance."

Sharon wanted to scream at her father that he couldn't do this, but she knew the truth. He could. She glanced at Danny, and his expression reflected her own. A fake marriage was bad enough, but a baby? "Give us time to think it over."

Mark smirked. "You're going to need it." He stood. "By the way, Bradley is a willing candidate, even with the baby clause."

I bet he is. "Goodbye, Father."

Neither of them spoke until after they heard the front door close.

"I can't do this, Sharon. I thought I could, but a baby? I won't bring a child into the world this way." Danny fell back against the couch.

"I know." She'd expected no less, and she had to agree with him. Marriage was already going to be a hurdle, but a baby? She'd never imagined having kids, her focus solely on obtaining her inheritance. Bringing a child into the world under a contract? Bile rose in her throat thinking about it. She wouldn't do that to Danny or herself. The realization that everything she'd ever wanted was being yanked away from her slammed into her like a wrecking ball into a building. The air around her became thinner, and she couldn't breathe. Her chest tightened and her legs felt numb. She tried to stand and rush to her room, but she couldn't move. Her throat constricted and her eyes burned like they were on fire. Before she could stop herself, she clutched her head and screamed until her throat couldn't scream anymore.

Danny wanted to rush to her and put his arms around her, but the pitch of the scream—and the fact that it didn't stop—kept him from moving. *She must be in shock.* He'd never seen her react so fiercely before. Her father had just given her an obstacle she wasn't willing to remove to get what she wanted.

A baby?

He still couldn't believe her father would do such a thing to his own daughter, and to make matters worse, suggest a man like Bradley was willing? As if a baby was simply another commodity to add to their agreement. What kind of man did that?

"I'm sorry," she whispered.

He moved closer and put his arms around her. "Don't be. It's not your fault."

"I never thought he'd take things this far. I'd hoped he would change his mind and give me my inheritance without getting married."

"Once he found out it was me?"

"Yes, and once he found out the truth about Bradley."

"What truth?"

"One of his girlfriends ended up in the hospital. My father didn't care."

"Shit!" What kind of man would marry his daughter off to someone like that? "You're better off without a father like that in your life," Danny assured her.

"Maybe, but it'd mean giving up everything I've ever wanted, and losing everything I tried to build."

"You've got this house, money in the bank. You wouldn't be starting from scratch."

"I would. Nothing belongs to me. Only the money I earned working for him. My car, home, investment accounts, most of my possessions—all belong to him."

"Is that even legal?"

"If I was smart, I would've walked away when I got out of college and started out on my own, but stupid me wanted to make my father proud and get what I thought was mine. Now I'm going to lose it all anyway. All those years...wasted."

He brushed a strand of hair away from her face. "Not wasted. Lessons."

"Those are some hard lessons." She managed a smile, but it quickly faded.

"I'm so sorry, Sharon."

"At first, I thought it was another hard lesson he was trying to teach me, but now I'm not so sure. He certainly doesn't want my cousin Carlton to take the seat, and Virginia implied something was going on with the board after Robert died."

"Couldn't you offer to give up your seat and take the inheritance and start on your own?"

"The contract requires me to get married to get my inheritance, so I'll lose everything if I don't get married, even if I offer to give up my seat. Trust me, Patrick and I have tried every scenario, but none of them gets me freedom, other than walking away, and even then, I risk my father sabotaging everything."

"Speak with Patrick again and see if there are any scenarios to get you out but stop your father from coming after any business you try to start. It's not much, but it's better than doing nothing."

Sharon chewed on her bottom lip. His suggestion meant walking away from everything she'd ever wanted and known, a decision that wouldn't come easy, but the alternative wasn't either.

"I'll talk to Patrick."

The silence stretched out before them. Danny stood. "I make a mean omelet."

"That would be great, except I haven't got anything in my fridge but water and premade meals."

He pulled her off the couch. "Then let's go shopping."

"At the supermarket?"

"Yes. It's a crazy concept, I know, but that is where they keep the food."

She laughed. "I know that, but I'm just used to having my meals delivered and eating out."

"I'm going to change all that."

"Umm. I don't know how to cook, Danny."

"I know, but that's an easy change." He grinned.

"Somehow I doubt that." They laughed.

Chapter 35

The phone on her nightstand buzzed, waking Sharon. Why the hell was Carlton calling her this time of night? "Hello?"

"My mother is dead," came from the other end of the phone.

Sharon shot up in bed. "What?"

Carlton's tone was broken. "She drove her car into a wall. I knew she was unsettled after my father died, but this..."

"Oh my god, Carlton. I'm so sorry. Is there anything I can do to help?"

"Can you come by the police station with me? I don't want to be there alone." Carlton gave her the name of the station.

"Of course. Give me a few minutes."

"Thank you, Sharon. With Robert dead, and now Virginia, there's no one left."

"You have me and Mark, Carlton. You're not alone." She shouldn't have spoken for her father, but she could speak for herself and knew she would be there to help Carlton through this difficult time of losing both parents.

"Thank you, Sharon."

Sharon jumped out of bed and dressed quickly and headed to the living room to wake Danny. He looked so peaceful she didn't want to wake him. She brushed a strand of hair away from his face and touched his skin. He was warm and she longed to curl up next to him. The news of Virginia's death was a reminder that life was short, and death came unexpectedly. Or did it? It did seem suspicious that both of

Carlton's parents were gone. What would that mean for the board? For Carlton? For her father?

Danny startled her when he grasped her hand and sat up. "What's wrong?"

"Virginia, Carlton's mother, is dead."

"Are you okay?"

"I'm not sure. We weren't close." Sharon shared the story of their last encounters with Danny and a wave of guilt washed over her. While Virginia could be cold and manipulative, she'd lost her husband and Sharon hadn't visited her once.

"Do you think her death is connected to Robert's?"

"I'm not sure. I hope not, but I do want to hear what the police have to say. Carlton asked me to meet him at the station."

"I'm coming with you. I don't want you going anywhere alone right now. Just to be safe."

"I agree. I'll wait for you in the kitchen." Danny rolled off the couch and stood shirtless and gorgeous. *Focus, Sharon!*

"I'll be right there." Danny headed into the room where his clothes were hidden.

Sharon started the coffee while she waited. It was four in the morning, and they were going to need it.

Coffee in a travel mug was waiting for Danny when he entered the kitchen.

"Thanks." He picked it up and they headed for the door.

When they arrived at the police station, shock showed on Carlton's face behind the glass doors. To her surprise, Bradley was there in the waiting area. *I thought they didn't like each other.*

Sharon addressed the officer at the front area, letting her know why she was there. "Please have a seat. He'll be finished with the officer shortly."

"What are you doing here?" Sharon asked when she and Danny took the seats next to Bradley. The station was quieter than she expected, with officers at their desks working on their computers or interviewing someone.

"I was with Virginia before her accident."

"With her?" Danny asked.

"I was talking to her and Carlton about Robert's role on the board and how I could support her and Carlton. I drove up shortly after the accident and called the police. I didn't think she was that fragile..." Bradley's voice trailed off, clearly shaken.

"What did you say to her in the meeting?" Danny asked.

"Nothing that would cause her to drive her car into a wall. The office said there were no brake marks. Why would she do this? I was only trying to help her and Carlton."

Sharon didn't know if he was at fault or not, but he was clearly upset. Seeing this side of him made her feel guilty for suspecting he could be involved in Robert's death. His hands shook, his face was sweating, and his distraught expression showed he was in shock. "How is Carlton doing? Have you spoken with him at all?"

"No. I was here when he arrived, but we didn't speak. He seemed upset. Who can blame him?"

"Yes. Losing a parent is hard. I couldn't imagine both." Sharon honestly didn't know how she'd react if her father died. She'd be sad, but the pain would be nothing like when her mother died.

"Yes. Hard." Bradley's gaze drifted to the other side of the room, as if he'd journeyed to another time and place.

An officer walked Carlton over to them.

Sharon hugged him. "Are you okay?"

He glanced between Bradley and Danny. "What are you two doing here? Neither of you are family!"

"Danny drove me here." Sharon didn't elaborate.

"I was the last one to see your mother alive. I came just after the accident. I'm so sorry. I didn't know she was so unstable."

Carlton's jawline jumped. "If she was unstable, it was because of what you said to her."

"All I did was offer to help you and her with the board. To make things easier for you both."

"Liar. You just want it all for yourself. You killed her, you bastard!" Carlton lunged at Bradley, knocking him to the ground and wrapping his fingers around his neck.

Bradley struggled to push Carlton off him without success, until Danny and other officers rushed to pull them apart. "You're crazy. I wasn't anywhere near your mother. I'm the one who called the police. Your mother killed herself from the grief."

"No. She wouldn't leave me." Carlton dropped to the ground and sobbed. Sharon rushed to him and pulled him off the floor and onto a chair. She stroked his back to calm him. Carlton's public reaction was unexpected. She hadn't realized the relationship with his mother was a close one, but those on the outside might've said the same thing about the one she had with her mother.

"Let us drive you home, Carlton."

"No. I want to be alone." He stood and rushed out of the police station. That was a reaction she was more familiar with.

"Should we go after him?" Danny asked.

"No, give him time. I'll call him later to check on him." Bradley was sitting in a chair, his head in his hands.

"What about him?"

Sharon felt sorry for him, but not sorry enough to offer him a ride home, given his reaction to her rejection. "Leave him."

Sharon and Danny walked out of the police station. Part of her felt guilty for leaving him there alone, but another part couldn't help wonder about the words that transpired between him and Carlton.

Chapter 36

The home was decorated from top to bottom with Christmas decorations, thanks to someone she'd hired at the last minute. Since her father stopped by, her mind had been occupied with the baby clause and finding ways to walk away. She wanted to cry every time she thought about it, so started avoiding the topic all together. It wasn't easy with her father, and Bradley, hovering by her office door every minute to see if she'd made her decision. They didn't ask outright, especially Bradley, but their eyes implied it.

Danny was supportive at first, but recently he'd been pressuring her to walk away, as if it were no big deal and she could start a new life. Easy for him to say, but taking that step was another story. Her stalker was keeping his distance, which she was happy for, but also annoyed her because it kept them in limbo. Danny insisted on staying with her, even though their contract was clearly null and void.

The dinner party was tonight. The women were scheduled to be there in an hour, and she was dreading it. Another boring dinner party talking about husbands, and trying to make connections or find out information about their family's business and political dealings.

The catering company she hired had two waitstaff downstairs setting up while she got dressed. Everything was in place, including her, when the doorbell rang and the first guest arrived. The conversation headed in the direction she expected by the time everyone had arrived and they were seated at the table. She imagined year after year passing like this if she got married and remained with her father's company. Things wouldn't change, even when her father died. The men on the board would see to that. She'd live her years in a perpetual cycle, day in and day out, surrounded by people just the same as her, behind their guarded walls while soldiers were sent out to get information to be used and manipulated by the men in charge. Sharon wanted to vomit. Gaining the seat and her inheritance was meant to change her life, but it wouldn't. It would merely pull her further and deeper into the world she was trying to change. A world that wasn't likely to change in her lifetime, or her children's. Is that the life she wanted for herself? *No!* She banged her hands on the table for emphasis. The women around her jumped and glared at her as if she'd lost her mind, or had too much to drink.

"Aren't you sick of this!? Playing their game and being part of their world? Don't you want something for yourselves other than planning and attending parties!?"

She began calling out the women's names, their accomplishments, and what they gave up after they got married. "They've turned powerful, brilliant women into arm candy," she said with disgust.

"You've got nannies, people to clean and cook, and you're still required to stay home? Why? So their egos can feel good about having a wife who isn't more successful than them? I say to hell with them all!"

There was rousing applause from all the women. She'd stirred up emotions. Woman after woman started sharing what they'd tried to achieve, only to have it shut down by their husbands.

"I say we start our own companies. Companies that can't be touched or shut down. I say we stand together and be the strong women they wanted and married, and to hell with their egos!"

A round of agreements came from everyone sitting at the table.

While Sharon had fired everyone up by the end of the night, she hoped she hadn't set anyone down on the path to divorce. Her mind was still racing and excitement pumping through her when Danny returned. He'd gone over to his parents for dinner and called to make sure the women were gone before he returned.

"How did it go?"

She was so excited, the only thing she could manage was to grab him by the shirt and kiss him soundly.

"I guess it went well," she heard him say as she rushed upstairs to bed.

Change was in the air, and she was excited for what lay ahead.

Chapter 37

"Are you sure you want to do this?" Danny asked while they sat in the car parked outside his parents' house.

"I'm sure. I promised. Besides, I wouldn't want to miss out on seeing you wear whatever horrible Christmas sweater your mother picked out for you."

"Don't laugh. She might have one for you, too, so you don't feel left out."

Sharon opened the door, "Unlike you, I relish the idea of wearing a horrible sweater." It helped fill the space missing from the special times she'd spent with her mother during the holidays. Her father's idea of Christmas tradition was making sure gifts were sent to all their clients and political connections. They hadn't had a Christmas together opening presents since her mother died. At first she thought it was too painful for him, but when he went about business as usual in other areas of his life, it was as if his wife's death meant nothing.

"I don't mind as long as I don't have to wear it anywhere else but their house." Danny grabbed the presents from the back seat.

She laughed and grabbed a couple of presents from the top of his pile. Shopping for Danny's parents hadn't been easy since she barely knew them, but Ryan had helped her with suggestions she'd gotten from Danny.

"You didn't have to buy my parents presents."

"I know, but I wanted to. They made me feel so welcome."

"They do that for all my future wives," he teased.

She chuckled, although truthfully it wasn't so funny, especially after her father's visit. But it was better to joke about it than dwell on what it meant.

"How did they feel about Teri?"

"They never met her. I tried to have her volunteer with me at the shelter so she could meet my mom, but…"

She could only imagine the horror on Teri's face. Her idea of charity was writing a check or unloading clothing she no longer wore. Getting her hands dirty wasn't her thing. "I'm sorry. I didn't mean to bring her up."

"It's okay. She's my past, and a lesson learned."

The door flew open before they could knock.

"Come in! I'm so glad you came." Rose greeted them both with hugs and a kiss on their cheeks. "I wasn't sure you were going to make it. I know how busy this time of year is for you, Sharon."

They stomped the snow off their shoes on the outside mat and stepped into the warm, cozy house. Everything was covered from top to bottom in decorations, with no theme that Sharon could see other than "Christmas." It was beautiful!

"Is that for me?" Rose asked of the poinsettia in her hand.

"Yes, but it appears you don't need it!" There were at least five plants in the living room alone.

"Nonsense!" She took the plant and placed it in an empty space. "There's always room for more."

Rose took the presents and placed them under the tree with the rest of the gifts while they removed their coats.

"Did you tell your parents anything?" Sharon whispered to Danny.

He shook his head.

She was grateful. Not telling them made sense since the baby clause her father threw at them. She liked Danny's parents and didn't want them thinking less of her, especially since she wasn't going to be around much longer. Those thoughts made her sad. While she could still see Rose at the homeless shelter on occasion, being part of their lives on a regular basis wasn't a good idea, or likely possible, depending on how things turned out.

John was in the kitchen setting up trays of Christmas cookies along with the ingredients to decorate them. "Hello, Sharon. Danny."

"So, we're here to work?" Danny observed.

"Of course." John removed his apron and handed it to Sharon.

"You have my usual fee?" Danny took another apron from a drawer and put it on.

"Two steaming cups of hot chocolate with extra marshmallows coming up."

Sharon put on the apron and got to work. She'd never decorated cookies before, but she could do damage to a gingerbread house. Surely cookies were easier.

An hour later, she changed her mind.

Both she and Danny were covered in frosting, sprinkles, and other decorations, partly thanks to Danny, whose idea of decorating meant getting it everywhere but on the cookies. She'd never laughed so hard or felt so at home with anyone else or anywhere else. Although Danny's parents kept a safe distance in the living room, they contributed to the camaraderie between her and Danny as she tried to help him decorate.

"Mine are masterpieces, while yours look like a train wreck," Sharon observed, wiping her hands on the apron, although it didn't help.

"Christmas cookies aren't about being pretty, they're about being delicious, and that's what mine are," he argued.

"How delicious are they going to be when someone cracks a tooth from everything you've got on the cookie?"

"Hey. No one's ever broken a tooth on my cookies before." He pointed a decorating pack at her. "What about you? No one wants to eat cookies from an amateur."

She picked up one of her pretty cookies and one of Danny's and held them side by side. "Which one would you prefer to eat?" The question was directed at John and Rose.

They raised their hands. "Don't bring us into this. We're here to sample all the cookies, regardless of who made them," John replied.

Sharon turned to Danny. "That's their way of saying they like mine better."

John and Rose laughed.

"Not even close," Danny said, throwing a pinch of flour at her.

"You just can't accept defeat." She returned the favor.

They'd both grabbed a handful of flour, ready to launch, when Rose interrupted. "Whatever mess you make in there, you're cleaning it up!"

Danny and Sharon looked at each other, at the kitchen—which was already a mess—and lowered their flour-filled hands.

"How about we let taste be the judge?" Danny handed her one of his cookies and took one of hers.

They took a bite at the same time.

"I think I just lost a tooth," Sharon teased.

"I can feel the sugar racing to my bloodstream," Danny added.

"But how do they taste?" Rose asked.

They switched cookies and took another bite. "Sweet as hell but good," Danny said first and Sharon nodded in agreement.

"That's why you need to have hot chocolate to wash them down with," John added.

"Yes, more sugar." Sharon laughed.

"You two clean up the kitchen and then we'll open presents," Rose said.

Sharon was covered in flour, frosting and other condiments, but Danny thought she looked beautiful. Her body was relaxed, and she was genuinely enjoying herself. He'd been hesitant to tell her about his parents' invitation, given all the madness in her life right now, but he sensed she needed a break, especially after her aunt's death and father's visit.

He made a final offer for her to back out tonight, but he was grateful she didn't. His parents adored her, and he knew the feeling was mutual. If only they'd found each other under normal circumstances. *Hell, Danny. You never would've met her under normal circumstances, and if you did, you wouldn't have gotten to know the real her.*

That was true. He and Sharon might've met each other because of their relationship with Patrick and Danny, but they would've never communicated past polite conversation. A conversation that would've been painfully obvious and showed that they had nothing in common. And meeting Sharon was something he'd never regret, only the circumstances that kept them apart.

Moments later, they were all seated in the living room, opening presents.

Sharon gave his parents a couple's session at the spa. His mother was thrilled, but his father looked terrified until Sharon assured him they would take good care of him.

They gave her a small home tool set and an ugly Christmas sweater. Sharon laughed and teared up.

The last two presents under the tree were their gifts to each other.

They headed onto the patio to enjoy another cup of hot chocolate and the Christmas lights and decorations his parents had set up in the backyard.

After lighting a fire in the pit, he sat next to her on the loveseat, accepting the blanket she held out for him. Half of their bodies were pressed together under two layers of blankets to stay warm. Sharon surprised him when she rested her head on his shoulder. He put his arm around her.

"Are you going to be all right?" The question was more about their contract, and the bomb her father dropped.

"I don't know," she answered honestly.

"You will, Sharon. You're a brilliant woman who got this far with all the obstacles you faced. You'll make it through. It might not seem like it now, but you will."

"Thank you." She pulled the blanket closer. "I know this on one level, but fear of what my father will do is what's making it difficult. And walking away from everything I've know my whole life is a little daunting."

"You'll make it, no matter what your father does. I'll help you get through it."

She grabbed his hand. "That means a lot to me Danny, but I think its best I keep my distance from you. I don't want you to be caught in the crossfire from my father and have it impact your business."

"You mean I'm not getting the two million dollars?" he teased.

She grinned. "No, sorry."

"Damn. I'd already spent it in my head."

When they stopped laughing, she glanced up at him. "I'm sorry about the money. I know what it meant for your business."

He shrugged. "It just means I'm back to my original business plan."

"Which is?"

"Work until the loans are paid off and the bills are paid."

"I'd recommend others in my circle to you, but I don't think I'll be welcome anywhere anytime soon."

"It's all good. Josie and I have a big job lined up for the new year, but I'll take a good review."

"Deal."

They sat there for several more moments enjoying each other's company, neither saying a word, afraid the spell would be broken and the real world would come crashing through his parents' French doors. In this moment, he could pretend she was with him, and they were spending the holidays with his parents and soon they'd go home and spend the evening together. Then they'd wake up and enjoy the rest of the holidays with each other in bed, having breakfast, lunch, and dinner, and doing all the normal things couples did this time of year.

The patio lighting glimmered with various Christmas lights, and they were surrounded by ornaments, statues, poinsettias, and other types of Christmas decorations his mother had collected over the years. The longer they stayed on the patio, the colder it got, but neither wanted to leave and break the spell.

"Danny?" Sharon glanced at him.

"Yes?"

She touched his cheek with her gloved hand and pulled his face toward hers.

"You two will freeze to the chair if you don't come inside soon," John's voice interrupted. "Oh, I'm sorry," he stammered when he saw them.

"It's all right, John. Time for us to go. I've got a long day ahead of me tomorrow, and things to wrap up before the end of the year." Sharon stood as she and Danny unwrapped themselves, and headed back into the house.

"Thank you so much for having me over." She hugged Rose and John goodbye.

"It was our pleasure, sweetheart! We hope to see you here next year," Rose said, glancing at Danny.

Sharon watched him say goodbye to his parents. John whispered in his ear, "Don't let her get away." He wished he could take the advice, but in the end, the choice would be Sharon's to make.

When they got in the car, she turned up the heat. "It was freezing on the patio."

He smiled and adjusted the vents. As he watched her pull out of the driveway, he longed to reach over and finish the kiss they almost had on the patio. He ached with wanting her lips against his, along with other parts of her body, but then what? Things were complicated between them as is.

He'd almost forgotten he was staying at Sharon's house until she pulled into the driveway and parked the car. They took the presents from the back seat and headed inside.

The renovations were done, so she was back in her room and he was in her guest room, and thankfully off the torturous couch. His back still ached from the time he'd slept on it. Sharon was leaning across the counter, her gaze fixed on the living room. No doubt her mind was racing with all the decisions she had to make, and the difficult road that lay ahead.

She straightened and walked around the counter to where he stood. Blood rushed through him at the speed of light until it thumped in his ears. Her arms went around his neck and she stood on her toes and kissed him. He stood with his arms by his side before pulling her away from him.

"Sharon, as much as I want this, it's not a good idea."

Her fingers went through the hair at the base of his neck. "I've regretted a lot of things in my life, Danny, and I don't want one of them to be not being with you, no matter how. I know things are complicated, but I want this. I want this moment with you, even if I never get it again."

An azure gaze met his and it was warm, open, and vulnerable.

He lifted her so she was pressed against him and kissed her. Then he returned her to the ground, took her hand, and guided her upstairs.

Chapter 38

"Your daughter is here to see you," his secretary announced.

Mark grinned. His ploy had worked, and she was coming to agree to Bradley. He may not be the best candidate, but he was acceptable, and she'd be able to keep him in line because of his past. As strong as she thought Bradley was, she was stronger. "Send her in."

There was no way he'd allow her to ruin her life by marrying some glorified carpenter. *She belongs with her family—and the company—with a man who'll fit into their world.* Danny knew nothing of their life and would only hold her back.

Adding a baby to the contract was the only thing he could think of to derail her plan to marry Danny. His financial situation wasn't dire enough to accept the baby clause, but from what he'd found out about him, and what Sharon shared with him, he'd backed out of the contract. As would Sharon. Her showing up today was evidence of that. He'd won. She'd fall in line, marry Bradley, and take her place in the company.

Sharon strode into his office, her hair down and dressed in clothing he'd never approve of. She was going to test his limits.

"Sit," he ordered.

She ignored his demand and remained standing. "I won't be here that long." She dropped an envelope on his desk. "Thanks for your offer, but Danny and I have declined to accept your change."

"I figured as much. So have you spoken to Bradley about an offer?"

"You misunderstand me. I'm not interested in any offer you plan to make, including the original contract for me to marry. I'm forfeiting everything. Everything you threatened to take away from me. I don't want any of it. I'll be moved out before January first."

"You'll never find another job."

"I don't care. I'd rather be homeless on the street than spend anymore of my life with you, this company, or these people."

"How dare——"

"I did everything I could to make you proud, to prove to you I deserved the respect, power and position your son would've gotten, but it was never enough for you. Being your child, your daughter, wasn't enough. I'm tired of trying to please you and be a part of a company and family who don't respect me."

"No business you start will take off," Mark threatened.

"Make whatever threats you want. Try and stop whatever plans I make, I don't care. I'm going to do what I've always done over the years. Keep going."

"How dare you defy me this way?!"

"It will be the last time. Consider this my notice. My last day is two weeks from today unless you'd like me to be escorted from the building sooner. I'll make sure to notify all my clients and direct them to you until someone is assigned to take them over."

She strode toward the door. "Once I leave the company, I don't want you to call me, or try to contact me. As far as I'm concerned, I'm no longer part of this family. That should make it easier for you. I know it will make it easier for me."

"Sharon."

"I don't want to be part of a family or have a father who'd rather marry me off to a man like Bradley. I'm done, and you're free of me."

Her voice hitched, but her eyes were clear of tears and her steps determined as she walked through the door of his office, leaving him with his thoughts.

Sharon headed to her office. "Ryan, please compile my complete client list and when you've got it, come into my office." She paused at the door. "If my father calls or comes by, tell him I'm in a meeting and can't be disturbed, or I'm on an important call."

"Yes, Sharon," Ryan stammered before his fingers returned to the keyboard.

She stormed into her office, tempted to slam the door. She took deep breaths to steady her nerves, and the fire that was coursing through her from the encounter with her father. It hadn't been as confrontational as she expected, but then she hadn't given him a lot of chances to speak. She'd wanted to get in and get out of his office before both their tempers flared.

What had he done next? Did he go to Bradley's office, the lawyers who handle board issues, or his own lawyer? Was he contacting her clients at that moment? He might even be hatching plans to sabotage her leave. It didn't matter what he had planned, she'd be gone in two weeks, or sooner.

Surprisingly, she felt more relief than anxiety, but that was likely because the reality of her actions hadn't sank in. Once it did, she'd be a wreck, but in the meantime, she enjoyed the weightlessness she felt imagining no longer being at the whim of her father, making decisions without worrying about the circumstances. All right, so that part would've changed, but for once she only had to worry about how it would affect her, and not her father or the board. The business and social fallout would be brutal, but she didn't care. She'd take one day at a time and pray she could find her own way without her father sabotaging everything she started.

The statement about being homeless wouldn't be far from the truth once she moved out of her home. She'd have the clothes on her back and the money she'd saved over the years from her salary, but little else. She could pawn the few pieces of jewelry her mother had left her, but that would only last so long. Fear descended, closing the space around her with endless words of doubt and what ifs and trying to convince her she'd be better off with Bradley.

Hell no! She'd made her choice and she'd stick to it. No matter what.

"Carlton is here to see you, Sharon. I told him you weren't available, but..."

"It's all right, Ryan. Send him in." Handing her clients to Carlton wouldn't be her first choice. She'd love to recommend Ryan, but her father would never agree.

"What can I do for you, Carlton?"

He strode into her office and paced before her. "I heard you didn't make Bradley an offer, you and turned down your seat on the board. Is that true?"

His mouth was practically salivating. Too bad he wasn't smart enough to realize Mark probably wouldn't give him her seat either, but maybe he was and that's why he was here.

"It's true."

"You gave up your seat? Charities? Everything?"

Carlton knew the seat on the board and charities were her passion, but from his expression, she guessed he didn't suspect she'd have to give up her home, car, and most of her investments. She nodded.

"Why?"

"You wouldn't understand."

He paced again and she could see him contemplating his next questions. "So does this mean I'll get your position?"

She laughed. "You'll have to take that up with my father and the board. It's up to them now, but I wouldn't hold my breath if I were you."

"But it should all be mine!"

"Yes, and it should've been mine, too."

"Damn stubborn man won't budge either, I bet."

She placed a hand on his shoulder. "You're a man, and the only person other than my father to take the seat, so maybe you'll get what you want. Maybe not tomorrow, but he can't say no forever, and he's not getting any younger. In the meantime, you should try living up to the position, like doing your job."

"I shouldn't have to live up to it. My name should be enough!"

That stupidity is what'll keep my father from giving you what you want. Sharon didn't respond. She had her own issues to deal with without having to worry about one of Carlton's tantrums that had obviously returned, even with his mother's death.

"I'm handing my clients over to Mark before I leave in two weeks."

"Why don't you give them to me?"

I'd rather send them boxes of thorns. "I told my father I'd give him the list, but I'll hand them over to you if you get it in writing."

Carlton's jawline jumped and his eyes shot daggers at her.

"You know I can't just hand them over, Carlton," she tried assuring him, but the daggers didn't stop. "Was there anything else?"

"No. When do you leave?"

"Two weeks."

"And you're sure you won't change your mind?"

"No."

"Maybe Uncle Mark will change his mind?"

"If he hasn't in the time I've been trying to convince him, it isn't likely to happen now, or anytime soon."

"You're right. He is a stubborn man." He headed to the door but turned before leaving. "Good luck, Sharon."

That was unexpected. "Thanks, Carlton."

Moments later, Ryan walked into the office. She told him about her resignation, and apologized because it would affect him.

"Are you sure I can't come with you?"

"I'll reach out to you when I'm settled." *If Father doesn't sabotage it.* "But you might like my replacement."

"Do you know who it is?"

"No. I doubt I'll know before I leave, but I'd like to make it easy for them to step in for the clients' sakes."

Ryan nodded. He knew how much her clients meant to her.

The rest of the day was spent preparing letters to clients, along with a list of personal cards and gifts to send them.

When she was ready to go home, she called a taxi to pick her up. She hadn't taken any chances since the attacks. Danny wasn't home when she got there, giving her time to think about what would happen with her attacker now that she'd given up her seat and was walking away from everything. Would he leave her alone?

She hadn't told her father about the attacks, figuring it wouldn't make a difference in his decision. If anything, she suspected he would use it as another reason for her to marry Bradley. There would be no marriage. There would be no more striving toward the dreams she'd wanted for as long as she could remember. Now she would have to find new dreams to chase.

Chapter 39

Danny was loading up his truck to leave the new site he was working at when a car pulled up behind him. At first he thought it was Sharon, since it was a luxury car, but Mark stepped out.

"We need to talk." His tone was harsh.

Oh, great. It's one of those talks. Danny hadn't seen Mark since he showed up at Sharon's home and made his baby announcement.

Danny checked his watch. "I've got a few minutes."

This annoyed Mark, but he didn't care. The man was an ass, and he didn't want to talk with him any longer than he had to.

"Did you put my daughter up to this?"

"Up to what?"

"Don't play games with me."

"You're the one who added a baby to your daughter's contract, and I'm the one playing games?"

"I did that so she'd come to her senses."

"And what? Marry a man known for beating up his girlfriends instead?"

"You're no better choice. You don't belong in our world."

"Neither does your daughter."

"She's a Donovan. That name alone says she belongs."

"Really? Then why have you made it so difficult for her?"

"I treat her the same as I would a son."

"Do you?"

Mark's face blistered in anger. "She's a woman. There's a certain expectation in my world."

"The expectation you're less?"

"You don't understand."

"I understand you've controlled and manipulated everything in her life, so she's felt unworthy and had to scrape for every success she had just to prove she was good enough, when you know damn well she was more than good enough to be part of your life, business, and she deserves that seat on the board."

Mark studied Danny for a moment before bursting into laughter. "You love her," he declared.

"She's a remarkable woman."

"I know, and that's why I want her to stay."

"Then change the contract so she doesn't have to get married."

"No. It's been that way for years for a reason."

"What reason?"

"To ensure the line continues."

"Is that why you added the baby clause? You were worried we'd marry in name only?"

"Yes, and I know my daughter. She wants to control as much as she can."

"I wonder where she gets that from?"

Mark grinned proudly. "Unfortunately, it makes for a difficult relationship."

"I didn't push your daughter into anything, Mr. Donovan. You did, by forcing her to do something she didn't want to."

Mark paced before him. "I suppose you'll continue to be in her life?"

"Yes." Honestly, they hadn't discussed it, but he hoped so, especially now that they had time to get to know each other without the weight of a contract and the conditions.

"I'll give you money to stay out of her life. Name your price!"

Was he serious? Mark already knew they weren't getting married, what reason was there? Was Mark that much of a snob, or was he worried the people in his circle would think his daughter gave up everything for a contractor?

"Why?"

"You've been a friend to Sharon, or perhaps more. I want her back with me, and that means removing all her support systems, and any possibility of her succeeding on her own."

Sharon had told him her father threatened her, but Danny thought it was just words said in anger to get her to do what he wanted. The fact that Mark was standing before him with this offer proved she knew her father well.

He wanted to tell Mark what he could do with his money, but instead said, "I don't want your money, and the harder you push, the farther away you're going to push her. She's not going to let you manipulate her anymore, and she isn't going to give up being on her own, no matter what you do."

"This is your doing."

"If you believe that, you're clueless about yourself and your daughter. You've been pushing her to this for years. She's stayed with you, hoping to change your mind and give her the respect she deserves, and all you've done is spit on her efforts and made it so difficult, she doesn't even want to be your daughter, or part of your world. And that's my fault? I've only known your daughter for three months, Mr. Donovan. You've known her for her entire life. Who do you think has a bigger impact?"

"If you continue a relationship with my daughter, I will ruin you, your business, and make the lives of you and your family a living hell," he threatened.

Danny shook his head in disbelief. "You're a piece of work." He jumped into his truck and left Mark standing in the driveway.

As he drove to Sharon's, he couldn't help but wonder if Mark was the one making the threats—another drastic attempt to bend her to his will. If he hadn't seen the side of Mark he just did, he never would've imagined it, but now?

The man was rich enough to hire someone, or powerful enough to influence someone. No wonder Sharon wanted to remove herself from him. It sucked that she had to give up what she'd worked so hard for because of it. He was confident Sharon would land on her feet, but how often she'd have to restart depended on how far her father would take things. After the encounter today, Danny was certain he'd take drastic measures.

When he pulled into Sharon's driveway twenty minutes later, her car was there and the lights were on in the kitchen. No one had tried to break in since he moved in, which was a good thing, but what would happen when she left the house? Would she be safe at her new place? She seemed sure that now that she had walked away, she was no longer in danger, but he also knew she took a cab to and from work instead of driving her car, so she wasn't 100 percent sure.

He wanted to ask her to move in with him, just until she was settled, but he suspected she'd turn him down. Then he considered asking his parents if she could stay with them, but that meant telling them, and Sharon was too proud and embarrassed to tell them. He couldn't blame her. When he walked into the kitchen, she was seated at the kitchen counter, a glass of wine next to her along with a stack of papers. "Still working?"

She glanced up from the papers, the weight of the world in her eyes. "Not exactly. I'm trying to figure about how much money is really mine and what I'll have to leave behind."

"That sucks!" He sat on the stool next to her. "You could stay with me until you get on your feet." *There.* He'd said it. "It's the least I could do."

She touched his cheek. "Thanks. That means a lot, but I can't. I need to do this on my own."

He swiveled the chair so it faced her. "You know the best part of having friends who care? You don't have to do it alone. I know that's what you're used to, Sharon, but it doesn't have to be that way. I'm here for you. My parents care about you, and I know Patrick and Josie would be happy to have you stay at their house while they're on their honeymoon. The point I'm trying to make is that you have options. You don't have to do it alone anymore."

Tears had pooled in her eyes, and she brushed them away quickly. "Thank you," she whispered. "No one has ever..."

He tucked a stray hair behind her ear. "I'm here for you no matter what you need, Sharon. Except for money. I just lost two million dollars so," he joked.

She hiccupped, then laughed before jumping out of her seat to hug him. "I love you, Danny."

From the expression on her face, it was obvious that had slipped out or was meant as an endearment and not a confession, but it still shook him right down to his toes. The silence was interrupted by the doorbell ringing. Relief reflected on both their faces before Sharon rushed out the kitchen to answer the door. There was a peep hole in the door so she could see who was outside.

Sharon opened the door, but he couldn't hear the conversation well enough to make out what was being said. Danny waited in the kitchen until Sharon and the guest made their way to the living room. From his spot in the kitchen, he could see them. He didn't recognize the man, but Sharon must've known him to let him inside. "Do you need privacy?"

Sharon nodded and mouthed *Thank you*. As much as he wanted to stay and find out who this man was to her, he stood to leave. "I'll be upstairs if you need me." Danny gave the man his most intimidating gaze before leaving them alone.

Sharon stared at the man, who'd been her mother's lawyer before she died. The man who'd told her the conditions of her family contract when she turned eighteen years old. The man who'd crushed her dreams of a having a normal life, even if it wasn't really his fault. He was just following orders, but it had felt personal at the time. What the hell was he coming to tell her now? She'd lost even more.

They sat and her heart was in her throat as he opened his briefcase and took out what she assumed was another contract. Had her father sent him? Had Mark found some way to stop her plans to leave before she could even execute them?

To her surprise, he turned on his laptop and turned the screen toward her and pressed Play.

Moments later, her mother came up on the screen. Tears pooled in her eyes at the sight of her. Sharon realized how much she'd missed her. She missed her guidance, advice, and even her hugs.

"Sharon, if you're watching this video, then it means you've stood up to your father and taken your first steps to freedom. I'm so proud of you. You were always a strong-willed child, but you always wanted your father's approval and to be part of his world, as was your right as his child. I'm so sorry he didn't change his mind about the marriage clause. I hoped he'd become so proud of your accomplishments he'd change it. The fact that you're watching this video says he didn't, and you've made the choice to go out on your own. A decision that I was never strong enough to make.

"Henry is here to give you your inheritance—the part of your inheritance I hid from your father all these years. The house is yours to keep, along with all the money in your bank accounts. You'll lose your stocks in the company, but I have other investments that have been even more successful. Investing was my talent your father never took advantage of. His loss, but your gain. You'll get everything that was mine before I married your father, including my seat on the charities we both loved. I know how much those meant to you. I hope they'll make up for losing the seat on the board of the company.

"I never had the courage to follow my own dreams, but you can, and I know you'll do great things, Sharon. Things your father can't take away from you anymore."

Tears flowed freely down her cheeks. Her mother had known the kind of man her father was and had taken steps to protect her. It was her final act of love.

"I hope you find the love and happiness you deserve, and that you'll open your heart to it when it comes. I love you, Sharon." She blew a kiss at the camera before the video ended.

Sharon sobbed, and Henry handed her his handkerchief. She wiped her face and handed it back to him.

"This is the entirety of your inheritance." He placed the papers before her.

She flipped through it, shocked by the amount of money and assets her mother had acquired before she married her father. It was substantial. Sharon laughed. She couldn't help herself. Her grandfather had been an investment banker, and his talents had obviously rubbed off on his daughter. What would her mother have achieved if she'd followed her own dreams? The trail stopped when she married Mark. She must've been afraid he would seize any funds she invested after they married. She had taken steps to hide the money and ensure Mark couldn't legally get his hands on it.

"Thank you, Henry."

"I'll leave these with you." He handed her his card. "Call me if you have any questions, or if you need anything else."

"I will." She stood and walked him to the door.

After locking the door, she stood in shock for several seconds before jumping up and down and dancing a jig. That was how Danny found her.

"I take it he came with good news. Your father changed his mind?"

"No. He was my mother's lawyer."

"Your mother?"

"Yes. She had a separate will that activated if I walked away from my family contract."

"Wow! That's wonderful. I take it it's enough for you to be on your own without having to worry about your father?"

"Yes, and I take over my mother's seat on the charities we set up. She knew how much they meant to me. Oh, and I get to keep the house!"

"That's good news. I worried the new owner would have me redo the renovations I just finished," Danny joked.

She threw herself at him and wrapped her arms around him and kissed him. She pulled away before he could kiss her back. "This calls for a celebration!"

"Chinese food?"

"Absolutely, and maybe even sushi?"

She laughed when Danny made a face. He didn't like sushi.

"How about you eat the sushi and I'll eat the Chinese food?"

"Deal."

Chapter 32

H is parents were going to kill him. They'd be happy he was getting married, but not under the circumstances, and not with it ending. They liked Sharon, but would they still like her when they heard about the arrangement? Danny snorted. If his mother had her say, he and Sharon would remain married and give her a couple of grandchildren. Warmth spread across him when he thought of waking up to Sharon every morning, and then her pregnant with their child. Did Sharon want kids? Somehow, he couldn't imagine her changing dirty diapers or putting their kids to bed. Working at a homeless shelter for a few hours was one thing, but taking care of kids every day? He doubted that fit into her CEO life.

Danny shivered as he thought about Mark being his father-in-law and grandfather to his kids. Over his dead body. Good thing kids weren't part of the plan. Talk about nightmarish Thanksgivings and Christmases.

Maybe speaking to his parents was the way to go. They'd talk some sense into him and give him alternative ideas than this crazy one. Danny changed his mind when his parents' faces appeared in his mind, their eyes filled with disappointment. No. If he decided to accept Sharon's offer, he had no intention of telling his parents the truth. Let them believe he'd found love, even if it was for a short while. It wasn't far from the truth.

Later, Danny pulled into the parking lot of Patrick's office. He set the alarm before leaving and told Sharon he'd be back in a couple of hours. He hated leaving her alone, but this had to be taken care of.

The building was smaller than he expected. He exited the car and went inside. The offices inside were richly decorated, except for Patrick's office. The design in his office had clean, modern lines with no extra frills, and Danny knew instantly that Josie had designed it for him. Patrick's assistant led Danny into his office and offered him something to drink. Danny declined and took the seat Patrick directed him to take.

"Good to see you again, Danny." Patrick shook his hand before sitting down. "What can I do for you?"

Danny pushed the contract across the desk to Patrick before he lost his nerve and left. "You weren't kidding when you said having a relationship with Sharon would mean drastic changes to my life."

"She told you." It was a statement. "I'm glad. You needed to know it wasn't just about you." Patrick pushed a button on his phone. "Cancel my 1:00 appointment, Betty."

"Thanks." Danny shifted his position on the chair. He'd tried reading through the contract himself, and while he understood some of it, there were parts too legalese for him, and why he wanted Patrick to look through. Did Patrick cancel his appointment because of the contract or because it was his contract? Whatever the reason, it couldn't be a good one.

Patrick leaned back in his chair when he finished reading. "Did you want me to read this because of changes you wanted to make, or because you wanted to make sure you weren't getting screwed?"

"Both." Danny hadn't thought about Sharon screwing him over, since the contract seemed straightforward, but better safe than sorry.

"Are you seriously considering this?"

"Yes. No. I'm not sure. My business could really use the money, but..." Danny raked a hand through his hair. He should've waited until he made up his mind before coming to see Patrick. He didn't want to waste his time. "I guess I wanted your advice and whether you thought this was a good idea."

"I can give you my advice, but only you can decide if signing this contract is a good idea."

Danny nodded.

"The contract itself looks good, but I would definitely recommend you adding an escape clause, and one that benefits you financially if things go south."

Spoken like a true lawyer. Danny appreciated it. Patrick and Sharon were friends, and he could've left the contract as is. "Would you add it for me and let me know the charge?"

"Sure, but it's on the house. I insist."

"I couldn't."

"Consider it done. Don't argue. It'll take me less than ten minutes to add it."

Danny was certain the time was an exaggeration, but he'd take it.

"If changes are suggested during the signing. Don't sign until I've looked the new contract over. All right?"

"You got it. So, what do you really think?"

Patrick leaned back in his chair and linked his fingers.

"I know Mark and how difficult it's been for Sharon to get what's she's entitled to, but I also know Sharon, and she can be ruthless when it comes to being a part of her family's business and getting her inheritance. I'm worried those two will go to war and you'll be caught in the crossfire."

Shit! Danny was so worried about the crossfire between him and Sharon, he hadn't thought about her father.

"On a personal note, you and Sharon seem to genuinely care about each other, and the two years could be time to truly get to know each other. You might find that you stay married. However, two years can be a lifetime if you don't like the person. Hence why I suggested the escape clause. She needs you so she won't object to the change, regardless of the money."

Was that a good thing? It sounded like it, but Danny had a feeling he'd need a shower to wash the dirt from his body after the contact was signed.

"I'll speak with Sharon about the contact changes, and I'll review the new contract to make sure all is good before you sign."

Danny stood. "Thanks, Patrick. I really appreciate you doing this."

"Don't thank me yet. Between Sharon and Mark, it's going to be one hell of a ride. One you might not enjoy."

"Tell me about it."

"What are you telling your parents?"

"I haven't decided yet, but whatever I tell them, they have to keep the truth a secret from Sharon's family."

"Good luck with that." Patrick stood and walked with Danny to the door.

"Thanks. I have a feeling I'm going to need it."

Danny and Patrick shook hands and Danny made his way to the exit.

A blast of cold air rushed over Danny, and he pulled his coat closer against his frame before getting in the car. The drive back home didn't give Danny the calm he thought would come after speaking with Patrick. He'd hoped that visit would make the decision easier. It hadn't.

Chapter 33

The contract on Sharon's kitchen counter loomed between them like spoiled food no one wanted to touch. This was what she asked for, but that didn't stop fear and dread from coursing through her veins in a way no other business deal had. Maybe because this wasn't just another business deal. This was her life. She cared about Danny a lot, but this was a huge step. She and Danny hadn't known each other long, and in the short time they'd gotten to know each other, he'd stirred up more emotions in her than any other person had. It was exhilarating and terrifying all at once. When they signed this contract, he'd be a regular part of her life for the next two years. Two years was a long time. A lot could happen in those two years. Sharon smiled when she remembered him wanting to add sex as part of the contract. He was bluffing and trying to point out the ridiculousness of her proposal, but she'd added it anyway.

The call from Patrick about the escape clause had been a surprise, not only that Danny had involved Patrick, but that Patrick hadn't tried to talk Danny out of it, or Josie, for that matter. Maybe they tried. Sharon was happy the money was going to him. "Did you have any questions?" Sharon asked, trying to break the ice of silence that had remained in the room when he saw the contracts.

Danny shook his head. "Did you make any changes other than the ones we spoke about?"

"No. I would've told you if I had."

He grabbed one of the contracts and skimmed through it. Danny paused on page five. It was the page with the sex clause.

"You didn't have to put this in." Amber-colored eyes locked on Sharon.

"I know, but I thought it should be there. Just in case." Her voice was a whisper.

"Are you sure it's a good idea? Sex complicates things."

How much more complicated could their relationship get? They were about to sign a contract to be married. "You don't need to ask for it, but it's there if you want it." *OMG! Did those words just come out of my mouth?*

Danny's gaze pierced her, heating the room. "You have the choice to ask yourself."

Heat raced to Sharon's cheeks and other parts of her body as she remembered his mouth and tongue against hers. What the hell was she thinking, including that clause? She managed to nod.

Danny continued reading the contract and picked up the pen to sign. His hand paused. "We must agree to be honest with each other if we're going to do this. And if anything changes between us, good or bad."

"Agreed. The escape clause covers that."

"The escape clause is just words on a page, Sharon."

He was right. In the end, while this contract bound them legally, it was just words. A marriage contract didn't guarantee a happy marriage. "I promise to be honest with you, no matter what happens between us."

Danny signed the contracts and pushed them toward her. She signed both copies. Sharon was still staring at her signature and didn't notice that Danny was standing next to her. When she met his gaze, the heat in his eyes made her gasp. He placed an arm around her waist and pulled her against him. Before she could say a word, his mouth crashed into her, hot and demanding, making her knees melt. Was he claiming his right in the sex clause now? Her mind raced with excitement and dread. He softened the kiss until it was as sweet as the first time they kissed. This kiss was more terrifying. It said he could take what he wanted, but he'd be gentle, passionate. Sharon didn't know whether to wrap her arms around him or run like hell. Her arms made the decision for her, clinging to his shirt, drawing Danny closer. His moan filled her mouth and her knees trembled when his hand dug into her back and he pressed closer, pushing her against the kitchen counter.

As quickly as the kiss started, it ended, leaving Sharon hot and satisfied and unsatisfied all at the same time. *I'm in big trouble.* She met his gaze, her eyes asking why he kissed her.

"I wanted to seal the deal another way," Danny mumbled, answering her question.

Sharon opened her mouth to speak, but what could she say? *Thank you?*

The sound of the guys arriving to start work saved her. She straightened and grabbed the contracts, closing them and stacking them neatly in a pile. "I'm going to work." *Of course you are, Sharon. You can't stick around here.*

"See you later." His heated gaze melted into a friendly one just as two crew members entered the kitchen to get the coffee Sharon always made.

319

"Happy working, fellas," Sharon said and waved goodbye, the contracts in hand. She grabbed her handbag at the end of the counter and headed out the front door. It was going to be a long day. As Sharon drove to work, she was trying to decide if she wanted Danny waiting for her to return and pick up where they left off. *Icing on the cake.* Those were the wrong words. What happened between them when they kissed wasn't icing, it was a damn volcano. Sharon just prayed she wouldn't get burned.

What the hell was that? Danny scolded himself when he heard the front door close. A kiss to close the deal? *The deal was the last thing on your mind while you were kissing Sharon.* He hadn't been able to stop thinking about the sex clause, and with Sharon standing across from him looking like she'd stepped out of a magazine, he couldn't help himself. He'd wanted his mouth on hers, his hands on her skin, even if it was just her arm. He resisted the urge to run a hand through her hair, knowing doing so would mess it up and make his guys, who were arriving any minute, wonder what they were up to.

Sharon's shock reflected in her eyes, but the way her body responded when their mouths and bodies met made him want to text the guys. Send them to another work site and keep Sharon home for the day. The words of the sex clause were there in black and white, and after he signed his name, it was all he could think about. Danny wished he was at home so he could take a cold shower and clear the memory of Sharon from his head and skin, but he had a full day of work ahead of him that couldn't be avoided.

It was done. The contract was signed, and he'd be tied to Sharon for the next two years, or at least after they were married. *Married.* The clause in the contract was about a simple ceremony with only close friends and family. Danny wondered if Mark would agree to those terms. Mark might not since he was the person his daughter was marrying and not some hotshot from their world.

Danny grinned as he imagined the discomfort on Mark's face when he heard the news. While he wasn't looking forward to Mark as his father-in-law, Danny was going to enjoy watching him squirm. When he was with Teri, he'd gone out of his way to fit into her world, sacrificing parts of himself to make her happy. He wasn't going to do that this time around. He was going to be himself and to hell with what anyone else thought. Sharon liked him the way he was; otherwise, she wouldn't have proposed to him. They'd had fun together, and he planned to keep it that way. Sharon needed fun in her life. She needed him.

Maybe that was another reason why he agreed, other than just keeping her safe. Sharon was a strong woman, but she needed someone to make her smile and forget about the world she lived in, and the people in it, who were cold as ice. She needed him to remind her that life could be fun. Sharon needed someone to pull her out of the office in the middle of the afternoon and screw her against the back of her door or on the kitchen counter. She needed someone to remind her there was more to life than work and the malicious people around her. She needed him.

Okay, he had to admit the sex part was mostly for him, but he'd gotten glimpses of the woman who smiled and laughed, and Danny liked her...a lot. He planned to see more of her over the next two years, with and without clothes on. As to what came after the two-year mark, he'd worry about it when the time came.

Chapter 34

Mark stood outside the front door when Sharon opened it. It had been two days since she and Danny had signed the contracts, and she'd left one on his desk. She'd expected him to come storming to her office after reading it, but he hadn't arrived. Sharon was certain he was planning how to break their contract.

"Is Danny here?"

"Yes. What do you want?"

"Can I come in?"

"Only if you don't plan to insult him."

"I've got thick skin, remember, Sharon?" Danny said.

She stepped away from the entrance so he could come inside. Mark followed them to the living room.

"I've read through the contract, and while I'm not happy with the arrangement, given Danny is not someone from our world, the choice is yours to make."

Sharon let out the breath she was holding. "I'm glad we agree on that." She'd expected him to storm in with fire and spit, but he was being reasonable. While she was relieved, something in the back of her mind remained on alert.

"The two years came as no surprise either, but the sex clause was."

They both blushed.

"Why are you here?"

His gaze shifted between them before settling on Sharon. "I've made an amendment to the contract, as is my right as your parent."

Her heartbeat slowed and her skin tingled, threatening to break out in a sweat.

"I've added a baby clause."

The word *baby* was a bomb exploding in the room as the silence stretched on for several moments.

"If there's no baby at the end of two years, Sharon, you forfeit your seat on all company boards, including your charities; the rest of your inheritance; and any property you've obtained. Danny gets to keep the deposit, but forfeits the balance."

Sharon wanted to scream at her father that he couldn't do this, but she knew the truth. He could. She glanced at Danny, and his expression reflected her own. A fake marriage was bad enough, but a baby? "Give us time to think it over."

Mark smirked. "You're going to need it." He stood. "By the way, Bradley is a willing candidate, even with the baby clause."

I bet he is. "Goodbye, Father."

Neither of them spoke until after they heard the front door close.

"I can't do this, Sharon. I thought I could, but a baby? I won't bring a child into the world this way." Danny fell back against the couch.

"I know." She'd expected no less, and she had to agree with him. Marriage was already going to be a hurdle, but a baby? She'd never imagined having kids, her focus solely on obtaining her inheritance. Bringing a child into the world under a contract? Bile rose in her throat thinking about it. She wouldn't do that to Danny or herself. The realization that everything she'd ever wanted was being yanked away from her slammed into her like a wrecking ball into a building. The air around her became thinner, and she couldn't breathe. Her chest tightened and her legs felt numb. She tried to stand and rush to her room, but she couldn't move. Her throat constricted and her eyes burned like they were on fire. Before she could stop herself, she clutched her head and screamed until her throat couldn't scream anymore.

Danny wanted to rush to her and put his arms around her, but the pitch of the scream—and the fact that it didn't stop—kept him from moving. *She must be in shock.* He'd never seen her react so fiercely before. Her father had just given her an obstacle she wasn't willing to remove to get what she wanted.

A baby?

He still couldn't believe her father would do such a thing to his own daughter, and to make matters worse, suggest a man like Bradley was willing? As if a baby was simply another commodity to add to their agreement. What kind of man did that?

"I'm sorry," she whispered.

He moved closer and put his arms around her. "Don't be. It's not your fault."

"I never thought he'd take things this far. I'd hoped he would change his mind and give me my inheritance without getting married."

"Once he found out it was me?"

"Yes, and once he found out the truth about Bradley."

"What truth?"

"One of his girlfriends ended up in the hospital. My father didn't care."

"Shit!" What kind of man would marry his daughter off to someone like that? "You're better off without a father like that in your life," Danny assured her.

"Maybe, but it'd mean giving up everything I've ever wanted, and losing everything I tried to build."

"You've got this house, money in the bank. You wouldn't be starting from scratch."

"I would. Nothing belongs to me. Only the money I earned working for him. My car, home, investment accounts, most of my possessions—all belong to him."

"Is that even legal?"

"If I was smart, I would've walked away when I got out of college and started out on my own, but stupid me wanted to make my father proud and get what I thought was mine. Now I'm going to lose it all anyway. All those years...wasted."

He brushed a strand of hair away from her face. "Not wasted. Lessons."

"Those are some hard lessons." She managed a smile, but it quickly faded.

"I'm so sorry, Sharon."

"At first, I thought it was another hard lesson he was trying to teach me, but now I'm not so sure. He certainly doesn't want my cousin Carlton to take the seat, and Virginia implied something was going on with the board after Robert died."

"Couldn't you offer to give up your seat and take the inheritance and start on your own?"

"The contract requires me to get married to get my inheritance, so I'll lose everything if I don't get married, even if I offer to give up my seat. Trust me, Patrick and I have tried every scenario, but none of them gets me freedom, other than walking away, and even then, I risk my father sabotaging everything."

"Speak with Patrick again and see if there are any scenarios to get you out but stop your father from coming after any business you try to start. It's not much, but it's better than doing nothing."

Sharon chewed on her bottom lip. His suggestion meant walking away from everything she'd ever wanted and known, a decision that wouldn't come easy, but the alternative wasn't either.

"I'll talk to Patrick."

The silence stretched out before them. Danny stood. "I make a mean omelet."

"That would be great, except I haven't got anything in my fridge but water and premade meals."

He pulled her off the couch. "Then let's go shopping."

"At the supermarket?"

"Yes. It's a crazy concept, I know, but that is where they keep the food."

She laughed. "I know that, but I'm just used to having my meals delivered and eating out."

"I'm going to change all that."

"Umm. I don't know how to cook, Danny."

"I know, but that's an easy change." He grinned.

"Somehow I doubt that." They laughed.

Chapter 35

The phone on her nightstand buzzed, waking Sharon. Why the hell was Carlton calling her this time of night? "Hello?"

"My mother is dead," came from the other end of the phone.

Sharon shot up in bed. "What?"

Carlton's tone was broken. "She drove her car into a wall. I knew she was unsettled after my father died, but this..."

"Oh my god, Carlton. I'm so sorry. Is there anything I can do to help?"

"Can you come by the police station with me? I don't want to be there alone." Carlton gave her the name of the station.

"Of course. Give me a few minutes."

"Thank you, Sharon. With Robert dead, and now Virginia, there's no one left."

"You have me and Mark, Carlton. You're not alone." She shouldn't have spoken for her father, but she could speak for herself and knew she would be there to help Carlton through this difficult time of losing both parents.

"Thank you, Sharon."

Sharon jumped out of bed and dressed quickly and headed to the living room to wake Danny. He looked so peaceful she didn't want to wake him. She brushed a strand of hair away from his face and touched his skin. He was warm and she longed to curl up next to him. The news of Virginia's death was a reminder that life was short, and death came unexpectedly. Or did it? It did seem suspicious that both of Carlton's parents were gone. What would that mean for the board? For Carlton? For her father?

Danny startled her when he grasped her hand and sat up. "What's wrong?"

"Virginia, Carlton's mother, is dead."

"Are you okay?"

"I'm not sure. We weren't close." Sharon shared the story of their last encounters with Danny and a wave of guilt washed over her. While Virginia could be cold and manipulative, she'd lost her husband and Sharon hadn't visited her once.

"Do you think her death is connected to Robert's?"

"I'm not sure. I hope not, but I do want to hear what the police have to say. Carlton asked me to meet him at the station."

"I'm coming with you. I don't want you going anywhere alone right now. Just to be safe."

"I agree. I'll wait for you in the kitchen." Danny rolled off the couch and stood shirtless and gorgeous. *Focus, Sharon!*

"I'll be right there." Danny headed into the room where his clothes were hidden.

Sharon started the coffee while she waited. It was four in the morning, and they were going to need it.

Coffee in a travel mug was waiting for Danny when he entered the kitchen.

"Thanks." He picked it up and they headed for the door.

When they arrived at the police station, shock showed on Carlton's face behind the glass doors. To her surprise,

Bradley was there in the waiting area. *I thought they didn't like each other.*

Sharon addressed the officer at the front area, letting her know why she was there. "Please have a seat. He'll be finished with the officer shortly."

"What are you doing here?" Sharon asked when she and Danny took the seats next to Bradley. The station was quieter than she expected, with officers at their desks working on their computers or interviewing someone.

"I was with Virginia before her accident."

"With her?" Danny asked.

"I was talking to her and Carlton about Robert's role on the board and how I could support her and Carlton. I drove up shortly after the accident and called the police. I didn't think she was that fragile..." Bradley's voice trailed off, clearly shaken.

"What did you say to her in the meeting?" Danny asked.

"Nothing that would cause her to drive her car into a wall. The office said there were no brake marks. Why would she do this? I was only trying to help her and Carlton."

Sharon didn't know if he was at fault or not, but he was clearly upset. Seeing this side of him made her feel guilty for suspecting he could be involved in Robert's death. His hands shook, his face was sweating, and his distraught expression showed he was in shock. "How is Carlton doing? Have you spoken with him at all?"

"No. I was here when he arrived, but we didn't speak. He seemed upset. Who can blame him?"

"Yes. Losing a parent is hard. I couldn't imagine both." Sharon honestly didn't know how she'd react if her father died. She'd be sad, but the pain would be nothing like when her mother died.

"Yes. Hard." Bradley's gaze drifted to the other side of the room, as if he'd journeyed to another time and place.

An officer walked Carlton over to them.

Sharon hugged him. "Are you okay?"

He glanced between Bradley and Danny. "What are you two doing here? Neither of you are family!"

"Danny drove me here." Sharon didn't elaborate.

"I was the last one to see your mother alive. I came just after the accident. I'm so sorry. I didn't know she was so unstable."

Carlton's jawline jumped. "If she was unstable, it was because of what you said to her."

"All I did was offer to help you and her with the board. To make things easier for you both."

"Liar. You just want it all for yourself. You killed her, you bastard!" Carlton lunged at Bradley, knocking him to the ground and wrapping his fingers around his neck.

Bradley struggled to push Carlton off him without success, until Danny and other officers rushed to pull them apart. "You're crazy. I wasn't anywhere near your mother. I'm the one who called the police. Your mother killed herself from the grief."

"No. She wouldn't leave me." Carlton dropped to the ground and sobbed. Sharon rushed to him and pulled him off the floor and onto a chair. She stroked his back to calm him. Carlton's public reaction was unexpected. She hadn't realized the relationship with his mother was a close one, but those on the outside might've said the same thing about the one she had with her mother.

"Let us drive you home, Carlton."

"No. I want to be alone." He stood and rushed out of the police station. That was a reaction she was more familiar with.

"Should we go after him?" Danny asked.

"No, give him time. I'll call him later to check on him."

Bradley was sitting in a chair, his head in his hands. "What about him?"

Sharon felt sorry for him, but not sorry enough to offer him a ride home, given his reaction to her rejection. "Leave him."

Sharon and Danny walked out of the police station. Part of her felt guilty for leaving him there alone, but another part couldn't help wonder about the words that transpired between him and Carlton.

Chapter 36

The home was decorated from top to bottom with Christmas decorations, thanks to someone she'd hired at the last minute. Since her father stopped by, her mind had been occupied with the baby clause and finding ways to walk away. She wanted to cry every time she thought about it, so started avoiding the topic all together. It wasn't easy with her father, and Bradley, hovering by her office door every minute to see if she'd made her decision. They didn't ask outright, especially Bradley, but their eyes implied it.

Danny was supportive at first, but recently he'd been pressuring her to walk away, as if it were no big deal and she could start a new life. Easy for him to say, but taking that step was another story. Her stalker was keeping his distance, which she was happy for, but also annoyed her because it kept them in limbo. Danny insisted on staying with her, even though their contract was clearly null and void.

The dinner party was tonight. The women were scheduled to be there in an hour, and she was dreading it. Another boring dinner party talking about husbands, and trying to make connections or find out information about their family's business and political dealings.

The catering company she hired had two waitstaff downstairs setting up while she got dressed. Everything was in place, including her, when the doorbell rang and the first guest arrived. The conversation headed in the direction she expected by the time everyone had arrived and they were seated at the table. She imagined year after year passing like this if she got married and remained with her father's company. Things wouldn't change, even when her father died. The men on the board would see to that. She'd live her years in a perpetual cycle, day in and day out, surrounded by people just the same as her, behind their guarded walls while soldiers were sent out to get information to be used and manipulated by the men in charge. Sharon wanted to vomit. Gaining the seat and her inheritance was meant to change her life, but it wouldn't. It would merely pull her further and deeper into the world she was trying to change. A world that wasn't likely to change in her lifetime, or her children's. Is that the life she wanted for herself? *No!* She banged her hands on the table for emphasis. The women around her jumped and glared at her as if she'd lost her mind, or had too much to drink.

"Aren't you sick of this!? Playing their game and being part of their world? Don't you want something for yourselves other than planning and attending parties!?"

She began calling out the women's names, their accomplishments, and what they gave up after they got married. "They've turned powerful, brilliant women into arm candy," she said with disgust.

"You've got nannies, people to clean and cook, and you're still required to stay home? Why? So their egos can feel good about having a wife who isn't more successful than them? I say to hell with them all!"

There was rousing applause from all the women. She'd stirred up emotions. Woman after woman started sharing what they'd tried to achieve, only to have it shut down by their husbands.

"I say we start our own companies. Companies that can't be touched or shut down. I say we stand together and be the strong women they wanted and married, and to hell with their egos!"

A round of agreements came from everyone sitting at the table.

While Sharon had fired everyone up by the end of the night, she hoped she hadn't set anyone down on the path to divorce. Her mind was still racing and excitement pumping through her when Danny returned. He'd gone over to his parents for dinner and called to make sure the women were gone before he returned.

"How did it go?"

She was so excited, the only thing she could manage was to grab him by the shirt and kiss him soundly.

"I guess it went well," she heard him say as she rushed upstairs to bed.

Change was in the air, and she was excited for what lay ahead.

Chapter 37

"**A**re you sure you want to do this?" Danny asked while they sat in the car parked outside his parents' house.

"I'm sure. I promised. Besides, I wouldn't want to miss out on seeing you wear whatever horrible Christmas sweater your mother picked out for you."

"Don't laugh. She might have one for you, too, so you don't feel left out."

Sharon opened the door, "Unlike you, I relish the idea of wearing a horrible sweater." It helped fill the space missing from the special times she'd spent with her mother during the holidays. Her father's idea of Christmas tradition was making sure gifts were sent to all their clients and political connections. They hadn't had a Christmas together opening presents since her mother died. At first she thought it was too painful for him, but when he went about business as usual in other areas of his life, it was as if his wife's death meant nothing.

"I don't mind as long as I don't have to wear it anywhere else but their house." Danny grabbed the presents from the back seat.

She laughed and grabbed a couple of presents from the top of his pile. Shopping for Danny's parents hadn't been easy since she barely knew them, but Ryan had helped her with suggestions she'd gotten from Danny.

"You didn't have to buy my parents presents."

"I know, but I wanted to. They made me feel so welcome."

"They do that for all my future wives," he teased.

She chuckled, although truthfully it wasn't so funny, especially after her father's visit. But it was better to joke about it than dwell on what it meant.

"How did they feel about Teri?"

"They never met her. I tried to have her volunteer with me at the shelter so she could meet my mom, but..."

She could only imagine the horror on Teri's face. Her idea of charity was writing a check or unloading clothing she no longer wore. Getting her hands dirty wasn't her thing. "I'm sorry. I didn't mean to bring her up."

"It's okay. She's my past, and a lesson learned."

The door flew open before they could knock.

"Come in! I'm so glad you came." Rose greeted them both with hugs and a kiss on their cheeks. "I wasn't sure you were going to make it. I know how busy this time of year is for you, Sharon."

They stomped the snow off their shoes on the outside mat and stepped into the warm, cozy house. Everything was covered from top to bottom in decorations, with no theme that Sharon could see other than "Christmas." It was beautiful!

"Is that for me?" Rose asked of the poinsettia in her hand.

"Yes, but it appears you don't need it!" There were at least five plants in the living room alone.

"Nonsense!" She took the plant and placed it in an empty space. "There's always room for more."

Rose took the presents and placed them under the tree with the rest of the gifts while they removed their coats.

"Did you tell your parents anything?" Sharon whispered to Danny.

He shook his head.

She was grateful. Not telling them made sense since the baby clause her father threw at them. She liked Danny's parents and didn't want them thinking less of her, especially since she wasn't going to be around much longer. Those thoughts made her sad. While she could still see Rose at the homeless shelter on occasion, being part of their lives on a regular basis wasn't a good idea, or likely possible, depending on how things turned out.

John was in the kitchen setting up trays of Christmas cookies along with the ingredients to decorate them. "Hello, Sharon. Danny."

"So, we're here to work?" Danny observed.

"Of course." John removed his apron and handed it to Sharon.

"You have my usual fee?" Danny took another apron from a drawer and put it on.

"Two steaming cups of hot chocolate with extra marshmallows coming up."

Sharon put on the apron and got to work. She'd never decorated cookies before, but she could do damage to a gingerbread house. Surely cookies were easier.

An hour later, she changed her mind.

Both she and Danny were covered in frosting, sprinkles, and other decorations, partly thanks to Danny, whose idea of decorating meant getting it everywhere but on the cookies. She'd never laughed so hard or felt so at home with anyone else or anywhere else. Although Danny's parents kept a safe distance in the living room, they contributed to the camaraderie between her and Danny as she tried to help him decorate.

"Mine are masterpieces, while yours look like a train wreck," Sharon observed, wiping her hands on the apron, although it didn't help.

"Christmas cookies aren't about being pretty, they're about being delicious, and that's what mine are," he argued.

"How delicious are they going to be when someone cracks a tooth from everything you've got on the cookie?"

"Hey. No one's ever broken a tooth on my cookies before." He pointed a decorating pack at her. "What about you? No one wants to eat cookies from an amateur."

She picked up one of her pretty cookies and one of Danny's and held them side by side. "Which one would you prefer to eat?" The question was directed at John and Rose.

They raised their hands. "Don't bring us into this. We're here to sample all the cookies, regardless of who made them," John replied.

Sharon turned to Danny. "That's their way of saying they like mine better."

John and Rose laughed.

"Not even close," Danny said, throwing a pinch of flour at her.

"You just can't accept defeat." She returned the favor.

They'd both grabbed a handful of flour, ready to launch, when Rose interrupted. "Whatever mess you make in there, you're cleaning it up!"

Danny and Sharon looked at each other, at the kitchen—which was already a mess—and lowered their flour-filled hands.

"How about we let taste be the judge?" Danny handed her one of his cookies and took one of hers.

They took a bite at the same time.

"I think I just lost a tooth," Sharon teased.

"I can feel the sugar racing to my bloodstream," Danny added.

"But how do they taste?" Rose asked.

They switched cookies and took another bite. "Sweet as hell but good," Danny said first and Sharon nodded in agreement.

"That's why you need to have hot chocolate to wash them down with," John added.

"Yes, more sugar." Sharon laughed.

"You two clean up the kitchen and then we'll open presents," Rose said.

Sharon was covered in flour, frosting and other condiments, but Danny thought she looked beautiful. Her body was relaxed, and she was genuinely enjoying herself. He'd been hesitant to tell her about his parents' invitation, given all the madness in her life right now, but he sensed she needed a break, especially after her aunt's death and father's visit.

He made a final offer for her to back out tonight, but he was grateful she didn't. His parents adored her, and he knew the feeling was mutual. If only they'd found each other under normal circumstances. *Hell, Danny. You never would've met her under normal circumstances, and if you did, you wouldn't have gotten to know the real her.*

That was true. He and Sharon might've met each other because of their relationship with Patrick and Danny, but they would've never communicated past polite conversation. A conversation that would've been painfully obvious and showed that they had nothing in common. And meeting Sharon was something he'd never regret, only the circumstances that kept them apart.

Moments later, they were all seated in the living room, opening presents.

Sharon gave his parents a couple's session at the spa. His mother was thrilled, but his father looked terrified until Sharon assured him they would take good care of him.

They gave her a small home tool set and an ugly Christmas sweater. Sharon laughed and teared up.

The last two presents under the tree were their gifts to each other.

They headed onto the patio to enjoy another cup of hot chocolate and the Christmas lights and decorations his parents had set up in the backyard.

After lighting a fire in the pit, he sat next to her on the loveseat, accepting the blanket she held out for him. Half of their bodies were pressed together under two layers of blankets to stay warm. Sharon surprised him when she rested her head on his shoulder. He put his arm around her.

"Are you going to be all right?" The question was more about their contract, and the bomb her father dropped.

"I don't know," she answered honestly.

"You will, Sharon. You're a brilliant woman who got this far with all the obstacles you faced. You'll make it through. It might not seem like it now, but you will."

"Thank you." She pulled the blanket closer. "I know this on one level, but fear of what my father will do is what's making it difficult. And walking away from everything I've know my whole life is a little daunting."

"You'll make it, no matter what your father does. I'll help you get through it."

She grabbed his hand. "That means a lot to me Danny, but I think its best I keep my distance from you. I don't want you to be caught in the crossfire from my father and have it impact your business."

"You mean I'm not getting the two million dollars?" he teased.

She grinned. "No, sorry."

"Damn. I'd already spent it in my head."

When they stopped laughing, she glanced up at him. "I'm sorry about the money. I know what it meant for your business."

He shrugged. "It just means I'm back to my original business plan."

"Which is?"

"Work until the loans are paid off and the bills are paid."

"I'd recommend others in my circle to you, but I don't think I'll be welcome anywhere anytime soon."

"It's all good. Josie and I have a big job lined up for the new year, but I'll take a good review."

"Deal."

They sat there for several more moments enjoying each other's company, neither saying a word, afraid the spell would be broken and the real world would come crashing through his parents' French doors. In this moment, he could pretend she was with him, and they were spending the holidays with his parents and soon they'd go home and spend the evening together. Then they'd wake up and enjoy the rest of the holidays with each other in bed, having breakfast, lunch, and dinner, and doing all the normal things couples did this time of year.

The patio lighting glimmered with various Christmas lights, and they were surrounded by ornaments, statues, poinsettias, and other types of Christmas decorations his mother had collected over the years. The longer they stayed on the patio, the colder it got, but neither wanted to leave and break the spell.

"Danny?" Sharon glanced at him.

"Yes?"

She touched his cheek with her gloved hand and pulled his face toward hers.

"You two will freeze to the chair if you don't come inside soon," John's voice interrupted. "Oh, I'm sorry," he stammered when he saw them.

"It's all right, John. Time for us to go. I've got a long day ahead of me tomorrow, and things to wrap up before the end of the year." Sharon stood as she and Danny unwrapped themselves, and headed back into the house.

"Thank you so much for having me over." She hugged Rose and John goodbye.

"It was our pleasure, sweetheart! We hope to see you here next year," Rose said, glancing at Danny.

Sharon watched him say goodbye to his parents. John whispered in his ear, "Don't let her get away." He wished he could take the advice, but in the end, the choice would be Sharon's to make.

When they got in the car, she turned up the heat. "It was freezing on the patio."

He smiled and adjusted the vents. As he watched her pull out of the driveway, he longed to reach over and finish the kiss they almost had on the patio. He ached with wanting her lips against his, along with other parts of her body, but then what? Things were complicated between them as is.

He'd almost forgotten he was staying at Sharon's house until she pulled into the driveway and parked the car. They took the presents from the back seat and headed inside.

The renovations were done, so she was back in her room and he was in her guest room, and thankfully off the torturous couch. His back still ached from the time he'd slept on it. Sharon was leaning across the counter, her gaze fixed on the living room. No doubt her mind was racing with all the decisions she had to make, and the difficult road that lay ahead.

She straightened and walked around the counter to where he stood. Blood rushed through him at the speed of light until it thumped in his ears. Her arms went around his neck and she stood on her toes and kissed him. He stood with his arms by his side before pulling her away from him.

"Sharon, as much as I want this, it's not a good idea."

Her fingers went through the hair at the base of his neck. "I've regretted a lot of things in my life, Danny, and I don't want one of them to be not being with you, no matter how. I know things are complicated, but I want this. I want this moment with you, even if I never get it again."

347

An azure gaze met his and it was warm, open, and vulnerable.

He lifted her so she was pressed against him and kissed her. Then he returned her to the ground, took her hand, and guided her upstairs.

Chapter 38

"**Y**our daughter is here to see you," his secretary announced.

Mark grinned. His ploy had worked, and she was coming to agree to Bradley. He may not be the best candidate, but he was acceptable, and she'd be able to keep him in line because of his past. As strong as she thought Bradley was, she was stronger. "Send her in."

There was no way he'd allow her to ruin her life by marrying some glorified carpenter. *She belongs with her family—and the company—with a man who'll fit into their world.* Danny knew nothing of their life and would only hold her back.

Adding a baby to the contract was the only thing he could think of to derail her plan to marry Danny. His financial situation wasn't dire enough to accept the baby clause, but from what he'd found out about him, and what Sharon shared with him, he'd backed out of the contract. As would Sharon. Her showing up today was evidence of that. He'd won. She'd fall in line, marry Bradley, and take her place in the company.

Sharon strode into his office, her hair down and dressed in clothing he'd never approve of. She was going to test his limits.

"Sit," he ordered.

She ignored his demand and remained standing. "I won't be here that long." She dropped an envelope on his desk. "Thanks for your offer, but Danny and I have declined to accept your change."

"I figured as much. So have you spoken to Bradley about an offer?"

"You misunderstand me. I'm not interested in any offer you plan to make, including the original contract for me to marry. I'm forfeiting everything. Everything you threatened to take away from me. I don't want any of it. I'll be moved out before January first."

"You'll never find another job."

"I don't care. I'd rather be homeless on the street than spend anymore of my life with you, this company, or these people."

"How dare—-"

"I did everything I could to make you proud, to prove to you I deserved the respect, power and position your son would've gotten, but it was never enough for you. Being your child, your daughter, wasn't enough. I'm tired of trying to please you and be a part of a company and family who don't respect me."

"No business you start will take off," Mark threatened.

"Make whatever threats you want. Try and stop whatever plans I make, I don't care. I'm going to do what I've always done over the years. Keep going."

"How dare you defy me this way?!"

"It will be the last time. Consider this my notice. My last day is two weeks from today unless you'd like me to be escorted from the building sooner. I'll make sure to notify all my clients and direct them to you until someone is assigned to take them over."

She strode toward the door. "Once I leave the company, I don't want you to call me, or try to contact me. As far as I'm concerned, I'm no longer part of this family. That should make it easier for you. I know it will make it easier for me."

"Sharon."

"I don't want to be part of a family or have a father who'd rather marry me off to a man like Bradley. I'm done, and you're free of me."

Her voice hitched, but her eyes were clear of tears and her steps determined as she walked through the door of his office, leaving him with his thoughts.

Sharon headed to her office. "Ryan, please compile my complete client list and when you've got it, come into my office." She paused at the door. "If my father calls or comes by, tell him I'm in a meeting and can't be disturbed, or I'm on an important call."

"Yes, Sharon," Ryan stammered before his fingers returned to the keyboard.

She stormed into her office, tempted to slam the door. She took deep breaths to steady her nerves, and the fire that was coursing through her from the encounter with her father. It hadn't been as confrontational as she expected, but then she hadn't given him a lot of chances to speak. She'd wanted to get in and get out of his office before both their tempers flared.

What had he done next? Did he go to Bradley's office, the lawyers who handle board issues, or his own lawyer? Was he contacting her clients at that moment? He might even be hatching plans to sabotage her leave. It didn't matter what he had planned, she'd be gone in two weeks, or sooner.

Surprisingly, she felt more relief than anxiety, but that was likely because the reality of her actions hadn't sank in. Once it did, she'd be a wreck, but in the meantime, she enjoyed the weightlessness she felt imagining no longer being at the whim of her father, making decisions without worrying about the circumstances. All right, so that part would've changed, but for once she only had to worry about how it would affect her, and not her father or the board. The business and social fallout would be brutal, but she didn't care. She'd take one day at a time and pray she could find her own way without her father sabotaging everything she started.

The statement about being homeless wouldn't be far from the truth once she moved out of her home. She'd have the clothes on her back and the money she'd saved over the years from her salary, but little else. She could pawn the few pieces of jewelry her mother had left her, but that would only last so long. Fear descended, closing the space around her with endless words of doubt and what ifs and trying to convince her she'd be better off with Bradley.

Hell no! She'd made her choice and she'd stick to it. No matter what.

"Carlton is here to see you, Sharon. I told him you weren't available, but..."

"It's all right, Ryan. Send him in." Handing her clients to Carlton wouldn't be her first choice. She'd love to recommend Ryan, but her father would never agree.

"What can I do for you, Carlton?"

He strode into her office and paced before her. "I heard you didn't make Bradley an offer, you and turned down your seat on the board. Is that true?"

His mouth was practically salivating. Too bad he wasn't smart enough to realize Mark probably wouldn't give him her seat either, but maybe he was and that's why he was here.

"It's true."

"You gave up your seat? Charities? Everything?"

Carlton knew the seat on the board and charities were her passion, but from his expression, she guessed he didn't suspect she'd have to give up her home, car, and most of her investments. She nodded.

"Why?"

"You wouldn't understand."

He paced again and she could see him contemplating his next questions. "So does this mean I'll get your position?"

She laughed. "You'll have to take that up with my father and the board. It's up to them now, but I wouldn't hold my breath if I were you."

"But it should all be mine!"

"Yes, and it should've been mine, too."

"Damn stubborn man won't budge either, I bet."

She placed a hand on his shoulder. "You're a man, and the only person other than my father to take the seat, so maybe you'll get what you want. Maybe not tomorrow, but he can't say no forever, and he's not getting any younger. In the meantime, you should try living up to the position, like doing your job."

"I shouldn't have to live up to it. My name should be enough!"

That stupidity is what'll keep my father from giving you what you want. Sharon didn't respond. She had her own issues to deal with without having to worry about one of Carlton's tantrums that had obviously returned, even with his mother's death.

"I'm handing my clients over to Mark before I leave in two weeks."

"Why don't you give them to me?"

I'd rather send them boxes of thorns. "I told my father I'd give him the list, but I'll hand them over to you if you get it in writing."

Carlton's jawline jumped and his eyes shot daggers at her.

"You know I can't just hand them over, Carlton," she tried assuring him, but the daggers didn't stop. "Was there anything else?"

"No. When do you leave?"

"Two weeks."

"And you're sure you won't change your mind?"

"No."

"Maybe Uncle Mark will change his mind?"

"If he hasn't in the time I've been trying to convince him, it isn't likely to happen now, or anytime soon."

"You're right. He is a stubborn man." He headed to the door but turned before leaving. "Good luck, Sharon."

That was unexpected. "Thanks, Carlton."

Moments later, Ryan walked into the office. She told him about her resignation, and apologized because it would affect him.

"Are you sure I can't come with you?"

"I'll reach out to you when I'm settled." *If Father doesn't sabotage it.* "But you might like my replacement."

"Do you know who it is?"

"No. I doubt I'll know before I leave, but I'd like to make it easy for them to step in for the clients' sakes."

Ryan nodded. He knew how much her clients meant to her.

The rest of the day was spent preparing letters to clients, along with a list of personal cards and gifts to send them.

When she was ready to go home, she called a taxi to pick her up. She hadn't taken any chances since the attacks. Danny wasn't home when she got there, giving her time to think about what would happen with her attacker now that she'd given up her seat and was walking away from everything. Would he leave her alone?

She hadn't told her father about the attacks, figuring it wouldn't make a difference in his decision. If anything, she suspected he would use it as another reason for her to marry Bradley. There would be no marriage. There would be no more striving toward the dreams she'd wanted for as long as she could remember. Now she would have to find new dreams to chase.

Chapter 39

D anny was loading up his truck to leave the new site he was working at when a car pulled up behind him. At first he thought it was Sharon, since it was a luxury car, but Mark stepped out.

"We need to talk." His tone was harsh.

Oh, great. It's one of those talks. Danny hadn't seen Mark since he showed up at Sharon's home and made his baby announcement.

Danny checked his watch. "I've got a few minutes."

This annoyed Mark, but he didn't care. The man was an ass, and he didn't want to talk with him any longer than he had to.

"Did you put my daughter up to this?"

"Up to what?"

"Don't play games with me."

"You're the one who added a baby to your daughter's contract, and I'm the one playing games?"

"I did that so she'd come to her senses."

"And what? Marry a man known for beating up his girlfriends instead?"

"You're no better choice. You don't belong in our world."

"Neither does your daughter."

"She's a Donovan. That name alone says she belongs."

"Really? Then why have you made it so difficult for her?"

"I treat her the same as I would a son."

"Do you?"

Mark's face blistered in anger. "She's a woman. There's a certain expectation in my world."

"The expectation you're less?"

"You don't understand."

"I understand you've controlled and manipulated everything in her life, so she's felt unworthy and had to scrape for every success she had just to prove she was good enough, when you know damn well she was more than good enough to be part of your life, business, and she deserves that seat on the board."

Mark studied Danny for a moment before bursting into laughter. "You love her," he declared.

"She's a remarkable woman."

"I know, and that's why I want her to stay."

"Then change the contract so she doesn't have to get married."

"No. It's been that way for years for a reason."

"What reason?"

"To ensure the line continues."

"Is that why you added the baby clause? You were worried we'd marry in name only?"

"Yes, and I know my daughter. She wants to control as much as she can."

"I wonder where she gets that from?"

Mark grinned proudly. "Unfortunately, it makes for a difficult relationship."

"I didn't push your daughter into anything, Mr. Donovan. You did, by forcing her to do something she didn't want to."

Mark paced before him. "I suppose you'll continue to be in her life?"

"Yes." Honestly, they hadn't discussed it, but he hoped so, especially now that they had time to get to know each other without the weight of a contract and the conditions.

"I'll give you money to stay out of her life. Name your price!"

Was he serious? Mark already knew they weren't getting married, what reason was there? Was Mark that much of a snob, or was he worried the people in his circle would think his daughter gave up everything for a contractor?

"Why?"

"You've been a friend to Sharon, or perhaps more. I want her back with me, and that means removing all her support systems, and any possibility of her succeeding on her own."

Sharon had told him her father threatened her, but Danny thought it was just words said in anger to get her to do what he wanted. The fact that Mark was standing before him with this offer proved she knew her father well.

He wanted to tell Mark what he could do with his money, but instead said, "I don't want your money, and the harder you push, the farther away you're going to push her. She's not going to let you manipulate her anymore, and she isn't going to give up being on her own, no matter what you do."

"This is your doing."

"If you believe that, you're clueless about yourself and your daughter. You've been pushing her to this for years. She's stayed with you, hoping to change your mind and give her the respect she deserves, and all you've done is spit on her efforts and made it so difficult, she doesn't even want to be your daughter, or part of your world. And that's my fault? I've only known your daughter for three months, Mr. Donovan. You've known her for her entire life. Who do you think has a bigger impact?"

"If you continue a relationship with my daughter, I will ruin you, your business, and make the lives of you and your family a living hell," he threatened.

Danny shook his head in disbelief. "You're a piece of work." He jumped into his truck and left Mark standing in the driveway.

As he drove to Sharon's, he couldn't help but wonder if Mark was the one making the threats—another drastic attempt to bend her to his will. If he hadn't seen the side of Mark he just did, he never would've imagined it, but now?

The man was rich enough to hire someone, or powerful enough to influence someone. No wonder Sharon wanted to remove herself from him. It sucked that she had to give up what she'd worked so hard for because of it. He was confident Sharon would land on her feet, but how often she'd have to restart depended on how far her father would take things. After the encounter today, Danny was certain he'd take drastic measures.

When he pulled into Sharon's driveway twenty minutes later, her car was there and the lights were on in the kitchen. No one had tried to break in since he moved in, which was a good thing, but what would happen when she left the house? Would she be safe at her new place? She seemed sure that now that she had walked away, she was no longer in danger, but he also knew she took a cab to and from work instead of driving her car, so she wasn't 100 percent sure.

He wanted to ask her to move in with him, just until she was settled, but he suspected she'd turn him down. Then he considered asking his parents if she could stay with them, but that meant telling them, and Sharon was too proud and embarrassed to tell them. He couldn't blame her. When he walked into the kitchen, she was seated at the kitchen counter, a glass of wine next to her along with a stack of papers. "Still working?"

She glanced up from the papers, the weight of the world in her eyes. "Not exactly. I'm trying to figure about how much money is really mine and what I'll have to leave behind."

"That sucks!" He sat on the stool next to her. "You could stay with me until you get on your feet." *There.* He'd said it. "It's the least I could do."

She touched his cheek. "Thanks. That means a lot, but I can't. I need to do this on my own."

He swiveled the chair so it faced her. "You know the best part of having friends who care? You don't have to do it alone. I know that's what you're used to, Sharon, but it doesn't have to be that way. I'm here for you. My parents care about you, and I know Patrick and Josie would be happy to have you stay at their house while they're on their honeymoon. The point I'm trying to make is that you have options. You don't have to do it alone anymore."

Tears had pooled in her eyes, and she brushed them away quickly. "Thank you," she whispered. "No one has ever..."

He tucked a stray hair behind her ear. "I'm here for you no matter what you need, Sharon. Except for money. I just lost two million dollars so," he joked.

She hiccupped, then laughed before jumping out of her seat to hug him. "I love you, Danny."

From the expression on her face, it was obvious that had slipped out or was meant as an endearment and not a confession, but it still shook him right down to his toes. The silence was interrupted by the doorbell ringing. Relief reflected on both their faces before Sharon rushed out the kitchen to answer the door. There was a peep hole in the door so she could see who was outside.

Sharon opened the door, but he couldn't hear the conversation well enough to make out what was being said. Danny waited in the kitchen until Sharon and the guest made their way to the living room. From his spot in the kitchen, he could see them. He didn't recognize the man, but Sharon must've known him to let him inside. "Do you need privacy?"

Sharon nodded and mouthed *Thank you.* As much as he wanted to stay and find out who this man was to her, he stood to leave. "I'll be upstairs if you need me." Danny gave the man his most intimidating gaze before leaving them alone.

Sharon stared at the man, who'd been her mother's lawyer before she died. The man who'd told her the conditions of her family contract when she turned eighteen years old. The man who'd crushed her dreams of a having a normal life, even if it wasn't really his fault. He was just following orders, but it had felt personal at the time. What the hell was he coming to tell her now? She'd lost even more.

They sat and her heart was in her throat as he opened his briefcase and took out what she assumed was another contract. Had her father sent him? Had Mark found some way to stop her plans to leave before she could even execute them?

To her surprise, he turned on his laptop and turned the screen toward her and pressed Play.

Moments later, her mother came up on the screen. Tears pooled in her eyes at the sight of her. Sharon realized how much she'd missed her. She missed her guidance, advice, and even her hugs.

"Sharon, if you're watching this video, then it means you've stood up to your father and taken your first steps to freedom. I'm so proud of you. You were always a strong-willed child, but you always wanted your father's approval and to be part of his world, as was your right as his child. I'm so sorry he didn't change his mind about the marriage clause. I hoped he'd become so proud of your accomplishments he'd change it. The fact that you're watching this video says he didn't, and you've made the choice to go out on your own. A decision that I was never strong enough to make.

"Henry is here to give you your inheritance—the part of your inheritance I hid from your father all these years. The house is yours to keep, along with all the money in your bank accounts. You'll lose your stocks in the company, but I have other investments that have been even more successful. Investing was my talent your father never took advantage of. His loss, but your gain. You'll get everything that was mine before I married your father, including my seat on the charities we both loved. I know how much those meant to you. I hope they'll make up for losing the seat on the board of the company.

"I never had the courage to follow my own dreams, but you can, and I know you'll do great things, Sharon. Things your father can't take away from you anymore."

Tears flowed freely down her cheeks. Her mother had known the kind of man her father was and had taken steps to protect her. It was her final act of love.

"I hope you find the love and happiness you deserve, and that you'll open your heart to it when it comes. I love you, Sharon." She blew a kiss at the camera before the video ended.

Sharon sobbed, and Henry handed her his handkerchief. She wiped her face and handed it back to him.

"This is the entirety of your inheritance." He placed the papers before her.

She flipped through it, shocked by the amount of money and assets her mother had acquired before she married her father. It was substantial. Sharon laughed. She couldn't help herself. Her grandfather had been an investment banker, and his talents had obviously rubbed off on his daughter. What would her mother have achieved if she'd followed her own dreams? The trail stopped when she married Mark. She must've been afraid he would seize any funds she invested after they married. She had taken steps to hide the money and ensure Mark couldn't legally get his hands on it.

"Thank you, Henry."

"I'll leave these with you." He handed her his card. "Call me if you have any questions, or if you need anything else."

"I will." She stood and walked him to the door.

After locking the door, she stood in shock for several seconds before jumping up and down and dancing a jig. That was how Danny found her.

"I take it he came with good news. Your father changed his mind?"

"No. He was my mother's lawyer."

"Your mother?"

"Yes. She had a separate will that activated if I walked away from my family contract."

"Wow! That's wonderful. I take it it's enough for you to be on your own without having to worry about your father?"

"Yes, and I take over my mother's seat on the charities we set up. She knew how much they meant to me. Oh, and I get to keep the house!"

"That's good news. I worried the new owner would have me redo the renovations I just finished," Danny joked.

She threw herself at him and wrapped her arms around him and kissed him. She pulled away before he could kiss her back. "This calls for a celebration!"

"Chinese food?"

"Absolutely, and maybe even sushi?"

She laughed when Danny made a face. He didn't like sushi.

"How about you eat the sushi and I'll eat the Chinese food?"

"Deal."

Chapter 40

Danny was already downstairs and brewing coffee. She was usually the first one down, especially since she was days away from leaving the company. She was usually up early working from home before heading into the office. She wanted to make sure everything was in order before she left, especially since her father still hadn't assigned anyone to replace her. She suspected he was holding out, thinking she'd change her mind. She hadn't told her father about her mother's will, but he suspected, especially since she could keep the house.

She'd expected him to come storming through her office door in a rage, but he hadn't shown up. *He's trying to figure out how to take away what her mother had done.*

Let him work until the cows came home. Henry assured her there wasn't anything he could do, and if he tried, he'd tie him up in court for years. Her mother had left money for the fees. Henry had grinned when he said the words, telling her he didn't like her father either.

"You're up early."

Danny smiled, which made her stomach flip-flop. Damn, he was sexy, especially since he hadn't brushed his hair, so it looked windblown, or the way it did the morning after they made love. Her cheeks heated as she thought of it. It was the first and last time, but it wasn't because she didn't want to.

Now that she had her freedom, and the threat of her father ruining Danny's business was gone, she was looking forward to their relationship blossoming.

"Yeah, I've got a job a couple hours away and I wanted to leave before traffic got bad, but I'd love to take you to dinner tonight. Somewhere beside the kitchen counter."

Yes! His invitation said he wanted the same thing she did for their relationship to continue. She wasn't sure he did, given everything that had happened with her family. She'd also blurted out she loved him—not exactly how she planned to tell him. His horrified expression matched her own, and an indication it was too soon. She was grateful those words and her father hadn't changed his mind.

"I think we should talk about the living arrangements. As much as I enjoyed staying here, I can't stay forever."

He wants to leave. *That isn't what I expected. Was dinner just a way for him to break it to me? What did you expect? He can't stay with you forever, Sharon.*

"Dinner would be fantastic! Sushi?" she teased, bypassing answering his statement.

"I was thinking of tacos," he shot back.

She was not a fan of tacos, and he knew it.

He filled his travel mug with coffee and she handed him a water bottle from the fridge. "Trying to get me healthy?" He grinned.

"Someone has to."

His hand was still covering hers that held the water. They were standing close, and he leaned down and kissed her. "I'll see you tonight."

His low sexy tone sent a shiver up her back. They hadn't talked about the night they made love, and Danny hadn't come to her room to ask, or made another move. *Another move, Sharon? You're the one who practically dragged him into bed.* He wasn't complaining.

"Keep looking at me with that expression, Sharon, and neither of us will make it to work."

Oh my! She cleared her throat and let go of the water bottle. He caught it before it dropped to the ground.

He chuckled and kissed her on the cheek before leaving.

Tonight was going to be interesting. She couldn't wait.

Twenty minutes after he left, she left for work. The entire drive, she couldn't stop thinking about their kiss and Danny's invitation to take her to dinner. It felt like a momentous moment in their relationship: a date with no strings attached, or being on display for people to wonder about and judge. The night would just be them having dinner and enjoying each other's company, like they did at her home. The difference was tonight they wouldn't be temporary roommates with him playing bodyguard. Tonight, they'd be on a date, and after dinner... She blushed thinking about it.

She was grinning when she arrived at work, excited to share the good news. When she called Ryan into her office and asked him to sit, he shifted uncomfortably in the chair.

"Don't worry, Ryan. This is a good meeting. I wanted to invite you to come to work for me. If you're interested."

After a moment of bulging eyes and an open mouth, he answered with an emphatic yes. She filled him in on her plan and asked for his input. "What changed?" Ryan asked.

"My mother had her own plans for me. Good ones."

"I'm so happy for you, Sharon. And I must admit, myself too. I've been having dreams about working for Bradley or Carlton." He visibly shivered.

She chuckled. "Luckily, we both escaped that nightmare."

He nodded in agreement. "Oh, speaking of Bradley. I found out something interesting about him."

"If it's about his old girlfriend, I already know."

"No, much juicier than that." Ryan went to her desk and picked up an envelope and handed it to her.

Sharon opened it, and her eyes widened in surprise before she laughed. She couldn't help it.

"I can't believe my father didn't find this out himself." Or maybe he knew and didn't care because it was leverage he could use against Bradley. "He's adopted. Who would've guessed? I wonder if he even knows himself."

Ryan shrugged. "Not sure. I didn't have time to dig more, but I figured this was something you could use against him if he tried to pressure you."

Sharon rested her hand on Ryan's. "Thanks for doing such a thorough job."

"You're very welcome. I just wish I could be there when you tell him. You are going to tell him, right?"

"Honestly, I'm not sure. I think I'd rather see the look on my father's face. Especially if he doesn't know."

"Yes, a much better choice."

An hour later, they were both laughing from sharing ideas and the excitement of a new business and the road ahead, along with their plan to contact Sharon's current clients. Ryan's was beaming when he returned to his desk. Tomorrow was her last day, and as much work as she'd done to get everything completed, there was still lots to do to make sure the person who came in after her could start without going through a huge learning curve.

"I'm heading out now." Ryan stuck his head in the door. "Unless you need to me to stay?"

"No, I'm almost done here. Did you write your letter?"

"It was the first thing I did." He grinned sheepishly.

Sharon smiled.

"It's so wonderful seeing you smile so often and laughing."

"I'm loving it too, Ryan."

"Does it have something to do with a certain someone named Danny?"

"Maybe."

"Whatever he's doing, it's working." He winked and waved good night.

She couldn't agree more. Ryan was getting comfortable with their relationship, and she was liking it to a great extent than she thought she would. They had a mutual respect and a good foundation of a working relationship, and she was looking forward to them working together to build a business. She'd shocked him—and herself—when she offered him a partnership.

Her phone buzzed in her purse. It was Danny. "Hello?"

"Hey, Sharon. I'm sorry, but I'm running late. We might need to reschedule our date."

She checked her watch and realized it was later than she thought. "It's okay. I'm still at the office. Why don't we plan for breakfast together tomorrow instead?"

"I'd like that. Don't stay too late. And make sure you take a cab home and call me when you get there."

"I won't. I've got a couple things to wrap up and then I'm leaving."

"See you later."

"Bye."

I should've invited him to breakfast in bed, she thought with a mischievous grin.

Chapter 41

An hour later, Sharon shut down her computer. When she opened the door to leave, Carlton was standing in the doorway. "What are you doing here?"

"I wanted to talk," he stammered. "I thought you could give me some advice about dealing with your dad."

She checked her watch. "Could we talk tomorrow?"

"I won't take much of your time. I promise," he pleaded. It was the first time she'd ever seen him look so vulnerable. She could sympathize with everything that had happened recently, especially losing both parents. "All right. Come in."

Carlton headed to the couch instead of her desk.

"I thought that when you walked away, your father would give me your position. He laughed in my face."

"He just needs time for you to prove yourself." Sharon sat back down at her desk.

"And now he told me your mother had another will, so you get what you want. You always get what you want."

Is he serious? He certainly hadn't heard anything she told him about her experiences with her father over the years.

"I may now, but that is only thanks to my mother."

He patted the seat next to him as an invitation. "Do you know the only person Mark—and even my father—bragged about was you? They told me how I should take the path you did if I wanted to have the success you did. Everything I did wasn't enough for them."

Robert and her father had bragged about her. She had no idea. "Mark treated me the same, Carlton. The man doesn't know the meaning of the word *praise*, or *appreciation*."

"They compared everything I did and didn't do to you."

"I'm sorry."

"Nothing was ever good enough, so I stopped trying. After all, I was family, and my seat was guaranteed, right?"

The harshness of his tone increased with each sentence he spoke. She'd always sensed Carlton didn't like her, but now she understood why.

"I thought I would get the seat after my father died without waiting until I was twenty-five, but no."

"And I gave up my seat, so that should be yours."

Carlton laughed but it held no humor. "I thought so too, especially since your mother made sure you could support yourself financially without your father. But no. The stubborn bastard thinks he can convince or force you to come back."

"I'm sorry, Carlton."

"I am, too. I tried everything I could think of, but now I'm left with only one option."

Carlton stood and headed to her office door.

What the hell is he talking about? Is he leaving? Chills spread across her chest. *Was he responsible for the threats?* She hadn't given much thought of it being him because of his mother's death.

Before he could lock it, Bradley walked in. Sharon let out a sigh of relief. Carlton wouldn't do whatever he planned with him there.

"Looks like I got here just in time." Bradley grinned evilly.

"I thought the threats would scare you, but I should've known better. You're too strong-willed to be swayed or frightened easily. Then there was Bradley." Carlton pointed in his direction. "But he couldn't convince you to marry him. Not that I could blame you. Not a nice guy."

"I'm really not," Bradley said with a maniacal laugh.

"But I thought..." *Bradley's part of this? Why?*

"You thought Bradley was picked by your father?" Carlton snorted.

"He only thought he did. So arrogant."

"I had Bradley whisper in his ear. Even with all his faults, your father admired him more than me." He gritted his teeth. "Bradley was supposed to convince you he'd let you keep the power you wanted so you'd marry him. Then he'd hand it over to me."

"How?"

"You'd meet with an accident once you were married. The power would go to Bradley and then to me. No one would suspect it was me, but I should've known better."

She stared at Carlton. He wasn't the fool he led everyone to believe. "But the night at the police station. You attacked Bradley. You thought he'd killed your mother."

Bradley and Carlton exchanged glances. "You mean OUR mother?" they said in unison.

Shock sliced through Sharon. *Virginia was Bradley's mother?* "I knew you were adopted, but..."

"She pawned me off to a family in her circle through blackmail. You didn't guess my mother was Virginia. No one did. Well, except for Robert. He uncovered the truth, and that's why he had to die. He was going to ruin our plan."

"You killed your own father?" Sharon glanced at Carlton.

Carlton laughed. "You should've seen the look on his face when he learned I wasn't the fool everyone thought, including him, before I shot him."

"Priceless," Bradley added.

"You two are crazy. But why would you kill Virginia?" The longer she kept them talking, the longer before they revealed what they had planned for her. It was nothing good if it was the same as Virginia and Robert's fate.

"She found out we killed Robert. She was beside herself, and was going to the police."

Carlton shrugged. "I never like her much anyway."

"She was your mother!" Sharon knew Carlton and Bradley were many things, but murderers weren't one of them.

"Virginia was nothing like your mother, Sharon. I grew up with nursemaids and her acting as the caring mother at dinner parties and in public. Behind closed doors, she was cold and manipulative."

"You were going to marry me knowing we are family?" Bile rose in her mouth.

Bradley chuckled. "Robert wasn't my father, so technically, not really blood related."

Much too close for her liking. Sharon's mind raced; how was she going to get away from them? She might've managed one of them, especially if it was Carlton, but Bradley too? There was only one way out of her office, and it was through the front door, close to where they were both standing. She'd never make it. *If only I'd taken Danny's advice about a gun.* A lump formed in her throat. She'd never see him again. All the fantasies she'd had about their future together would never happen.

"Looks like we'll have to get our hands dirty again." Carlton's menacing gaze raked over her.

"You won't get away with it here." Her mind raced with options to evade them. Would they shoot her like they had Robert? Strangle her? Throw her out a window? There couldn't be a lot of options in the office without raising suspicions. Maybe she could make it to the door if she could get them to move. She slipped off her heels to make it easier to run.

The malicious grin that tugged at his mouth gave her a glimpse of the real Carlton. All this time she thought he was an insolent, selfish man–child, and all along he was plotting to get the power no one would give him.

"I can and I will," he said calmly. "Just like with Robert."

"We'll be each other's alibi again," Bradley stated.

Sharon shifted her chair away from her desk. "I'm surprised you didn't try to take my father's seat."

Carlton smirked. "It would just go to you. Without you..." His words trailed off, leaving her to interpret the meaning.

Her breath hitched in her throat. "Won't the police get suspicious of two deaths in the same office?"

"We thought about having someone else do it, but we couldn't take the risk of someone blackmailing us later. Making threats is one thing, but murder? That is another story."

Murder. The word was out there. Even though she knew that was their intention, hearing the word out loud sent a chill straight to her stomach and caused trembling in her knees. *Oh, God. Oh, God! Think, Sharon!* Her thoughts were nothing but a jumbled mess as Carlton strode toward her. She pushed the chair away from her desk and stood, ready to run for the door. How close could she let him get to her before she tried to run? Too close and she'd never make it.

Before she had time to think of it, he rushed toward her. She ran for the front door, but Bradley stepped in front of it, blocking her. An arm went around her neck and mouth, silencing her scream. Was it Bradley? Carlton? It didn't matter. She tried to twist out of the grasp, but he was too strong. Both of his arms were holding her as he wrestled her to the carpeted floor.

She stilled when she felt a cold blade on her neck. It was Carlton. "Please. Don't do this."

"You left me no choice."

"There's always a choice, Carlton."

The jiggle of the door handle and a knock on the door caused him to pause.

"Sharon?" Danny called out.

"Are you in there?" Ryan added.

It was Danny and Ryan. They were outside. She shoved her entire weight against Carlton to shift the knife away from her neck, and then screamed Danny's name. She managed to kick herself away from Carlton and scramble to her feet before darting behind her desk to put some distance between her and Carlton.

In the distance, she heard Danny and Ryan yelling her name and banging against the door without any luck.

"Danny! Help me! It's Carlton and—" Bradley grabbed her and put his hand over her mouth before she could say his name.

"I told you we should've used a gun again, and not a knife," Bradley hissed.

"That would draw more suspicion. What the hell is Danny doing here? He's supposed to be on a job."

"How the hell should I know? I thought Ryan left. I saw him leave myself. We should've taken them both at the house. Made it look like a robbery gone bad. Now thanks to you, we're going to jail."

"Shut up and let me think. There's two of them and two of us."

"You've got a knife and I've got nothing."

Carlton rolled his eyes. "We've got her, you idiot!"

The banging stopped, and for a moment, Sharon thought they were gone. No. Danny would never leave her alone knowing she was in danger.

"It's over. There's no getting out of this now." Bradley's voice was panicked and his hands sweaty against her mouth.

"We'll have to kill everyone."

"You can't be serious. There's no way that won't draw the attention of the police!"

"We'll be each other's alibis again."

Did Danny call the police? Did they go for help?

Sharon glanced around, looking for something she could defend herself with. A glass tower award was on the shelf next to her desk. She bit Bradley's hand, grabbed the tower, and swung it. It hit his head with a loud *thwack* and he fell to the floor.

"Bradley!" Carlton rushed toward her, his eyes filled with rage.

Loud crunching sounds ricocheted through the room and moments later, her large office door opened and Danny, Ryan, and a security guard rushed in.

Danny zeroed in on Carlton and charged him. Carlton tensed and poised the knife, ready to strike. With Carlton distracted, Sharon rushed behind him and smashed him over his head with the glass tower. Carlton crumpled to the ground; the knife skittered across the carpet next to him.

Danny kicked it farther away and rushed to Sharon, checking her from head to toe to make sure she wasn't injured. "Are you okay?" He wrapped his arms around her tightly.

"No, but I will be." She hugged him back just as fiercely.

"I thought I'd lost you," he whispered.

"I thought they were going to kill me." Tears pooled in her eyes.

"They?"

Sharon pointed to Bradley's body slumped on the floor behind her desk. "It's a very long story."

"It's over. I called the police. They should be here soon."

She raised her head. "I thought you were working late."

"Ryan called and told me about Bradley's adoption. I just had a bad feeling it was him, so I rushed over here and asked Ryan to meet me. Just to be safe."

"Thank you, Ryan."

"It's the least I could do for my future business partner." Ryan said. "But seriously, I'm glad we got here in time."

"Me too! How did you get in?"

"I smashed the case for the ax. I tried kicking the door in and ramming it, but nothing worked. I think I dislocated my shoulder." He winced when he tried to move it. "Totally worth it."

She shared with them everything that had happened up to the moment they arrived. The police arrived as she finished, and thankfully Carlton and Bradley were still knocked out. They revived and cuffed them.

"Do you want to call your father?" Danny asked hours later as he drove her home.

She shook her head. Her body was numb as the reality of the night's events slowly sank in. Carlton and Bradley had tried to kill her, and for what? A seat? It wasn't just the seat, but the power and money that came with it. But compared to her life, it seemed trivial. She felt foolish for clinging to it for so long, but she'd wanted her father's approval. She wanted him to say she'd worked hard and deserved it, but the words had never come. Carlton's life was over, and the seat would remain empty for now. The best thing was that she had everything she wanted—money to start her own company, a home, friends, and someone to love.

She glanced over at Danny. Yes, she loved him. It was crazy, since they'd only know each other for a few short months, but the peace in her heart whenever she looked at him was evidence. From the moment they met, he'd brought so much to her life. Laughter, friendship, support, care, what a real family looks like. All she never thought possible until he showed her.

She took his hand and put it against her cheek.

Her life wasn't taking the road she'd planned, but the road she was on was a much better one, where she'd be happy and loved.

Acknowledgements:

To Susan Uttendorfsky from Adirondack Editing (http://www.adirondackediting.com/) who's been with me from the start and is an amazing editor who fixes my writing flaws but lets me keep my voice. To LeAnn F. Stout from Quick Feather Writing Service. (leannstout83@gmail.com) who loved my story and helped to make it better.

Special thanks to my fans. I can't tell you enough how much I appreciate your support and love for my stories. You continue to inspire me!

My fellow CayWriters, whose enthusiasm for literature drives my passion. To Lorraine Carey who's been a trusted friend and an amazing writer herself. Thank you for your advice and support I could not live without.

To my beta readers for their love of reading, especially my stories. I appreciate you more than you know!

Thanks to my kids who put up with me talking about writing and my story ideas while having to make their own food so I can focus on writing. For keeping quiet (mostly) while I'm doing videos, and making me laugh with the faces you make. I love you guys!

About the Author:

Elke Feuer was born and raised in Grand Cayman. She moved to Florida in 2015 and lives there with her two kids (one of each) who keep her on her toes. She has a sarcastic/quirky sense of humor not everyone gets and loves using checklists for just about everything.

She stumbled into writing suspense and found she really enjoyed it along with writing about serial killers. She writes in other genres to even out her dark side, but no genre is safe because characters keep telling her their crazy stories and she's a sucker for a crazy story.

For more information about Elke and her upcoming books, visit her at: www.elkefeuer.com

Also By Elke Feuer:

For The Love of Jazz

Deadly Bloodlines, Deadly Series Book 1

Deadly Race, Deadly Series Book 2

Deadly Family, Deadly Series Book 3

Persuading Lola

Connect with Me:

FaceBook:

https://www.facebook.com/elkefeuer.author

Instagram:

https://www.instagram.com/elke_feuer/

YouTube:

https://www.youtube.com/@ElkeFeuer/featured

Email:

elkeafeuer@yahoo.com

Download a free book from my website:
www.elkefeuer.com

www.ingramcontent.com/pod-product-compliance
Lightning Source LLC
Chambersburg PA
CBHW050917030726
47503CB00007BB/2335